From A Distance

Gloria Cook

CANELO

First published in the United Kingdom in 2004 by Severn House

This edition published in the United Kingdom in 2018 by

Canelo Digital Publishing Limited
57 Shepherds Lane
Beaconsfield, Bucks HP9 2DU
United Kingdom

A CIP catalogue record for this book is available from the British Library.

Print ISBN 978 1 78863 131 0
Ebook ISBN 978 1 78863 066 5

Look for more great books at www.canelo.co

Printed and bound in Great Britain by Clays Ltd, Elcograf S.p.A.

To Una and Rod Searle, good friends and a blessing

Chapter One

It was only three o'clock in the afternoon but already nearly as dark as night. A gale had been raging all day from the south-west and, like some malevolent monster, it was still lashing rain against the windows and walls of Ford Farm. The house, the animal sheds and storage buildings had not been spared. Slates, chimney pots and guttering had been hurled down and smashed on the cobbles and flagstones. Debris was embedded in areas of thick mud. Ripped-out thatch danced at crazy heights in miniature whirlwinds. Howling in banshee tones, the wind was indiscriminately bringing down branch after branch of the trees around the farm perimeter and in the woods at the bottom of the valley behind the property. Loose objects like flower pots were being tossed about, and gates, fences and even the washing-line posts had been brought down.

An enormous gust of wind made the oldest timbers, eighteenth-century in origin, the working part of the huge, rambling farmhouse, creak and heave noisily, making it seem to shudder on its thick stone foundations. Emilia Harvey was filling Thermos flasks with hot tea and paused to look anxiously towards the kitchen door, willing her husband, the farm owner, and her father, the manager, and the farmhands outside in the uproar to stay safe. In boots, gaiters and weatherproofs, they would be having a tough time securing the stock, specially the ewes – it was lambing season – and in making repairs thought urgent to hedges, and ensuring the lanes were safe to pass through to the nearby village of Hennaford. Also, her sons would be cycling home about now from the boys' grammar school in Truro. The day had started off with just a swift wind, and although it was late spring there had been a wintry feel and a peculiar tension in the air. She had wondered if Will and Tom should attend today – but at the ages of thirteen and twelve they saw themselves as young adults and had poured scorn on her disquiet; and they had rugby today, it would take more than a threatening storm to keep them at home. The match would have been abandoned, but there was still the six-mile ride back to negotiate through any amount of missiles and fallen wreckage and deep pools of muddy water. Emilia took comfort in Tom's sensible nature. Hopefully he would keep his more reckless brother out of any danger.

Despite her concern, Emilia smiled. There, kneeling up on one of the window seats, was the source of her most constant joy, her five-year-old daughter, Lottie, who was watching the wilful machinations of the fierce weather with animated glee.

There came a juddering crash and a prolonged splintering from outside. Lottie, who was much given to drama, squealed loudly and clapped her hands. 'That's another slate down.'

'All very well for you to say, young lady, but Daddy's going to have to see to an awful lot of repairs.'

'And you,' Lottie said, without taking her eyes off the exciting scene outside. 'You do as much work as he do. More sometimes.'

'Perhaps. I've going out to the dairy to help prepare for the milking in a little while, and,' Emilia stressed, 'you, my love, will have to trot along to the sitting room and stay with Granny and Tilda. No mischief, Lottie. Promise me.'

Lottie wasn't listening. 'Uh, uh, oh…' She was watching her doll's pram, new and shiny, a recent birthday present, being driven on its little rubber wheels by the gale. It hit a corner of the horses' concrete drinking trough with such force that the front of the little grand carriage was staved in. 'Oh! Dulcie! She's in there!'

Emilia dropped the huge iron, copper-spouted kettle back down on the hob of the range. 'What's happened? Lottie, what are you talking about?'

Lottie jumped down from the window seat and shot towards the back kitchen.

'Lottie!' Emilia dashed across the room and stopped her opening the door. 'You can't go outside. There are things flying about everywhere. It's too dangerous.'

'Mummy! I have to go. I have to rescue her!' Lottie used desperate expressions on her mulish little face and raised her grubby hands. Taller and more statuesque than the average child her age, she looked fearless. Like Emilia, she was resolute and direct, but her boldness and spontaneity sometimes gave the inhabitants of the farm cause to fear for her safety. 'Dulcie will be dead else.'

Emilia reached for Lottie's hand with the intention of taking her to the window so she could see for herself why she was fussing about one of her dolls. Although Lottie returned her mother's adoration it didn't mean she was more obedient towards her, and she set her tiny red mouth in a tight line, glared out of her dark brown eyes and clamped her hands behind her back. 'I've got no time for this,' Emilia said, and hefted her up underarm and carried her to the window.

'See?' Lottie bawled indignantly, struggling to get free. 'My pram's broke. Dulcie's in grave danger.'

Emilia peered through the darkness and chaos and saw the pram being rammed against the trough, then it toppled over on to its side. The doll and covers were already spewed across the yard. 'Oh, Lottie, this really is too bad.' She was cross with Lottie for disregarding her order the day before to bring all her toys inside. Lottie didn't really care about the doll, and was not at all impressed that it wasn't of the usual girly sort but a felt-bodied googly-eyed doll. She preferred boys' toys and she was constantly being reprimanded for hiding away games and other possessions of her two brothers. Emilia knew her daughter was only longing to go outside so she could boast to Will and Tom that she had made a daring rescue in one of the worst gales that had ever hit Hennaford. 'What's Daddy's going to say? He chose the pram specially for you. You are a naughty little girl.'

Lottie stopped struggling and Emilia put her down. Lottie changed her look to one that was designed to be sweetly appealing. It worked with most people for she was captivating and amusing. 'If we bring it inside, Mum, we could mend it. He'd never know. I like mending things. I want to be a motor mechanic when I grow up.'

'I'm afraid the damage is too obvious. I'll slip outside and put it in one of the outhouses. You'll go to bed early tonight for this, Lottie. I'll tell your Daddy about it.' Wryly, Emilia pulled in her lower lip. Many a mother would have smacked her child's leg or sent her to her room over such a misdemeanour, but Lottie's birth into the Harvey family was extra special, so she was unwearyingly pandered to by most of them.

'He'll send me to bed early for a whole week. Again!' Lottie shrieked in hard-done-by tones.

'What's the matter with our little maid then?' Emilia's mother, Dolly Rowse, had come through from the sitting room, which was in the building's fine Victorian extension, set at a right angle and facing the road. With the farm's housekeeper, Tilda Lawry, she had been cleaning up soot blasted down the chimney by the wind. 'Why was she screaming, Emilia?'

Mournful and long-faced, Lottie dragged her feet to her grandmother and complained about her future punishment as if it wasn't her fault her pram was damaged. Dolly Rowse, in her usual hairnet and wrap-around apron, owned a forbidding brow and an often alarming, candid nature. She could be tart with Emilia but, while she insisted her grandsons be respectful and quiet in the house, she had unending patience for Lottie. Dolly picked her up, kissed her and colluded with Emilia in an indulgent smile. 'Well, my handsome, you shouldn't have left Dulcie outside, but as long as you're not out there getting hurt that's all that matters. You come with Granny and she'll look in her handbag and see if she's got a nice bar of chocolate just the right size for a pretty little girl.'

Lottie was swept away, chuckling in delight, and Emilia smiled after them.

The sky was suddenly lit up in eerie shades of yellow, green and gold, and very shortly afterwards came a drawn-out threatening rumble. 'I wondered when you lot were going to make yourself known,' Emilia muttered about the thunder and lightning. 'Now, to get that pram.'

She was worried about Alec's reaction to the broken doll's pram. Eight years ago they had lost a daughter at only three and a half weeks old, born prematurely and blind and deaf, with cerebral palsy and a weak heart. Alec had adored Jenna. Her death had devastated him. A quiet, deeply thoughtful man, sometimes given to periods of brooding, he refused to give up the belief that somehow he should have prevented Jenna's tragic condition, that he should have protected her, and Emilia knew the loss had left him floundering for explanations that were unattainable. Alec had hardly dared look at Lottie or hold her until she had started talking and walking, until it was clear she could see and hear perfectly and had normal intelligence. Emilia had wanted to call her Anna, but Alec had insisted her first name be Charlotte, after his grandmother who had lived to the good age of eighty-six, and immediately he had called the baby Lottie, as the old lady had been known. While grateful that his daughter was as healthy and apparently as strong as his sons, he wanted her to be feminine, something of a delicate lady, as it had seemed Jenna was going to be, and he did not approve of her mutiny against the usual pastimes of little girls.

Emilia made a mental note to go after Lottie and make sure she had a clean dress on, that her short hair was brushed and her socks pulled up, in case Alec arrived home unexpectedly. He was a gentleman farmer, he had a large workforce, and although he worked most days for long hours on the land, he sometimes suddenly appeared at home. Once he had turned up in a sort of daze and had sat motionless in his den, and when she had asked him why he had come home he had shrugged and replied he didn't really know. Alec was getting more and more absent-minded, and from being kind and patient was turning unaccustomedly irritable. He had always been frustrated with business matters that involved paperwork, due to a condition which meant he couldn't read or write properly, but now he was getting testy about issues he formerly would have not cared about.

While the wind and rain continued their battering and complaining, and the flashes and crashes in the heavens came ever closer, Emilia, praying the lightning wouldn't bring down the newly erected electricity power lines, hurried to the back kitchen and carried the oil lamps through to the kitchen table in case they were needed. She put on her boots and mackintosh, thinking about how complicated it was nowadays to read Alec's moods. He had always been cynical of the usual order of things, like class observances – she had been a dairy maid here but he had chosen her to become his second wife. Of a powerful build and noble bearing, he had taken lately to walking with his head down, either because keeping it upright was becoming a bother to him or he was signalling for even more remoteness.

Sometimes when Alec looked at her, ever since the time she herself had come to terms with Jenna's death, Emilia got the uneasy feeling that he thought he had lost part of her too. In the most significant way he had, but she was always on her guard to conceal it. The truth would destroy Alec, and he in no way deserved that.

There was a sudden clatter and a burst of young excited voices outside the door. Startled out of her musings, Emilia was relieved to hear her sons safely home. No doubt they had enjoyed the ride, which must have been in some ways hazardous. They were typical boys who would rather play games or lark about than get on with their homework or see to their chores, but today they would be eager to change their clothes and clear the yard of debris, seeing it as a daring deed rather than a duty.

She opened the door to them and heard Tom – sensitive, dignified and shrewd Tom – mutedly agree with his careless, energetic older brother's boastful claim that the ride up the hill at Devil's Arch was 'just like fighting through a battlefield but a heck of a lot more fun.' Emilia didn't kiss Will, it would have embarrassed him, but Tom instantly returned her affectionate hug, laughing as his dripping arms and wet face made her wet too. 'Did you know Lottie's pram is battered to death out there, Mum?' he said seriously, knowing there was tension ahead, and some rebellious shouting on his little sister's part. And probably screaming. Lottie screamed for ages when she got started.

'I'm just about to steal it away into the cart house,' Emilia whispered, as if in part of a conspiracy. 'Tom, will you see what you can do with it tomorrow?'

'Of course,' he said. 'Don't worry.'

'It's only fit for the scrap heap now,' Will scoffed. 'She'll be in for it from Father. She'd better not have put anything of mine inside the pram.'

Emilia sighed.

Leaving pools of water on the linoleum the boys flung off their outdoor things and went into the kitchen, then after raiding the cake tin they went upstairs to dry themselves and change. Emilia overheard Will state in his uncompromising way, 'Lottie had better not plead to come outside with us.' She knew it was a warning to Tom, who, even though he wouldn't agree to allow Lottie to join them in the adverse conditions, would want to stay and give his little sister a drawn-out explanation on the wisdom of her staying inside and promise her all manner of treats in compensation.

Emilia was reaching once more for the door latch when it was opened and Alec stepped over the threshold, the abandoned, ruined doll held up in one accusing hand. He let it drop with a thud on the draining board. Emilia lowered her gaze. She couldn't help feeling guilty and this unsettled her. Alec's annoyance had never made her feel this way before, and there was not the slightest need for it. Alec had never been dictatorial or demanding. Only her great secret, something she cherished although she shouldn't, made her suffer this guilt.

'I take it she hasn't been playing outside today.' Alec's frustration and hurt was evident in his strong voice. 'I've put the pram, what's left of it, in the cart house.'

Emilia looked up at him. 'She's with Mother and Tilda in the sitting room. Alec, Lottie is sorry about the pram. I called her in for tea yesterday and after that it was dark and she must have simply forgotten about it. The boys are safely home. I've made flasks of hot tea. Would you like some?'

Alec gazed back and Emilia dropped her eyes again. He knew she was making excuses for Lottie. 'I know the boys are back. Their bikes are cleaned and oiled and properly stowed away. Be careful, Emilia, when going across the yard. I've come to escort you. I'll get the flasks. Listen…'

'What is it?' She glanced out of the window, alarmed. What was the gale about to wreak on them now?

'The wind has dropped.'

'Oh, thank goodness. Now we can start getting things back to normal. How much damage is there out and about, darling?'

'It's pretty bad.'

Next instant she was blinded and it was as if the house was rocked from roof to ground – the world seemed to be falling down all around her. Emilia screamed and flung out a hand to grab at the nearest thing, the huge cloam sink.

Alec met her panicked expression with something akin to shock, then he thrust open the door.

'Be careful, Alec! What on earth's happened?'

'Lightning's hit the roof of the cart house. It's caved in. I was inside there only a minute ago.' He touched the St Christopher medal around his neck, then superstitiously he touched the door; touched wood. 'I was lucky. I'll have to make sure the walls are safe.'

'I'll come with you.'

'No, darling. The boys can help me. You see to the milking, and be careful.'

When he'd gone back outside, she whispered to herself, 'You're such a good husband to me, Alec.' After fourteen years of marriage they were still in love. There was much to admire about Alec. Because he was polite and receptive to women his company was sought after by those of all ages and backgrounds. His good looks and enticing masculinity was remarked on often. At forty-one, ten years her senior, his tumbling, coal-black hair was silvering in a distinguished way, and this new habit of his of stooping a little, rather than diminishing his attraction, was bringing out the desire in his admirers to care for him. Emilia would have everything she could ever want in Alec if not for – she closed her eyes tight to forbid a vision. Of another man.

Why did her thoughts go so often to him? She had not seen him for eight years, so why did it feel as if he had left Hennaford, left Cornwall, only yesterday? It would help if they didn't keep in touch. But she could not bear that. She kept his Christmas and Easter greeting cards and secreted them away to pore over in private moments. To imagine him writing the simple polite words that were usual to cards. *To Emilia, Alec and family. With every good wish, Perry and Libby Bosweld.* To everyone else it was just a formal message from one of the estate's former tenants and his young daughter. Occasionally it had been pondered on by others in the family, why the disabled, one-time army surgeon bothered to keep sending cards, especially as the Boswelds had left Hennaford after a scandal involving Perry's promiscuous sister, Selina, but to Emilia it meant everything. For the deep love for Perry, which she had not sought but which had grown inside her, had not diminished one tiny bit by time or distance. And on Perry's cards, and the ones she sent to him, were roses. Roses were special to them. And by this she knew he still loved her.

Fetching the flasks, Emilia stepped out into the cold. Mercifully the rain had also eased and now fell only in a pathetic drizzle. Alec was up on a ladder, removing the remaining loose grey slates of the cart-house roof. She wanted to shout to him to be careful, in recompense for thinking about Perry. For still loving Perry, for loving him more than she could ever love Alec. But that might startle Alec and cause him to fall off the ladder.

Will and Tom came either side of her, the elder a typical strapping black-haired Harvey, the younger, rangy and his head topped with rich coppery-brown locks, like hers and Lottie's.

'Blood and bones! What a mess.' Will beat his fists together, eager to get to work. He was always the first of the brothers to speak. He was chuckling inside because he had secretly threatened Lottie that he'd lock her in the cupboard under the stairs if she didn't stop bothering him to be allowed to come outside. One thing she was afraid of was the dark.

He wouldn't ever do it, but it was the best way to make her shut up.

Tom always measured his thoughts before he spoke. 'There's damage all over the West Country according to the news on the wireless. No mention of anyone getting hurt, thank goodness.'

'Good,' Emilia said, smiling at Tom. 'But the storm's not over yet for others, it's shifting south-east. You boys feed the horses, then clear the paths to the outhouses. We don't want anyone tripping over wreckage. You know what to do with anything useful for firewood.'

'Dad!' Tom yelled suddenly and was dashing towards the cart house.

'What? Oh, my dear God!' Emilia froze. The top of the wall that Alec was up against was rocking as if by some unseen giant hand. There was nothing she could do. The large granite stones came hurtling down. Alec was swept off the ladder and buried under the rubble.

Chapter Two

Ben Harvey, Alec's youngest brother, who owned property on the other side of the village, was pleased to find only a few regulars in the village pub that night. He was in no mood for company and welcomed the dim light and subdued atmosphere. He offered a quick hello to Gilbert Eathorne, the shopkeeper and postmaster, who was perched on a stool at the bar with his brother Sidney, who owned the butcher's shop and had his well-trained border collie with him. Ben hoped the red-faced, cheery, nosy pair, who looked as if they were about to pounce on him with, no doubt, some exaggerated gossip about the consequences of the storm, would take the hint that he wanted only a quiet drink. He nodded to deaf old Mr Quick, who was scrunched up in his usual seat at a barrel table beside the crackling log fire, and received a trembly headshake in reply.

On his way to the bar he felt another pair of eyes on him. Unfriendly eyes. Due to an accident in his youth Ben was partially sighted in his left eye, and when he turned to look in that direction he was annoyed to see another drinker. He ignored the well-built, fair-haired young man stretched out in a territorial manner in a dark corner and puffing out a cloud of cigarette smoke. He and Jim Killigrew had despised each other from the time Jim had worked as a labourer on

Ford Farm, and it was not unknown for them to be involved in a fist fight.

'Your usual, Mr Ben?' The landlady, Ruby Brokenshaw, a good-natured but no-nonsense war-widow, nearing middle age in a plump yet stylish manner, made straight for a bottle of single malt.

'Make it a double please, Ruby.' His voice was full of sighs. 'What a day.'

'You're telling me. It's quiet in here tonight what with so many mopping up after the gale,' Ruby said, putting the glass of whisky and a jug of water in front of him. She took the ten-shilling note Ben proffered. He waved away the change and pushed away the water. 'And for that poor soul to die like that. Terrible!'

Puzzled, Ben raised the dark brows of his strongly contoured face and took his time bringing out a gold cigar case and lighter from the inside breast pocket of his coat. The Eathornes, portly and short, in ancient raincoats, were on their feet and moving in on him, their habitual wide-toothed grins missing as they stared at him for his reaction. They could damn well wait. Ben lit the small, fragrant cigar. While Alec saw most people as equals, inviting all to call him by his Christian name, Ben did not. He believed money counted in one's standing and good breeding counted even more. He had a proud bearing and towered over his brothers, and with the milky pea-sized spot in his damaged eye, he seemed like some fine battle-scarred warrior. He had great presence, which he had carefully cultivated, and which like now, even when he wasn't seeking to, ensured that he was usually central to the scene. Alec might own more land in and around Hennaford, but he, through his various businesses, including the local garage and filling station, was now the wealthier, and he wanted everyone to acknowledge it. At last he said, 'But my brother didn't die in the accident. He's suffered a broken leg and broken ribs and cuts and bruises. He should be released from the infirmary in a day or two. I've just driven Mrs Harvey home from there. The roads are still in a fine old mess.'

Ruby Brokenshaw's pink-lipsticked mouth opened in shock. 'I wasn't talking about the squire! Had no idea he was hurt. It's Leslie Annear I'm on about. He was struck down by lightning outside his own workshop. Killed instantly.'

'What? That's terrible.' Ben dropped the cigar in a brass ashtray, shaking his dark head in disbelief. The Annear carpenter workshop was half a mile further along Back Lane from where he himself lived; all part of the former Tremore estate. Leslie Annear had rented a cottage and a small piece of land off him. 'I was in Truro on business when I heard about my brother's accident, otherwise I would have heard about this. What's happened to the Annear children? I feel a responsibility towards them.'

Gilbert Eathorne answered in the lowered tones of an actor narrating a tragic play on the wireless. 'The young'uns have been taken in for now by Miss Rawley, but one'd expect nothing less from that dear fine lady. Ill-fated family, the Annears. Young Isaac was killed in the Great War. The parents were both took in the terrible 'flu epidemic just after that. Leslie was their last surviving child. His little wife died of cancer just last autumn. Now he's gone too. A sorry story, if ever there was one.'

'What happened to the squire then?' Sidney jumped in. 'Get caught out in the storm too, did he? Anything we can do?'

To avoid too many questions Ben pulled on his cigar and gave a brief outline of how Alec had been injured.

'So lightning got him too!' Gilbert gasped, his crinkled eyes wide in astonishment. 'It hit the village twice. Well, twice as far as we know. You never know what's going to happen.'

Sidney thumbed, with a disapproving glare, at Jim Killigrew. 'According to he there, our brother's farm got off lightly, but that's where young Killigrew should be now, on Druzel land. Must be a lot of clearing up to do. Leaves everything to Eustace and young Wally, he does. Just because his sister's married to Wally and he's moved in with 'em, he thinks it gives him leave to sit back on his laurels. Hope the rest of your property didn't fare too badly. Eh, Mr Ben?'

Ben wasn't given the chance to answer that all his other concerns had mainly been spared.

'You can mind your own damned business, Sidney Eathorne!' Jim Killigrew tossed down the butt of his cigarette, then rose swiftly and gulped down the last of his pint of bitter. 'I'd only just got here, remember? I'm off. Trouble with my life is I can't get away from you ruddy Eathornes. G'night, Ruby.' Before thrusting his way out of the Ploughshare, he tossed enough copper coins on old Mr Quick's barrel for the pensioner to buy himself drinks for the rest of the night.

'Thanking you kindly, boy,' old Mr Quick said, gathering up the money in his bony, arthritic fingers, his slowness of wit making him unaware of the bad feelings. In his worn flat cap and topcoat, once both a good fit but now overwhelming his small, wasted form, he gazed at the slammed door, puzzled and disappointed that he was to drink alone.

Jim Killigrew was usually a sociable young fellow. He had formed a way of communicating with him. Most people selfishly left him to abide on his own in his silent world.

'I'll thank you not to drive my customers away, Sidney Eathorne,' Ruby Brokenshaw said sharply. Her sister Effie was married to Gilbert. Gilbert had some good qualities but Sidney had few, and she was suspicious that he cheated with his meat measures. 'I've got to pay someone to replace the blown-down slates on my roof, you know. Jim weren't hurting. He always sits quietly. And I, for one, believe he's a hard worker. Make some maid a good catch, he would.'

'The boy gets above himself. Don't hurt to remind him where he come from. The workhouse.' Sidney was unrepentant and a malicious gleam showed in his pale eyes. 'If you ask me, all's not well on Druzel Farm. In fact we know it isn't, don't we, Gilbert?'

'We do,' Gilbert agreed. 'Thing is, Wally's soon to be a father again and the house is getting cramped. Killigrew's in the way.'

'Well, I like Jim.' Ruby was equally defiant. 'And he's hardly a boy now, must be all of twenty-seven.'

'Well, we know why women like him.' Gilbert made a knowing face before raising his nose sanctimoniously.

'I won't have that sort of talk in here! It was only rumours about him and that dreadful BoHweld woman anyway. It was someone's husband she was involved with,' Ruby huffed, then carried another half of mild to old Mr Quick. After the Harveys, the Eathornes were the most well placed in the parish, and to her mind the Eathornes were becoming pride-ridden snobs. They had no upper-middle-class blood in them as the Harveys did. Instead of returning to her side of the bar she went up to Ben and asked quietly, 'How's your little girl, Mr Ben? Wasn't too frightened by the gale, I hope.'

'I haven't seen her since breakfast. She's in good health, thank you, Ruby.' Talk involving his daughter reminded Ben why he hadn't gone straight home after dropping Emilia back at the farm. He loved seven-year-old Faye but was frustrated over his wife's two subsequent miscarriages and her reluctance to become pregnant again. The atmosphere at home was as gloomy as in here, and as charged as when Jim Killigrew had stormed out. He wanted a son and couldn't see why he shouldn't have one. But Brooke had come to the conclusion that she couldn't face another disappointment and that he should be happy with just Faye and herself as family. Why couldn't Brooke understand that a son and heir was important to him? Alec had two sons – Brooke had accused him of being jealous of Alec. It was true that in most things Alec had more than him, but if Alec had three daughters and not Will and Tom, he'd still want to have a son. Brooke should understand this. His other older brother Tristan had a daughter born the same year as Faye, and even he, the calm, content one of the family, had said that he was proud that his first born, by his first wife, was a son.

It wouldn't be so bad if Faye was more like Lottie, or Emilia. But his daughter was soft and fluffy and loved things like ballet and clothes; a career man's wife in the making. Brooke was an American, from Wyoming, but there was no pioneering stock in her or her daughter. He had nothing to look forward to. His injured eye had caused him to miss out on the army career he had coveted. He would probably have been killed in the war to end all wars. He wished he had. A hero's death and eternal veneration would have been preferable to this half life he was living.

He rubbed his brow. He was getting a headache. And he was being unfair to Brooke. She was a good wife. His recent harsh moods, his inconsideration, might kill off her feelings for him if he didn't change. He should go home and tell Brooke about Alec's condition. She would be worried about him, and worried about how safe the roads were for the journey home from Truro. It struck him then how much he had enjoyed the journey home with Emilia. Always a woman of strong feelings, she had been distraught over Alec's near death. For some moments, so she had said, she had thought Alec was dead as she and the boys had frantically pulled the rubble off him. 'I can't tell you how I felt at hearing him breathe. I couldn't bear it if I lost him, Ben.'

Would Brooke feel the same way if he had nearly been killed by a collapsing wall? And if he did die, would she sell everything he had worked so hard for and move back to America? He gulped down his whisky, relishing the comforting burn down his throat to his stomach. He should go. But Emilia had probably phoned Brooke with news of Alec. There was no need to hurry. Brooke would guess he was here. She was probably vexed with him. She would show this by an irritating polite quietness, the ruse she employed to keep him from making loving approaches. Emilia would tackle Alec over such a thing the moment he got inside the door. Ben would prefer this to passive sulking.

He had been engaged once to his spirited sister-in-law. He should have married her instead of blaming her, unfairly, and causing years of estrangement, over the loss of his sight. Emilia was strong-willed and tough. She hadn't been afraid to have another baby after Jenna's death and that was far more tragic than a couple of early miscarriages. Alec was going to need a lot of attention in the next few weeks but Emilia would manage. She'd cope with Alec and with running the farm. Pity Brooke wasn't more like her.

He finished the cigar and pushed his empty glass forward on the highly polished mahogany bar top. 'I'm ready for another, Ruby.' He would leave his sporty motor car here and walk home.

'Double again?'

'Yes, please, and whatever you and the others are having. And Mr Quick must have a packet of Gold Flake for his pipe.' He met the Eathorne brothers' grateful grins with a melancholy smile. 'Let's drink to the memory of Leslie Annear.'

Chapter Three

The funeral cortège left from Ford House, the home of Elena Rawley, the custodian of the two Annear children. While making the arrangements for today, she had told Emilia, 'I couldn't let the children go back to their home. Alan witnessed his father's death, and he and Martha had sat beside the body for hours before the tragedy was discovered.'

Elena's late father, once Hennaford's Methodist minister, had bought the grand four-bedroomed property for his retirement, cheaply from Alec. Alec had been glad to get rid of it – tragedy and troubles had beleaguered many a member of the Harvey family in the house. Elena knew of the house's history but avowed she found it peaceful. The villagers put this down to her character. She was modest and humble. She was old-fashioned in dress and in some of her views but never judgemental. She lived on the proceeds of a small trust fund, carrying on with her life as she had always done, serving those in need with understanding and without prejudice, and for this she was highly respected and was known as the heart and angel of the village.

It was the custom for few women to attend a funeral, but the sadness of the occasion ensured as many women as men were at the church and the wake afterwards at Ford House. As Elena greeted the mourners at her front door, with four- year-old Alan and infant Martha clinging nervously to her long tweed skirt, she was unaware that her home held differing memories for some of the arrivals.

While Emilia was relieved and thankful she didn't have a funeral to arrange – Alec's – her thoughts turned to Perry the instant she entered the house. He and his family had been its last tenants. It was here in the dining room, which had been turned into a bedroom back then for Perry, who had lost a leg during war service, that he and a doctor friend of his, at her request, had examined Jenna and she had learned the full horror of her condition. She stood motionless before the table, laid with ham, and egg and cress sandwiches and the usual fare consumed at funeral teas, recalling how in this room she had also shared her first kiss with Perry.

'No sherry, but one doesn't expect to be served a decent drink in this household.' Ben nudged her arm. 'Good spread though, but all the village chipped in with the refreshments. Brooke sent over those chocolate biscuits. She calls them cookies. Try some, Em.'

'What? Oh, I'm not hungry, Ben.'

His wide-shouldered, black suit was of finer quality than any other man's present, his tie was silk, and he cut an excellent figure. Under the guise of fussing to locate his handkerchief he looked Emilia up and down. She was tall and in perfect feminine shape, vigorous and healthy and, as always, a little stately. She was also a picture of winsome sorrow in a cross-over, fur-collared coat and a small pull-on hat. This was one of the rare occasions she wore stockings and high heels. It was a treat to see her divine legs and neat ankles, but he liked her too in working clothes when she wore a shirt and trousers. When her hat came off, her hair would spring back in chin-length coppery waves. 'Are you fretting about Alec? He's got enough people dancing attendance on him, surely? He'll knit together soon enough. Harveys are made of rock and steel. Is he being difficult?'

'You know Alec never makes a fuss. Sometimes I wish he would, to show me his spirit is returning. He lies on the couch most of the time, staring out of the bedroom window. I just feel sad, that's all. This is a sad house.'

Ben joined her in a silent moment, their minds going back down the years to when Tristan Harvey, the third Harvey brother, then an army captain away fighting in the war, had owned the house and his first wife, Ursula, had died here in childbirth, the baby sired by her lover. He and Emilia had sat through that terrible occasion and were linked unendingly by her deathbed wish, the promise they had made to ensure her baby would be well cared for. A promise that had turned into a secret shared also by Alec, a very reluctant Tristan, the medical attendants and the baby's adoptive aunt. Ben wanted to say that there weren't only bad memories for him here. During their brief engagement, when he had loved Emilia so much, she had willingly gone upstairs with him and they had made love. The first time for both of them, a special time. Since their reconciliation, brought about by Jenna's death, he had returned to cherishing that sweet occasion. He wished there had been more. What he liked best about Emilia was her earthiness and independent spirit. Emilia was a fighter, she got on with things, she was stoical and unfussy. He knew then that he would never stop wanting her. He reached out and touched her hand. 'Em...'

'What is it?' She was puzzled by the tremendous depth of emotion in the greyness of his eyes.

'Oh, nothing. I suppose at times like this one likes to feel safe.' Long ago Emilia had made him feel safe. And alive and valued in a way no other had since. He longed to feel like that again.

Jim Killigrew hadn't intended to come to Ford House. It had an unfortunate history for him too. Perry Bosweld's cruel, amoral sister, Selina, had seduced him here. Jim had thought he had fallen in love with her. He had become obsessed with her. But she had entertained many lovers and had spitefully thrown him over, laughing at him. Her way of sex had involved pain and humiliation. He didn't like to think of those times, even though, despite his attempts to keep his association with Selina Bosweld a secret, people had suspected there had been an involvement, and women tended to think he was some kind of stud, and men either congratulated him or were jealous of him. Righteous parents kept their daughters away from him, even though the war had left a chronic shortage of husband material. But he was here because he wanted to speak to, of all people, Ben Harvey, and he hadn't got the chance after the interment. Elena Rawley's kind personal invitation had given him the courage to come, because although he wasn't in any way a coward, he needed a sort of courage if he was to get the insufferably pompous toff to listen to him.

Emilia caught him during a moment when he was looking sympathetically at the Annear children. 'Jim's remembering what it was like when he and Sara were left orphans. Elena will have to make up her mind soon about what to do with Alan and Martha. She's been trying to trace their relatives but there don't seem to be any.'

Ben did not consider Jim Killigrew worthy of a comment. 'Perhaps someone will take them in.' He considered it himself. If he wasn't to get a son from his loins he could adopt one. Alan Annear was young enough to be moulded into different expectations. The girl could amuse Faye. But Brooke was unlikely to countenance such a proposal. She had refused to come to the funeral, pleading a headache and saying she would be of better use minding Lottie and Faye and tending to Alec, so the staff of both households, who had known Leslie Annear better than she had, could attend the funeral. Next moment Ben rejected the idea. There was still plenty of time to produce a son. Brooke would probably come round eventually.

Elena had a daily help. When the Annear children began to rub their eyes and threaten to cry, Maisie Clennick, an ordinary young housewife and a relative of Mrs Eathorne from the shop, took them upstairs for a nap. Elena made her way to Emilia and Ben. Her pure-toned voice was sad and contained. 'Poor things. It was getting too much for them. Emilia, I'd like to thank you for helping with the fund that's been set up for Alan and Martha.' She omitted that it was she herself who had started the fund. 'I think a few words needs to be said about it. I wonder, Mr Harvey, could I prevail upon you to call for order and read out this little speech I've written on this notepaper? I'm not really any good at that sort of thing.'

'Of course, Miss Rawley. It will be my pleasure.' Ben smiled down on her, comparing her sweet unassuming looks and shy, faltering manner to Emilia's unconscious magnetic sensuality. Elena Rawley had only a year's advantage on Em but her old-fashioned respectability made her seem older. Her trim figure was buried by a quantity of unflattering clothes of serviceable quality, a deliberate decision, no doubt. He gazed at her long enough to make her blush and turn to Emilia as if looking for reassurance.

Emilia tilted her face so Elena could not see her hiss at him. 'Get on with it, Ben!'

He grinned back, showing amusement at her annoyance over his attempt to charm the dear little spinster. As children, even though at that time her father had held the lower position of Alec's cowman, Emilia had been bossy with him, refusing to take into account his superior position. It was good to be back on familiar ground with her.

Ben picked up a serving spoon and banged it on the table. A hush descended almost at once. His speech was well received as he confirmed the grief of the occasion and thanked all those who had contributed to the Annear children's fund, which stood, so far, at nearly fifty pounds; a generous amount during these times when recession and uncertainty were looming in the country. 'I'm sure everyone will agree that Miss Rawley will know best about what to do with the money and all else concerning the children's interests. I'm also sure that you'll all agree that Miss Rawley deserves to be congratulated for her splendid efforts and that we should resolve to support her in every way.'

A wave of accord went round from those in the room and those listening out in the hall. Elena thanked him and looked a little lost. Emilia squeezed her hand. She didn't have a close friendship with the saintly Miss Rawley but she had total respect for her. 'Don't worry. You'll do the right thing.'

'Yes,' Elena said bravely. 'All that's required is to wait on the Lord. I'm afraid I haven't had the time to enquire yet about Mr Harvey. How is he?'

'Well, the district nurse is pleased with his progress.' While the women fell into conversation, with others listening in about Alec's injuries and what was required in nursing him, Ben excused himself and went outside for a smoke.

Jim took the opportunity of following him round the back of the house, where there was a good view up the valley to Ford Farm. At first Jim pretended not to notice his quarry. He lit a cigarette, as if he too had simply slipped outside with the same intention. Then he approached the arrogant Ben Harvey, who had never welcomed him and his twin coming to Ford Farm. Ben Harvey was observing him through narrowed eyes, as if he was something disgusting.

Jim braced himself to be humble and subservient. It was necessary if he was going to succeed in his plan to get away from Druzel Farm and the suffocating presence of the Eathornes. He'd encouraged his sister to accept Wally Eathorne's interest in her, thinking the apparently amiable farmer's son and his settled father would allow him to have a say in the running of the little farm, but he hadn't been prepared for the Eathornes' territorial passion for the scrap of land that had been farmed by generations of their fore-bears. He loathed them. Sara always took her husband's side, leaving him feeling small and rejected, and he was beginning to loathe her too.

One answer to his problem was to ask the squire for his old job back on the far larger bordering land, but that would be too humiliating. He had been thinking of moving away from the area, and then Leslie Annear had been killed. The Annear cottage and workshop would soon be cleared out and lying empty. Although not a trained craftsman, Jim was good with his hands. He was an expert at drystone walling and he could turn his hand to general building work. He was sure that with hard graft and careful planning he could build up a successful business. He had made extra money this week making good the storm damage at several addresses – but he had rebuilt old Mr Quick's garden shed for free as the pensioner was one of the few locals who paid him any civility.

A new future beckoned. All he had to do was get over this one huge hurdle. And it meant going cap in hand to a man he hated to ask if he could take over Leslie Annear's tenancy.

'Mr Harvey.' Jim slightly bowed his head as he spoke. 'Can I have a word with you?'

Ben sneered. He would have told Killigrew to skulk off, using a choice swear word, if not for being at a wake. He blew out cigar smoke lazily between his lips. 'I don't think so.'

'Please,' Jim returned quickly, fearing someone would witness him humbling himself as well as in eagerness to say his piece. He couldn't prevent the hope shining out of his deep blue eyes. 'I know we don't get along, but please hear me out. I know this is hardly the time and place but I'd like to put in a request to take over the Annear place. I've got money for the rent. I save. I can pay you three months' rent in advance. More if you want. And I'd give the Annear kids a good price for their father's furniture and tools.'

'You must be mad, Killigrew, if you'd think I'd have you living on my land. I wouldn't rent you a cup of dirty water if you were on fire. Now clear off. Get back to shovelling cow shit, where you belong.'

Jim's instinct was to lunge across the few feet of paved path and punch his old enemy in the face. He felt he had been delivered a physical blow to the guts. He thought he would choke on the bile rising in his throat. He drew desperately on his pride; he wouldn't allow this man to see him grovel, see him wounded and bitter. 'Well.' He brought his cigarette up to his mouth, only his shaking hand betraying his discomfort and fury. 'I'd an idea you'd say that. It was just a thought, that's all.'

'You've never had a decent thought in your life, Killigrew.'

'Nor have you, Ben Harvey,' Jim seethed. 'Some day someone will bring you down. Watch out it isn't me, I'd enjoy that pleasure. But with your rotten ways 'tis more likely you'll do it all by yourself.'

Chapter Four

Alec woke with a start as something was rammed between his teeth. He instinctively fended off the intrusion and groaned as pain cut through his ribs and where his hand had rubbed a cut near his mouth. 'What the... ?'

He tried to focus but it was some time before his sight cleared. Then he saw Lottie in her nurse's play clothes. Faye was with her, a tidy little thing in a knitted dress and embroidered cardigan, her black hair shiny and sleek, staying back shyly from the bed.

'Daddy! Keep still.' With determination, Lottie lowered a pencil towards his face. 'Be a good patient. I'm trying to take your temp'ture.'

'What? For goodness sake! Get out, Lottie! Go downstairs. Where's your mother?' Alec hadn't meant to bawl so loudly. Lottie jumped back from the couch, her reaction hurt and sulky, then she fled from the bedroom with Faye scampering after her. Alec was sorry about his anger, but he was also peeved his daughter hadn't been kept under control.

'God in heaven, what have I done to deserve this?' he muttered, reaching out from the couch for a drink of water to soothe his horribly dry and bitter palate. The doctor said it was the result of shock. Sometimes it was worse than his aches and pain. The food that Emilia and the district nurse insisted he eat, broths, savoury jellies, stews, eggs and milk puddings, all tasted foul. He was dizzy and every small movement was an effort. The migraines he got were enough to blast his head open. He moaned as he got a grip on the glass. He saw two glasses. He blinked, startled. Then shouted and swore as his fingers slipped and the water spilled over his neck and the glass crashed to the floor. The glass did not break but it rolled back and forwards on the carpet, as if mocking him.

Brooke hurried into the room. 'Alec. I'm sorry if the girls were annoying you. They've raced off to Lottie's room.' The concern in her mild American accent softened even more. 'Oh my goodness! Don't worry. I'll soon mop you up.'

Alec liked Brooke. She was without airs and thought herself no better than any other housewife in Hennaford. She put the latest fashions on her neat, sparely shaped body but wore them without show. She'd kept her gold-flecked, light-brown hair in the same short bob from when she'd first met Ben in Ypres, Belgium, where they had been paying homage to the war graves of relatives. 'Thanks,' he said, his voice husky and raw, after she had put the glass up on the veneered davenport and dried his skin carefully with a towel. 'Where's Emilia?'

'She's gone to Leslie Annear's funeral, remember? I'm in sole charge. Sorry for neglecting you. You'll need a dry shirt.'

She went to his double wardrobe. All the furniture in this, the master bedroom in the Victorian part, were gems of the period in walnut or mahogany. The chairs had pierced carved backs and slender cabriole legs and, like the couch, were upholstered in powder-blue velvet. The huge tester bed had gold and ivory floral needlework friezes and luxurious flowing drapes. Brooke liked this house with its dual personality, its thick uneven walls and ceiling rafters in the original quarters and the smooth half-panelled walls and moulded ceilings in the newer part, far better than her own modern furnished home. She was beginning to like Alec more than Ben. Alec might be getting a bit grumpy – and scatty, as the locals would say – but he was a man of principle, of genuine kindness, who had taken many an underdog under his protection, while Ben, she had come to see more and more, was shallow and selfish.

'I forgot about the funeral. I seem to forget a lot of things these days.'

'What you need, Alec, is a holiday. Ben and I go to Paris twice a year and we often go up to London and elsewhere. Last year we had that fantastic fortnight in my homeland and then we went on to New York. Faye loved it. We were away for months. I lost my second baby on the ship on the way back.' Her last words were delivered slowly and sadly, then she shook her head as if to dismiss her loss as nothing.

'You're still grieving for both your babies, aren't you? I know how you feel.'

The pain in her heart showed in the wistfulness and bewilderment of her expression. 'It can't be anything as bad as when you lost Jenna, but I'd liked to have had two little bodies to bury. Somewhere to go to remember them. Names on headstones to prove they'd actually once existed. Ben thinks… well, I mustn't get maudlin.'

'And the funeral today, even though it's for an adult, has made it hard for you. I understand that too.'

'That's what I like about you, Alec,' she said, bringing the fresh shirt to him. 'You're such a deep thinker and that makes you more perceptive than the average man. Come on then, sit up. I'll help you pull off your wet things.'

Alec clamped his hands across his body. 'I can't ask you to do that, Brooke.'

'Don't be silly. I'm a married woman and you're my brother-in-law, so it's hardly improper.' She laughed. 'Sometimes you're a little old-fashioned.'

'I'm not,' he protested good-humouredly, letting his hands fall away in free sweeping movements. 'I'll let you sign your name on my plaster.' Brooke was an uplifting sort of woman and for the first time since his accident he felt encouraged. The moment his strength returned he'd be able to get about with the pair of wooden crutches waiting for his use.

'Now that's something more of the way Emilia would like to see you look. She's been anxious about you. Thinks you're too quiet even for someone recovering from a bad accident. In a way, she'd have been pleased to witness your fit of temper just now. Shows you're feeling a little less apathetic. She felt bad about leaving you today for so long. Emilia's devoted to you.'

Alec said nothing for a while. Emilia gave him every consideration. Sometimes she behaved as if she was over-compensating for something and it didn't feel right. It made him uneasy and this worried him because he couldn't understand why. Their happy marriage was often remarked on, in the village and socially when they mixed with more influential people in Truro and further abroad. 'She wouldn't be happy about the way I shouted at Lottie.' He struggled to sit up straight, wincing as he reached for his shirt buttons. 'She spoils her.'

'Don't you? Here, let me do that for you.'

'Of course, sometimes. But Lottie's as hard as nails. She doesn't need fussing over.'

'She's certainly a lot different to Faye. I think Ben wishes our daughter was more of a tomboy.' Brooke started unfastening the buttons of his shirt. She felt his skin was hot and feverish where her fingers brushed his chest and arms. 'I don't think you're drinking enough. I'll see you get some water after this.'

'You should have been a nurse. You're gentler than the district nurse is. She's pretty fierce. And the questions she asks me.' He rolled his soft grey eyes. 'She's enough to embarrass a soldier.'

'I'm sure Emilia's gentle with you. And I bet you enjoy having all this female attention.' Brooke thought he'd be more comfortable if he was helped to freshen up but it would be out of order for her to suggest it. He could only shift a fraction at a time and she patiently guided his movements. His badly bruised chest was thick with crisp dark hairs and was broader and more muscled than Ben's. There was something splendidly animal about him, and despite his injuries he exuded virility and a noble strength. Suddenly she was aware that she was keeping her brother-in-law half naked, wearing just socks and trousers, the cloth of the left leg cut from ankle nearly to the thigh and fastened with large safety pins to accommodate the plaster around his broken leg. For the moment he was vulnerable and under her power. This new sense excited her. She had never felt this way with Ben. Ben had always been good to her but he had always been the master in their marriage, making all the important decisions, and lately because she was unwilling to be fully intimate with him in case she got pregnant, she had been feeling defenceless and inferior. This new awareness of Alec would be disturbing if she didn't welcome it.

Alec showed no signs of noticing anything different about her. She was pleased about this as she slid the sleeves of the clean shirt up over his arms, folded the collar and secured the buttons down his front, for if he attempted to flirt with her she thought she just might reciprocate with eagerness. In the same way as with the wet shirt, he wasn't bothering with cufflinks. He started to fold up the sleeves. 'Are you going to be warm enough? I'm know you're hot but if the temperature drops you might feel cold. I don't want you getting a chill. Shall I drape a sweater round your shoulders?'

'No, thanks. I'm roasting,' he said emphatically. 'But how about one of my mother-in-law's shawls?'

It was unusual for Alec to bother with funny witticisms and she laughed. 'I'll pour you a full glass of water, then in a little while I'll go downstairs and make us both a nice cup of tea. How does that sound?'

'Oh, I think I can manage that. And just to please you I'll eat a slice of cake. I'm suddenly tempted by the lingering aroma of cinnamon from Tilda's baking this morning.'

Lottie edged into the room, with Faye her shadow. 'I've done you a drawing, Daddy,' she whispered uncertainly. 'To make you feel better.'

'Bring it here, darling. It's working already. I am feeling better.' It was Brooke whom Alec was smiling and looking at while he spoke.

Chapter Five

Emilia was driving along the Newquay coast road. 'You've gone very quiet, my love.' She glanced at Lottie, who was sitting rigidly beside her, her arms crossed in front of her sturdy body, her fingers gripping the opposite sleeves of her cardigan. 'You were chatting all the way until we saw the sea.'

Lottie did not answer. She was refusing to answer. The telltale signs were her drawn brows and the stubborn tightening of her lips. If Emilia's mother was with them she would have remarked, with the pride and indulgence given only to grandparents, and which would encourage Lottie in her wilfulness, 'There that dear maid goes again. You wouldn't get she to budge now no more 'n if she was old Tolly's ox!'

Emilia changed gear to drive down the steep hill of Watergate Bay. She watched the road carefully but her main concern was to cheer up her daughter and get her out of her mood before they arrived at Roskerne, the home of Alec's brother Tristan. It was where Alec had been recuperating for the last two weeks. One trick with Lottie was to begin a process of elimination. 'Has someone upset you?'

The little scowl hardened.

'Was it Will?'

Last evening, Will had threatened to hold Lottie upside down and shake her to retrieve the spent matchsticks for the model ship he was making and which she had snatched up and clung on to within the confines of her skirt pocket. 'Mum!' he had wailed, when Emilia had reprimanded him over his thunderous threat. 'She won't give them back.'

'She's just a little girl, Will.' This was one of Emilia's stock answers on such an occasion. She hated Lottie being excluded from anything. 'Let her pass the matches to you or something.'

'Why should I? She always gets her own way.' In a temper inherited from Alec's difficult, unkind father, Will had blazed, 'You're turning her into a spoiled brat!'

Dolly and Edwin Rowse, and Tilda Lawry, who had been bringing in a tray of tea to the sitting room, had all laughed at his exasperation. Will had continued, 'You all are, except Father. I bet he's glad to be away from Lottie and is getting some peace and quiet.'

Lottie had smirked at Will but had gone off to play in her room, unusually quiet.

'It can't be Tom. You never get cross with Tom,' Emilia said. 'Did someone upset you at school today?'

Impatient huff.

'Is it—'

'I wish I hadn't come! Daddy won't want to see me,' Lottie blurted out, pouting and thumping her fists on the thick leather upholstery of the old, reliable Ford Coupe.

'Lottie! Of course he will.' They were climbing the steep hill up past the Watergate Bay Hotel, which was near to the cliff edge and overlooked a beach of fine golden-grey sand, on which heavy, frothy white waves of the Atlantic Ocean were charging and breaking like a conquering horde. The surrounding land, apart from the occasional dwelling, was wild with springy turf, golden gorse and pink and purple heather, and spread with creamy yellow primroses.

'Daddy doesn't love me.' Lottie's head was bowed. 'Granny's cross with him.'

'Of course he loves you. You mustn't carry tales to Granny, Lottie. It's not fair to Daddy. He's been through a lot, you know.' Emilia was worried. In this state Lottie would either throw a tremendous tantrum and refuse to get out the car when they stopped, or she would sob as if in the greatest distress. And there was some cause for Lottie to be upset with her father. When Emilia telephoned Roskerne every evening to ask Alec how he was and update him on the events of the farm, Lottie always fussed to speak to him. She would shriek excitedly down the receiver and Alec always chided her. Emilia had tried explaining to Lottie that Daddy was unwell and at the moment couldn't stand shrill noises, but last evening, when Will had got to the telephone first and complained about his sister's behaviour, Alec had refused to speak to Lottie afterwards, saying he had no time for a naughty little girl.

Emilia prayed Lottie wouldn't spoil the visit to Roskerne. She had missed Alec and was eager to join him for the weekend and then take him home. This fortnight had been the longest they had spent apart.

'You're looking forward to playing with Adele, aren't you? If the sun's out tomorrow I'm sure Vera Rose will take you both to play down on the beach.'

'I suppose so.' Lottie straightened out her dark expression a little. 'Will Jonny be there? He's my favourite cousin. He's funny, more fun than anyone I know.'

'Jonny's studying at Oxford, remember? You'll enjoy yourself, sweetheart. You love Uncle Tris. And Aunty Winnie is going to make your favourite strawberry blancmange. Daddy does love you, Lottie, and he will be pleased to see you. Please be a good girl. For Mummy's sake? Eh?'

Lottie eyed her sideways. 'Are you trying to bribe me?'

'Lottie! Where on earth did you get a phrase like that?'

The little girl was giggling now and chewing at the ends of her hair. 'It's something I heard a girl say once to Jonny. I think he wanted to kiss her.'

'Look, nearly there,' Emilia cheerily changed the subject. Eighteen-year-old Jonathan Harvey, Tristan's son from his first marriage, a somewhat uncontrolled individual with handsome film-star looks, had discovered the delights of the fairer sex at an early age and was a diligent pursuer of conquests.

Tristan Harvey had made a very successful second marriage to a war-widowed Harvey cousin. He and Winifred, their child Adele, and Vera Rose Stockley, the sporty, good-natured teenaged daughter from Winifred's first marriage, were waiting for them at the bottom of the steps of Roskerne. It was a solitary, imposing building, a fine example of Victorian flair and innovation. It had been run-down from roof to grounds when Tristan had married Winifred eight years ago but he had brought it all up to excellent order. Only the gardens, exposed here to salt-laden winds, refused to balance the order by providing flourishing trees and healthy blooms.

'How's my little ragamuffin?' Tristan swept Lottie up in his arms. 'You should have brought Faye with you. We'd have had three little girls to amuse us.'

'Yes, yes, Uncle Tris.' Lottie nearly throttled him with a tight hug round his neck. 'Faye could've danced in her tutu. Adele could've read one of her poems. And I could've acted a play for you. Tom pretends he's Long John Silver and me, I'm Cap'n Flint. I make a good parrot.'

'I'm sure you do, poppet. You and Adele can perform something for us anyway before dinner tonight. Hello, Em. It's good to see you.' Tristan was as dark in colouring as his brothers but, unlike Alec and Ben, he was lean in body. Of the three he was the calmest and the friendliest. A neat moustache covered some of the scars he had received from the wounds that had nearly taken his life at Passchendaele. Emilia felt an affinity with Tristan. He had been an officer over her brother, Billy, who had died in battle. He kissed Emilia on both cheeks. 'You're looking a bit stretched. Isn't she, Winnie? Hope you've not been fretting about his nibs in there.'

'How is Alec?' Emilia asked, climbing the wide stone steps.

'As quiet as usual but he's progressing well,' Winifred said, taking her arm and leading her inside the house. 'And I don't just mean that in medical talk. Alec's a wizard on his crutches now and he's been out and about quite a lot. In the gardens, along the cliff path and even down on the beach with Tris, taking photographs by the dozen.'

Emilia was cheered and hopeful. 'Where is he?'

'There.'

Emilia's keen brown eyes followed Winifred's pointing hand. Alec was heading for her from the drawing room, his crutches and good leg conveying him almost as fast as his normal long stride. He was looking better, not so pale and wan. 'Darling!' She ran to him, arms open wide, throwing herself against his broad chest, clinging to him tight.

Relieving himself of one crutch, using her for balance, Alec brought his mouth down on her offered lips. He kissed her as soundly, as intimately, as if they were alone. 'I've missed you,' he whispered, passion and meaning in his words. 'I've missed you so much.'

'Ahem!' Tristan coughed merrily. Vera Rose and the two girls were giggling. Old-fashioned in nature, Winifred was looking down demurely but she was pleased with the exchange of affection. 'Shall we go in for high tea? Emilia, I'm eager to learn how your roses are progressing. I suppose they'll win first prize again at all the horticultural shows this year.'

'Of course they will,' Alec said, regaining his crutch, his gaze still on Emilia and transmitting his desire that she stay close. 'Well, Lottie,' he called to his daughter. 'You're an untidy little mess, as usual. I've missed you too. Let Daddy sit down, then you must give me a hug. I've got something for you. From your uncle's shop. You'll love it.'

'What it is?' Lottie demanded, jigging along at his side, her earlier pique forgotten at the promise of a treat. Uncle Tristan's antique shop in Newquay stocked things called 'curios and collectables', all magical and fascinating to her imaginative mind.

—

'I don't think she liked it,' Alec said, that night in bed. Emilia was just drifting off to sleep, facing him. He had his arm over her and he brushed his fingertips all the way down her bare back, and lower.

'Mmmm?' Emilia murmured dreamily, coming closer for more caresses. 'Again, darling? Did you say something about Lottie?'

He nuzzled her neck, whispering in her ear, making her shiver deliciously. 'I like us having to be more adventurous with me having this plaster on my leg. Lottie? Yes. I don't think she liked the porcelain shoe I gave her. I thought it would make the start of a collection for her.'

Emilia wound her arms around his neck. 'Perhaps it's something she'll appreciate more when she gets older.'

Alec kissed her lips. 'So she was disappointed?'

'She loved those enamel dog brooches she saw in Tris's shop last time we were here. Perhaps she thought you'd got her one of those.' She reached for his mouth.

'There's no pleasing that child.'

'What?' Emilia let her arms fall away from him. Alec had made the remark with irritation and accusation. As a mother defending her young she demanded crossly, 'Is that all that matters to you? It's only a piece of old china. An ornament. Don't Lottie's feelings count?'

'What the hell does that mean?' Alec shied away from her. 'Of course my daughter means everything to me. I can't believe you've just said that.'

'What I'm trying to say, Alec, is that sometimes you behave as if Lottie is something of annoyance to you.' Emilia sounded stern. She didn't want an argument with Alec, but it was time this issue was fully aired.

'Oh, you've been thinking that, have you?' His anger almost scorched the air between them. With as much ease and quickness as his plastered leg would allow he thrust the covers aside and edged himself gingerly to the brink of the bed. 'Bloody charming, I call that, Emilia. Having bad thoughts stewing away inside your head against me.'

Emilia yanked the covers in tightly under her arms so she wasn't exposed to him. It was time Alec was faced with his impatient and indifferent attitude towards Lottie and if he didn't like it, that was too bad. She could feel his anger increasing and the more it did, so was hers. 'You've got no justification in getting all self-righteous, Alec. Think about it, sometimes you act like Lottie doesn't exist. You shut her out. You treat her differently to the boys and to the way you behaved with Jenna. I'm not making a fuss over nothing. Lottie's noticed how grouchy you get with her. You're making her very unhappy.'

'You're talking rubbish! How dare you!' he raged. 'I can't believe you've just said all that. It was here in this room where Jenna first stopped breathing, where we first thought we'd lost her. Never in all my life had I felt at such a loss, had been so scared. Not long afterwards we actually did lose our little girl. And now you're seriously accusing me of not loving our next child? You bitch!'

'What?' Emilia was up on her knees trying to get a grip on him, but he shrugged her off. 'Alec, I'm sorry. I went too far.' She saw that now. Her adoration of Lottie had made her overprotective, and too hard on those who took her precious daughter to task over her persistent mischief. 'I shouldn't have said all that. I'm sorry. I was trying to make you understand how Lottie feels, that's all. How sometimes you seem a little distant to her.'

'Distant? If it's distance you want then you can bloody well have it.' He struggled up on to his good foot and while leaning against the bedpost he pulled on his dressing gown, then reached for his crutches.

Stunned at what she had done, sorry and guilty over his hurt, Emilia wrapped the quilt around her body and hastened round the bed to him. 'Where are you going?'

'Out of this room and far away from you. I need a cigarette.' He was clutching the top of his head. 'I've got a terrible headache now, thanks to you!'

'You can't hobble downstairs at this time of night.' She reached for her negligee. 'Have your cigarette on the balcony. I'll fetch you some aspirin, and then I'll sleep with Lottie. Alec—' She stretched out a hand but didn't dare touch him. He was trembling in a shuddering sort of way. 'I really am sorry.'

Next day Alec refused to talk about the quarrel or leave the room. Sensing she was the cause of the bad feeling, Lottie refused to go in to him. Emilia packed hers and Lottie's things and they went home on their own.

Chapter Six

Upstairs in his house in Cheyne Walk, London, Perry Bosweld had already been busy at his desk for a couple of hours when his housekeeper waddled into his office and laid a wad of morning post down beside him. Also in plodded his daughter's neglected black Labrador cross, Casper, who for some years had taken up refuge with the housekeeper in the kitchen. 'Anything interesting, Mrs Nicholson?'

'Looks like the usual three or four letters you get every day from your charities, inviting you to give talks at meetings and raise funds for 'em. You work too hard, Mr B.' In her bright floral overall, her hand-knitted, multi-coloured, sleeveless cardigan, a paisley headscarf restraining her dove-grey hair, and beige lisle stockings and sturdy flat shoes, Mrs Nicholson began her day's prattlings. 'There's one from the local archery club. 'Tis time you went out again and contended a tournament. Haven't polished a new trophy of yours in ages. Want to lose your championship, do you? That'd be a shame. Miss Libby likes to watch you, you know that. You could get her up from that boarding school for a weekend. Give her something to look forward to, it would. I don't think she likes it there. Mind you, she didn't like any of the schools you've put her in. That girl, bless her, doesn't know what she wants and is never likely to. There's a letter from the merry widow Mrs Irene Farley, that painted Jezebel from Sloane Square; she's put her name on the envelope. She's been after you for ages. Well, can't blame her, you're a fine-looking, eligible young man. Hope you'll take no notice of her. I can't stand her and Miss Libby hates her. All glitter and no brains, that woman. There's a letter from the Rose Growers' Association by the look of it. I suppose that's why you're up bright and early, to get out to the greenhouse before this spot of sunshine goes. Forecast's none too good, mind.

'Dr Bosweld's written at last. About time. Anyone'd think Donegal was at the other end of the world and not just 'cross the Irish sea. Pretty stamp. She dashed the letter off quick, her writing's a scrawl, enough to make you think a spider fell in the ink. Envelope's light, so she couldn't have bothered with more than one page. Just to say she's arrived safely and settled into her new practice, I s'pose. Don't know how long she'll last there. Six months would be a record for her. I s'pose 'tisn't all her fault, there's lots of prejudice against women doctors, I've heard her getting cross about it. Shame, it is. Good doctors are needed everywhere. Oh, well, she's always busy, busy that one. I s'pose she'll be begging you and Miss Libby to jump on a ship and visit her. Be a good thing if you did. The both of you need a change of scene. You're wasting away 'cause you refuse to let me feed you up and the young lady's always as pale as a wet weekend. There's some lovely countryside over there, you know, 'tis said to be as green as grass. Well, I mean it's got lots of grass. Think there's an invitation to dinner somewhere among that lot. It's a very formal-looking affair. Now, Mr B, I'll have a full cooked breakfast ready in fifteen minutes. Along to the table with you by then, you understand? Can't be doing with having to climb the stairs and to keep calling you. Can we,

Casper? I'm piling up your plate this morning and I won't be accepting anything less than an empty plate. Understand?'

'I do. Thank you, Mrs Nicholson,' Perry said absently, having barely taken in a word, as was the norm.

As she passed through the doorway of the Queen Anne house, Mrs Nicholson cheerfully threw over her stout shoulder, 'Oh, and there's a letter from Cornwall.'

'What?' Perry threw down his fountain pen and rifled through the pile of letters, making some hit the floor, until he found what he was hoping for. Yes! The ordinary white envelope had Emilia's handwriting on it. He tore it open. The letter began, *Dear Perry.* He read the greeting twice. This was the first time she had written to him only and not included Libby. He feverishly sought for clues as to why, going on past the usual *I hope you and Libby are well,* etc... *Did you read in the newspapers about the gale that hit the West Country last month? Cornwall fared the worse and Hennaford suffered a tragedy.* There was an account of the death of the local carpenter Leslie Annear. Perry remembered the likeable young father. *Alec was injured just after the wind and rain eased off. He suffered...* Perry read about Alec's injuries and how he was recuperating at Roskerne. *Of course you may possibly have heard about this from Tristan.* Tristan Harvey was involved in some of the same ex-servicemen's charities as Perry; Perry was chairman or president of half a dozen. There was the mention of roses. On their last meeting alone Perry had given her a mass of multi-coloured roses. *I'm expecting a wonderful season with my roses and I'm planning to exhibit Crimson Sun in this year's village show.* Perry's gorgeous smile could have lit up every room in every house in Cheyne Walk. He had sent the original shrub rose as a bare-root to Emilia to plant. It was of the deepest red, the colour that epitomized love, and had a velvety property, with a strong, haunting traditional rose scent.

The letter was signed, *Yours sincerely, Emilia Harvey*. Perry pressed the letter to his lips. To other eyes it was just a letter from a friend relating some sad circumstances and information about a hobby, but to him it was what he had been waiting for during eight lonely, soul-leeching years. Emilia had only sent cards with a short note enclosed in them before and they were always signed from *Alec and Emilia Harvey*. Alec's name was not included this time. Perry sensed loneliness in the letter today. Emilia was lonely. It was a sign he had been waiting for, hoping for, longing for. He loved Emilia more than the breath in his body, but when he had left Ford House he had vowed to himself that he would not return to Cornwall or do anything to try to break up her happy marriage unless he was sure she needed him. Obviously her marriage wasn't as happy as before. Emilia was at the farm and Alec was taking a prolonged stay at Roskerne, fourteen miles away – too far for easy visits. It was unusual for Alec to stay away from home. He didn't socialize much and went down to the village pub just once a week. Something had changed. It might be a temporary thing and he sensed Emilia – his Em, his darling, wonderful Em – was confused, so he wouldn't pack himself off down to the beautiful Celtic county at the bottom of the country immediately. He'd wait for one more sign. And pray that he'd get it. Then he would go to Emilia. Without delay.

Chapter Seven

The night was disturbed by a cacophony of terrible, chilling proportions. Emilia, sleepless and brooding about Alec, and wondering how Perry had found her letter, leapt out of bed. The terror and cackling that had been unleashed could come from only one place and the urgent, ferocious barking of the dogs meant only one thing. In her dressing gown and the first pair of shoes she grabbed, Emilia tore down to the den, snatched up a shotgun and ran to the henhouses.

She reached what she was dreading to see, a mindless carnage, and had the shotgun loaded and ready to kill the creature decimating her poultry. Her rage knew no limits. This was all so unnecessary. Someone – Will, for he had been responsible last evening for making sure every door of the henhouses were securely latched – had made a terrible and costly lapse in his duty.

Her father was there beside her in his pyjamas, holding up a lantern. Dozens of hens were dead, their heads bitten off, their feathers scattered in bloodied heaps, and many more needed to be humanely finished off. The smell of death and fear and blood hung heavily in the air. The sheepdog and the Jack Russells ran about the vicinity, sniffing and watchful, excited and agitated.

'He's still about here somewhere,' Emilia whispered, referring to the dog fox who had caused the slaughter. This was not the work of a vixen. A vixen was more likely to slip in during daylight and daringly snatch an unsuspecting bird and steal away with it to feed her cubs.

She looked to all sides and Edwin Rowse swung the lantern in time with her for the telltale signs of a pair of sharp, vicious, glassy eyes. He didn't speak, he just stared, hoping to see the culprit that was suspected also of raiding Druzel Farm in the same manner two nights before, and he didn't try to take the shotgun from his daughter. Emilia was a keen shot, and light and fast on her feet. If anyone could pick off the fox, she could. Will and Tom and Dolly were there now, keeping back out of the way.

Suddenly there was a terrified squawk. One of the Jack Russells leapt straight across Emilia's path. She whirled in that direction and hared after it. She saw the fox running, coming out from where it had hidden behind a coop, a live hen dangling from its mouth. After a few seconds she halted, stood stock still, raised the gun to her shoulder, aimed and fired.

The fox dropped.

Dead.

She 'broke' the gun safely and hurried across the few yards of ground and in one swift, efficient movement put the young hen out of its misery. Sighing in anger, she shook her head over the brownish-red, bushy-tailed, larger body. This sort of occurrence wasn't rare on a farm and it was something all farmers hated, but in her case, with one of the horses lame and more cattle than usual recently needing to be 'drenched' for digestive troubles, it made her feel that she wasn't coping without Alec. Damn the fox! Damn Alec! In daylight she would shoot other pests to the remaining poultry, carrion crows and magpies, and hang them up as a sign to their friends to beware!

Edwin tapped on her shoulder. 'It's all over, maid. That was a good shot. You got him clean through the heart.'

Emilia tilted her head and when she saw her father's kindly, rugged face the tension went out of her. He was a small, stooped man, his weathered face adorned with old-fashioned side whiskers, his hair donkey-grey. He wasn't rattled at all by what had happened: it was just another of nature's vagaries to him. And although he had hurried from his bed, he had swept on his worn-out tweed cap, and his hooded brown eyes exuded reassuring strength. The farm was being managed very well; there was nothing for Alec to be concerned about or for her to chide herself over. And although foxes like this one were a pain and a nuisance, she enjoyed the sight of a family of cubs playing near their earths, and the occasional sleek, proud-faced creature that might be encountered in the lanes or padding as a free spirit through the meadows.

The boys and Dolly were gathering up the carcasses of the hens. 'I'll speak to you later, Will,' she said to her elder son, who for once kept his dark head down, guilty-fashion.

She drew Dolly away. 'Mother, you don't have to help with this.'

'I've not gone soft. I'm not an old woman yet.' Dolly wrinkled her formidable brow, and in the silvery light of the dawn, she looked as if this or nothing else would disgust or alarm her. She wasn't an emotional woman and she surprised Emilia the next moment by displaying a glitter of tears and having a shake in her voice. 'You haven't got your husband with you and I know you're worrying over him. We're all worried about Alec. His behaviour towards Lottie is strange considering he's lost a child. You and I bear the mark of that loss too, as we do your brother, Billy. Lottie needs you more now because her daddy seems aloof to her, and you need plenty of support. I'm here to help you, Emilia, dear, whenever and wherever you need it. A good mother will do anything for her children. Anything at all to make sure they're happy.'

Chapter Eight

Jim Killigrew was taking his employer's cob to the village blacksmith to be re-shod. When he trotted past Ford Farm, where he had been treated kindly, and more as a member of the family than the way his sister did now, he was tempted again to turn into the yard and ask for his old job back. Or he could ask Alec to recommend him to another farmer next market day, somewhere far away from Hennaford.

But Jim had always solved his own problems and he was on the point of trying something entirely different, perhaps the merchant navy. He could become a sailor, like his father had been. He ought to branch out, see something of the world. It was an exciting prospect. He'd never have stayed in Hennaford if it weren't for Sara anyway. Her preoccupation with her new family, her declaration that she owed the faithful, plodding Wally Eathorne everything for marrying her, cut deeply into Jim. She owed *Wally Eathorne* everything? Who the hell had been looking after her between the time of their parents' deaths and her marriage?

Before he left Hennaford he'd like just one chance to show those he worked and lodged with, and certain villagers, like the other snobbish Eathorne brothers and the egotistical Ben Harvey, that he could make something of himself, that he was a worthy individual. He had been inclined to be confrontational in his youth and some people had expected him to get into trouble, by fighting and perhaps stealing and even being sent to prison. Once or twice he had nearly strayed down a thorny road but, apart from his fist fight with Ben Harvey, something – his pride, he guessed, a streak more stubborn than his temperamental-ness – had stopped him.

A heavy smoker, Jim lit a cigarette on the ride down the short, steep hill after Ford Farm. At the bottom was the ford and the horse's big-hoofed, short legs barely made a splash through the trickle of dull water, which was ferried by leats through the high hedgerows. Then he came to a fork in the rough-paved lane. To the right was a narrow, twisting way, the shortest route into the village. To the left, round a bend and up a short climb, was Ford House. Jim's thoughts didn't often go to others but they drifted to Elena Rawley and her two orphaned charges. Village opinion was that she was doing a good job with them. He respected her for that.

While waiting for the blacksmith to complete his work Jim called in at the shop to buy cigarettes. The doorbell had a merry tinkle. The shop was a cosy place full of homely smells, where just about every type of commodity could be bought or ordered; a much-loved local meeting place, but Jim had never felt he belonged here. He waited behind Ben Harvey's attractive foreign wife to be served. Brooke Wilder Harvey always exchanged a greeting with him. Jim always addressed her back respectfully, but as if her equal. It irked him to observe how subservient Gilbert Eathorne was as he carried her shopping basket to the door.

'*Why don't you use your nasty gossiping tongue to lick the floor before her every step?*' Jim whispered to himself.

Gilbert Eathorne was back behind the counter in double quick time. 'Busy on the farm, are they?' he asked with an interrogatory lift of bushy brows.

'Forty Players Weights,' Jim snapped. It seemed to him the shopkeeper was eyeing him as if suspicious he had lifted something. Jim had had his hands in his corduroy trouser pockets when Eathorne had gone to the door and he had not moved – it must be obvious. Seething over this and the high-handed presumption that he was slacking on Druzel Farm, he snatched up the cigarettes and change and banged his way out of the shop. On the way down the wide, mismatched granite steps he used the side of his boot to push the Eathorne's ageing, slumbering ginger cat over the edge of the penultimate step. The cat was unhurt – Jim would never hurt an animal – and it hit the ground on its four paws with an affronted hiss. 'Bugger off!' Jim hissed back. Lighting up again, he resolved that from now on he would get his cigarettes, and everything else he needed, in Truro and deny the Eathornes his custom. That cheered him.

Across the road was another favourite meeting place. Surrounded on three sides by cottages owned by Alec Harvey was a concrete court, in the middle of which was an ornate, cast-iron pump where the housewives met up most days to get their water supply. Two women were there now, dumpy and plain, in pinnies, slippers and headscarves over their curlers. Jim didn't call a word to them. Apart from old Mr Quick, he didn't feel he had a friend among anyone in Hennaford. Years ago old Mr Quick had lost his wallet after drawing his pension, and without thinking twice Jim, who had found it under the village seat opposite the pub, had returned it to him. The old man had returned his honesty with genuine friendship. It meant a lot to Jim. Before returning to the forge he would call on the old boy, have a mug of tea with him, see if he wanted any little jobs done. Wally and his miserable father could complain as much as they liked at how long it had taken him to take the cob to and from the blacksmith.

On the ride back, in the lane he saw a pair of small, fair-haired, well-dressed children, hand in hand and heads down, hurrying towards him. It was Alan and Martha Annear. Without looking up they made to skirt round the cob. Jim reined in and jumped down on the dusty, animal-fouled ground. 'Where're you two off to then?'

'Home,' Alan said bluffly, scowling, drawing his sister, whose thin infant legs were already finding the trek hard to cope with, slightly behind him. They reminded Jim of the times he had been forced to protect Sara and himself in the workhouse, but back then he and his twin had, a little more fortunately, been orphaned a few years older than this pair.

Jim bent from the waist to speak to them. 'I'm afraid you haven't got your old home any longer, my handsomes. Your daddy's in heaven. Up there with your mother. You'll have to go back to Miss Rawley.' He didn't have the heart to tell them someone else was now living in their former home.

Tears welled up in Alan's puckered eyes and Martha squeezed in tighter behind him. 'I broked a window. I didn't mean to.'

'You've got nothing to worry about there. Miss Rawley's a kind lady. She'll understand, she won't mind. But she'll get worried if she finds you're gone missing. Tell you what, how'd you both like to ride back on Cuby? I'll lead her reins. We'll have you there in no time.'

Alan nodded. He shrank back, however, when Jim made to lift him up, and Martha shrieked. Jim spent another two minutes reassuring them. Then he gathered them up together and positioned a child on each of his broad shoulders. 'Right then. You can still hold on to each other. Cuby will follow on after us. Let's make a game of it, shall we? You count up to ten and we'll see how far we've gone.'

Jim's head was almost crushed as the children clung round him to each other. He could hear Alan counting under his breath. When he got to ten, he stayed silent. Jim said, 'Well, you must have a good view up there. What can you see?'

'Cows,' Alan said after a long hesitation.

'Good. Anything else?'

'Trees. Hills. The ford!' Alan exclaimed, becoming more confident.

'Flows,' Martha said in a whispery voice. Jim assumed she meant flowers. The hedges and verges were fully fledged with primroses, celandines, wild violets, pink campion, bluebells.

'Aunty,' Alan said nervously, his small body becoming rigid.

'Who?'

'Aunty 'Lena.'

The worried calls and light running steps of Elena Rawley could be heard, presumably echoing down the hill from Ford House. 'Alan! Martha! Dears, where are you?'

Jim rounded the last bend and there was the fork in the lane. Elena Rawley pelted round the bend at the bottom of the hill and cried with relief. 'Oh! Mr Killigrew! How wonderful. Thank you so much. Alan, Martha, you've had me so worried. I was afraid you'd got lost.'

'Alan told me about the broken window,' Jim said, amused at the sight of the demure young lady pink-faced and puffing and her well-worn clothes somewhat in disarray.

She wore her glossy, mid-brown hair in an unbecoming bun and pins were sticking out of it – a few lengths had escaped altogether. 'I've explained how you won't be cross with them.'

'Of course I'm not cross, Alan and Martha.' Elena was breathing heavily. It had only been a short run but her anxiety had chewed up all her energy. 'It was an accident. Listen, Maisie has baked you some fairy cakes. Would you like one, with a glass of milk?'

'Yes, please,' Alan said. His sister nodded, and as Jim tilted his blond head he was pleased to see Martha smiling. He was aware of the good influence Elena Rawley had over the children from Alan's good manners. Alan added, 'Can we ride the horse now?'

'Course you can,' Jim said, swinging the children towards the dark brown creature's strong back.

'Can we ride the horse now, please?' Elena corrected in a kind tone.

Jim inspected the broken lower sash window of the parlour while Elena settled the children in the back garden with their promised treat. She came to him, standing back a little, all gratefulness and shy smiles. 'I've telephoned the glazier. I'm afraid he can't come until tomorrow. I thought I'd put up a piece of wood or something until then. There should be something appropriate in the shed, I'm sure.'

'I'll do it for you. Weather's good, something of the right size taped up will do. Save banging nails into your window frame. I'll sweep up the glass and put it in the dustbin.'

'Thank you, Mr Killigrew. That would be a relief. I'll pay you for your time and trouble.'

He gazed at for her some moments, liking the way that the more he stared the more she blushed. She swallowed and he watched her throat move, a throat as white as lilies and as smooth as silk, he reckoned. Then he remembered she was one of the few people who showed him respect, the only one to call him Mr Killigrew. 'I wouldn't dream of taking money. Be neighbourly, that's what the Good Book says, doesn't it? I've been looking at your perimeter wall. It needs some attention. I'm a dab hand at drystone walling. Matter of a little rebuilding, that's all. I'll do that for you too, in a few days' time, for a small charge.'

'How very kind of you.' Elena gave a brief smile, ducked her head and blushed again. 'Thank you very much. Can I fetch you a cup of tea?'

Jim was already on his way to the shed. 'I'll come to the kitchen when I'm done.' Knowing its way home, Cuby the cob had trotted off. Wally and Eustace Eathorne would be angry. Too bad. Jim had been up and grafting before dawn and if it pleased him he'd stay out until milking time. They could dock his miserable wages for all he cared.

Elena's insides had turned to water. It felt as if a surging sea was frothing away inside her. She put the kettle on the hob and hurried into the parlour to brush up the few splinters of glass on the windowsill and carpet, hoping, praying as ardently as when in chapel or last thing at night, that she would be finished before Jim Killigrew arrived on the other side of the window and she found herself under his keen, blue-eyed scrutiny again.

She had seldom given any thought to men in respect of romance or gaining a husband. While her father was alive she had felt protected and settled. Now if there was an occasion in which she found herself alone with a man, she didn't know how to behave. And as Jim Killigrew was a single young man, just a few years her junior, a strong-bodied, attractive man, and supposedly a sort of Rudolph Valentino – irresistible to women, apparently – she felt horribly exposed and vulnerable. Some men in the village had no time for him, but most of the single girls were happy to encourage him and some mothers considered him a prospective son-in-law. It hadn't occurred to Elena that if Jim was an ardent womanizer he was keeping his activities outside the village, for he had dated no one locally nor, as of yet, had taken a girl home to Druzel Farm; the gossips would have known. She had also forgotten that the only female inhabitant of Hennaford he had ever publicly shown an interest in was she herself, years ago, when her father had stamped it out.

If only she could take Jim's tea outside to him, thank him again, and he would leave. She felt guilty then, feeling her wish to be uncharitable. She guessed he would prefer his tea in a mug and she put one on the big, round kitchen table, and a tea plate and a plate of cakes. She thought to call the children inside, at least then she wouldn't be alone with him, but usually they were fretful and clingy and now, for once, they were playing happily with the toys she had bought for them from their fund, so she left them to it.

She was correct in assuming that her unanticipated handyman wouldn't take long in finding the materials he needed and in completing the makeshift repair and the clearing up, so she made the tea and left it to brew. Elena's heart beat a fast march while she listened to him washing his hands at the back kitchen sink. It nearly leapt out of her chest when he knocked, two loud raps, on the connecting door.

She was forced to clear her throat. 'C-come in.'

Jim entered. He had taken off his boots. 'All done.' He put a handful of hairpins on the pretty pink and yellow floral oilcloth over the table, then bent down to retrieve two more from the tiled floor. 'Here. If ever you get lost the search party'd only have to follow a trail of these.'

She turned red and smiled faintly, gulping in embarrassment. She could cope better with this if he wasn't so... she didn't know what the right expression was but supposed it had something to do with the Great Unmentionable. 'Thank you... um, do sit down.'

He pulled out a Windsor chair and sat with his legs stretched out to the side of the table. His cigarettes and matches were uncomfortable in his trouser pocket and he pulled them out and laid them on the table.

'I'll get an ashtray...' She dithered. 'I have one somewhere.'

Jim raised a hand. Elena found her eyes rooted on it. It was a large, tough hand, clean after the scrub he'd given it, but calloused and dark. 'My sister won't allow me to smoke indoors. I wouldn't expect to in someone else's house.' He paused. 'Not yours anyway. It's a grand house. The third grandest house in Hennaford. You keep it nice.'

'Do I?' She gazed at him, somehow mesmerized, coming to with a sickening jolt for he was smiling at her. A deep smile. 'Tea!'

She poured from the biggest pot she had, which was covered with a knitted cosy bought at one of the numerous bazaars she had organized, her lips pulled in, concentrating, trying to stop her hand from trembling and trying not to pour tea on the table.

'A dash of milk. I'll help myself to sugar, three lumps,' Jim said, taking her discomfort as eagerness to be hospitable.

'What? I mean, I beg your pardon?' Elena said miserably. She poured tea for herself, it was only polite to join him. She sat down at an angle where she hoped her burning face was not on display.

Jim helped himself from the glass sugar bowl and the little blue and white china jug. He stirred his tea thoughtfully. 'The children are quiet. Are they all right?'

From where she was sitting, Elena could see them through the window. 'Th-they're building a camp.' Oh, why couldn't she speak normally? And must her face keep burning? She was sure she must be a terrible shade of scarlet. A few more moments of this agony and she'd spontaneously combust.

'All kids do that. I've made a tree house for my sister's kids. They have a lot of fun in it.' It struck Jim then that children liked him. He had a way with them. He used to play wild laughing games with his nieces and nephew before Sara put a stop to it. She always liked them to be tidy in case someone called at the farm. Overcompensating for her poor origins. Jim could understand that, but kids needed to run riot every now and then. It was natural. He could weep sometimes over the things he had missed out on as a child. All he could remember was regimental training and harsh rules and forever being told he should be grateful for what he got.

Alan and Martha could be heard laughing now. Elena smiled nervously over her teacup.

'They feel safe here,' Jim said. 'You've done 'em well.'

'I hope so, Mr Killigrew.' Elena forced herself to meet his eyes. 'Do have a fairy cake. Or – or perhaps you'd care for something more substantial. I've got a very nice slab of cherry and walnut in the pantry. Would you—?'

'What are you going to do about them?' Suddenly Jim was burning to know the fate of the Annear children.

'Pardon? Who?'

'Alan and Martha. You're not thinking of giving them up to an institution, I hope. No kid deserves that.'

Elena's eyes widened. Jim Killigrew was leaning forward over the table. One quick reach of his long arms and he could grab her if he wished. There was something different about him now. The overt masculinity, and the suspicion and edginess that was a part of him and made some people a little wary of him was still there, but added to it was a sense of something superior and judgemental. She felt it was vital she give the right answer. 'The question of the children's future is on my mind day and night, Mr Killigrew.'

'And?'

'I'll do my very best for them.' Her words came out fast. 'I'll do whatever's right for them. I swear.'

'Good.' He picked up his mug. His expression softened. It softened a lot and Elena scolded herself for thinking him a little frightening. 'I knew you'd say that. You're one of the few people in the world folk can depend on. If you need any help, you only have to ask me. I'll build Alan and Martha a tree house or anything else you'd like for 'em. Yes, a piece of that cake sounds good. Please.'

He was smiling at her. Smiling warmly. Elena got up on feet that felt they were about to disintegrate for she had to walk past him. In the walk-in pantry it took her a few moments to reason what she wanted there. It was good that Jim felt so concerned about Alan and Martha, but what would he say when he learned that she had never planned to keep them, and even if she wanted to – and during these last few weeks she had grown enormously fond of them – she couldn't afford to support herself and two children?

When she brought the cake tin to the table, Jim was quietly gazing down at the floor. He was a planner, always looking ahead, sifting through possibilities. 'I've got Saturday afternoon off. I'll come then and fix your wall. Don't feel shy at asking if you want anything else done as well.'

Trying not to show how unsettling she found his presence, she cut him a large slice of cake. She was thinking about her limited means. She was going to have to pay the glazier, and Alan had wet his bed so often it needed a new mattress. 'Thank you. I was wondering, how much will it cost to have the wall repaired?'

Jim watched a tiny nerve twitch on her forehead. Her skin was bright red. She was round the other side of the table but he fancied he could feel the heat emanating off her. How different she was to Selina Bosweld, his seductress, who had wielded such cruel power over him. Elena was childlike, an innocent. She was a pretty little thing, despite her boring hairstyle and frumpy clothes. 'I'm making you feel uncomfortable. I'll eat and drink outside. I need a smoke anyway.'

'Mr Killigrew...' she said, when he reached the door.

'I know. You don't have to keep saying thank you. There'll be no charge for the wall. I can pick up enough new stone on the moor. It'll be my way of helping you out for what you're doing for the kids. Call me Jim. See you soon, Miss Rawley.'

Chapter Nine

Emilia had also been to the village shop that morning, to choose a birthday card for Perry Bosweld's daughter. She had decided on one with few words, *To wish you a Happy Birthday.* She would simply write in it, *To Libby, Best Wishes from the Harvey Family.* The front of the card had white and red, gold-edged roses and would send a message to Perry too. A clear message that she still loved him. She would add a note, stating that Alec was still at Roskerne. She wanted the comfort of hinting to Perry that she was lonely, and missing him so much.

Their parting had been inevitable. Leaving aside Perry's sister Selina's spiteful, promiscuous behaviour which had caused them to be hounded out of the village, Emilia could never leave Alec, her children or her life at the farm. She had tried, all those years ago, not to fall in love with Perry. She had tried to stop loving him since they'd been apart, but her feelings were too strong and the part of her heart and soul that was Perry's was raw and empty. All she could do was to go on with her life with Alec, loving him with a lesser love, and keep some sort of vague hope.

She had only to close her eyes and she could see Perry as if he was actually with her. She did this now, as she sat on the wooden bench near the Wesleyan chapel, across the road from the Ploughshare, with its deep cobbled court, made pretty by half-barrels of daffodils, hyacinths and polyanthus in full bloom. Perry was unbelievably handsome, his hair dark, his eyes of the deepest blue, but it wasn't his looks she had fallen for. Perry was good and sensitive, open and gregarious. He understood people and would never knowingly hurt anyone's feelings. Libby was in fact Selina's child, her father unknown even by her mother, but to protect his sister and her baby Perry had adopted Libby and loved her as her real father. He had patiently borne Selina's selfish ways. It was easy to like Perry, who never complained about his disablement, his lost right leg and the unsteadiness of his hand that had denied him his surgeon's career. Emilia had formed a bond with him over her dying baby, and while Alec had sought solace after Jenna's death by constant visits to young Louisa Hetherton-Andrews, the daughter of Tristan's tragic first wife (the child's origins unknown to Louisa herself, and Jonny, her half-brother), Emilia had turned to Libby Bosweld, and Perry. Libby had been devastated by the way the villagers had, to her young mind, for no apparent reason unfairly disparaged her aunt, and she never acknowledged the cards sent to her. Perry did, and it was wonderful to see his familiar writing on an envelope two or three times a year. Emilia took a moment more on the bench to remember his beautiful smile and tender touch.

'When's the squire coming home then, maid?'

Emilia opened her eyes to see old Mr Quick shuffling to sit next to her. Most of the older villagers still referred to her in the same terms as when she was a seventeen-year-old dairymaid living among them, and it was how she preferred it. She would have guided old Mr Quick down but she was sensitive to his pride. He leaned his knobbly walking stick against the low garden hedge behind them.

'I'm not sure, Mr Quick.' She raised her voice close to his ear, angling her face under his cloth cap. Old Mr Quick was flushed and seemed feverish and she would have enquired about his health, but he wouldn't appreciate a fuss. 'When he feels he's recuperated enough, I suppose.' She did not want to talk about Alec. He was refusing to forgive her over her accusation about his manner with Lottie and was merely cool when she telephoned him each evening. She had not bothered to telephone him last evening and there had been no call from him. He could wallow in self-pity or indignation or whatever else he liked. His memory was getting so poor, or deliberately untrained, perhaps he had forgotten he had a family and responsibilities. He'd certainly forgotten that Lottie was a little girl with bruised feelings. No matter. Neither Lottie nor she herself was missing him at the moment.

Later today she and her father and the cowman were to put a ring through the nose of the new bull, and they were perfectly capable of doing so without Alec's help. Alec should be treated to a running noose, a pair of forceps and a nose ring and dragged back home! No, he shouldn't. Alec didn't have a stubborn neck or a pair of horns – he was no way a devil – and he didn't need to be led anywhere. She knew her husband. Alec wasn't well. It was Tris's opinion too. It was best to leave him to come round quietly. As soon as she got home she'd ring him, make some cheerful excuse for yesterday's lapse and tell him she and Lottie were missing him.

'Must have been a bad fall he had,' Mr Quick said. He was gazing across the road, licking his thin, raddled lips, relishing his first half-pint of the day. 'Young Jim Killigrew called on me again just now. He's a good boy. Not appreciated by they Eathornes, if you ask me. I think he regrets moving out of the squire's. Never thought that sister of his would turn against him, she makes him feel he's in the way. Still, I suppose we all got to make our own way in the world. It's what Jim needs to do. He don't say nothing much to me, mind. It's just that I get the gist of him being unhappy.'

'I think you're right, Mr Quick,' Emilia replied loudly. She felt sorry for Jim, but it had been obvious that while he had ruthlessly kept all other suitors away from Sara, he had pushed her in Wally Eathorne's direction while planning to take over Druzel Farm. Jim was a complicated young man. He had suffered a lot of hard knocks and harboured a certain amount of bitterness and jealousy. At least old Mr Quick was a steadying influence on him. And when Jim respected someone he gave them his total loyalty.

Old Mr Quick suddenly gave a queer sigh. His head fell forward. Emilia swung her head round to look up in under his cap. 'Are you all right, Mr Quick? Mr Quick!'

His eyes were shut. He blinked and formed a small smile. 'I don't half feel strange, maid.'

Without another word, old Mr Quick died.

–

Alec was in the summer house at Roskerne. The tumbling Atlantic Ocean was stretched out before him, fifty feet below the cliff, which was fenced off at the end of the garden. His dark-grey, brooding eyes were aimed at the black and white tiled floor. It was down there where he had first made love to Emilia. Wasn't it? Why couldn't he remember something so vital and such a wonderful occasion? He had wanted Emilia so much back then. He'd needed her. Her and her strong, direct, sensible ways, and the peace and calmness she'd had to go with her independent spirit. He had called her his angel. She had been his angel. And so had Jenna, his tiny, beautiful little angel with a fairy-like face. She would have been eight years old now.

A movement on the long, sweeping lawn caught his eye. There was a little girl. It wasn't Adele. She was dancing on the grass in a white floating dress, her delicate feet bare. She didn't have wings but she was like an angel or a fairy. Her hair streamed down her back in exquisite crinkly waves and was the colour of Emilia's. She was beautiful, ethereal, unworldly. He couldn't take his eyes off her. She stopped dancing and turned and faced him. Her eyes gazed straight into his, eyes as grey as his own.

Jenna?

She disappeared. She had been there and suddenly she was gone.

'Don't go!'

He couldn't get up quickly with the plaster on his leg and he flung out his arms to where she had been. His camera was on the wrought-iron bench beside him and he sent it crashing down. Someone seized and saved it or it would surely have been broken, but he had no notion of it.

'Alec? Are you all right? Who were you talking to?'

He turned his head slowly. Shook it as if waking up from a long, deep sleep. 'Oh… Brooke.'

'It was a good thing I turned up. You were miles away, Alec, in another world.'

'No. Another world came to me.'

'Alec, have you been out in the sun too long?' Brooke crouched and took his hands. They were warm and strong, although she had expected them to be cold and weak. 'You look so strange.'

'Sorry. I suppose I'm spending too much time on my own.' He looked over Brooke's head to where he was sure he had seen his daughter, not as a tiny baby but how she would be now.

'Have you been taking snaps?'

'No, I don't think so.'

'Let me take one of you,' she said to distract him, to bring him to a more conscious level. She was sure he'd refuse her request, afraid she might break or ruin his precious gadget. 'You're always behind a camera, rarely in front of it.'

'Do you know how it works?' He nodded at the camera, safe again on the bench.

'I do.' There were cameras in plenty at Tremore House. Ben had to have everything Alec had, and the latest model. He didn't like her touching his things, but she did when he wasn't around. Alec used a Kodak single-lens reflex camera with a ground-glass focusing screen, and she was familiar with the model. She moved to an angle on the summer house steps where she could get a clear upper body shot of him. Alec had his own darkroom. She'd have to wait until he went home to see her handiwork.

'It's good to see you, Brooke,' he said as she took the photograph. Because he wasn't posing, Brooke was sure it would be an excellent natural likeness of him, revealing him relaxed, his mind drifting, his eyes fixed on the lawn. 'Have you brought Faye? How's Ben?'

'Faye's at school. Ben's in Paris.' The flash seemed to hurt Alec's eyes. Brooke put the camera carefully down on the round table, where a tall glass of barley water was left untouched.

'You've not gone with Ben this time?' At last Alec took his gaze from the spot where he'd seen the vision of Jenna and looked at Brooke.

'I didn't fancy a trip away.' Brooke sighed softly, but there were tones of dejection. Two nights ago Ben had accused her of no longer fancying him.

'It's not that, darling,' she had pleaded. 'It's just—oh, why can't I make you understand?'

'That you're not willing to contemplate another baby yet? OK, OK!' He had kicked back the bedcovers and fetched his wallet. 'You don't trust me to be careful, but as far as I'm concerned there's no point in making love at all if we have to use one of these horrid things again.'

'Ben! How can you be so cold? If it's not going to be a loving experience then I don't want to be with you.'

He had pulled on his pyjama trousers and then flung himself down on the couch and shrugged his shoulders. 'I'm sorry, Brooke. I don't know what else to suggest. We've always had a good love life. I don't want it ruined. I love you. I love being with you. Damn it, Brooke! I'm a young man. I didn't come near you for three whole months after the last miscarriage. Am I supposed to take a vow of celibacy? And surely I have got the right to have a son.'

She had sat up in bed, sobbing. 'I'm sorry too, Ben. I don't know what the answer is either. I just...'

'Just what, for heavens sake? You're not the first woman to have lost a pregnancy, even more than one. I said last week if you lose one more then I'd be willing to give up. Adopt a son or something. I don't think I can be more reasonable than that!'

'Stop shouting, Ben, please. You'll wake Faye and the servants. I understand your point of view. I do. I'm sorry.

I know this isn't fair to you and you've been more than reasonable. I think what I want is for you to understand that to me it wasn't just the end of two early pregnancies but two babies. They were my children, Ben. As real to me as Faye is.'

Ben paced the luxurious bedroom, his feet silent on the deep-pile carpet. He lit a cigar, drawing on it impatiently. He pulled back the silk curtains and the voile drapes inside them, and the moonlight had gleamed on his chest, making his skin gleam like burnished bronze. Watching the powerful movements of his perfectly aligned body, she had wondered how she could resist him. In a low, defeated voice, he had, at last, said, 'What do you want to do?'

'I don't know.' She had stayed in bed, the covers pulled up to her chin, shivering, dreading what he would say next.

He'd turned to her, stubbing out the cigar. 'I suppose we all take different lengths of time to get over something. I can't entirely sympathize with you. There are men who came back from the front in ruins. There's one in the village left an imbecile. Wives back then lost babies at the shock of their husbands' deaths. You need to find some courage, Brooke. I can't imagine Em going to pieces over something similar.' He went to his dressing room. 'It's still early. I think I'll drive to Truro and call on Dougie Blend. Tomorrow, I'll go up to London and fly on to Paris. Then take a tour around the vineyards and look for some new wines. I take it you don't want to come with me?'

She had shaken her head, and cried the night away. Ben had made her feel small and guilty and selfish. He measured everything she did by Emilia's level, and because his partially blinded eye had denied him war service, he measured everything else by the horrors and sufferings of that. Dougie

Blend was his business associate, a wine merchant, a seedy individual, and some of the business Ben conducted with him was not legal. Brooke behaved as if she did not know this.

'Alec,' she said. 'Do you think I'm self-centred? That I should be made of stronger stuff, like Emilia?'

He smiled at her, a philosophical smile. 'There's only one Emilia and there's not enough of her to go round. I know what you're saying about yourself, Brooke. Of course you're not self-seeking. You're mourning. I'm sorry, because although I sympathize I can't help you. I'll never get over Jenna's death. I haven't really made the effort to and now I don't think I can.'

'Are you afraid?'

'I don't know.' He frowned, rubbing his brow at the threat of another headache; they were creeping up on him more frequently and with greater intensity. Sometimes lights sparked and marred his vision, sometimes the pressure inside his head made him think his brain was about to implode. Winifred had given him some of the analgesic she used for her occasional migraines but it hadn't made any difference. 'I don't seem to be able to take anything in any more. Do you think I'm going mad?'

'Of course not. You and I have a bad habit, that's all,' she smiled in understanding. 'We think too much. Others would advise us to do something new, find a distraction, but neither of us have the energy or the inclination to. I'd never have believed I could feel this way. I'm glad there's you, who identifies with how I feel.'

Alec held out his hand. Brooke put hers into it. 'So am I.'

They stayed as they were, words no longer needed.

Chapter Ten

Laden with a box of farm produce, Emilia knocked on the front of Wynne Cottage, which had been old Mr Quick's home all his life.

Jim answered. 'Mrs Em! Surprised to see someone at this door. Don't suppose it's hardly ever been used. Come in.'

'I sort of wanted to christen your new home, Jim.'

'Thanks.' He took the box from her. 'This is very kind of you. Sit down. I'll put the kettle on.'

'How are you?' She gazed about. Everything was in the same tidy order that old Mr Quick had left it in. Jim had been living here since hearing the news of old Mr Quick's death. Emilia had gone to Druzel Farm herself to tell Jim, interrupting a hostile quarrel between him and Eustace Eathorne. Jim had immediately gone to Wynne Cottage, where he had begun a vigil over the old man's coffin, ensuring that Mr Quick was laid out in his best suit.

Old Mr Quick had no living relatives and Jim had walked behind the bier and pair of black horses all the way to the church. The mourners had joined in the procession as it had wended its way past houses, smallholdings and farms. In respect of his age and lengthy associations in the village quite a few women went to the funeral. Ruby Brokenshaw had walked behind Jim, and when the cortège had got as far as Ford Farm, as wife of the squire, Mr Quick's landlord, Emilia had stepped in front of her. No one looked to take over the lead from Jim, not even those who usually denounced him. Elena Rawley attended every such Anglican occasion and had stayed circumspectly in the background.

'Are you going to the wake?' Emilia had asked Jim after the burial in the churchyard. The wake was to be held in Gilbert Eathorne's front room, adjoining the shop. Jim had taken no interest in its planning, even though Gilbert had come across the road to invite him specially, saying in reverential tones that his brother Sidney was 'going to do the old boy proud with a nice hunk of ham.'

'No,' Jim had replied to Emilia. 'I'd like to stay here for a while.'

'Jim, I need to speak to you. Mr Quick had entrusted some papers to Alec's care. What they contain concerns you. Will you come to the farm later today?'

He'd nodded, seeming much like when she'd first seen him, a lost, woeful fourteen-year-old, brought out of the workhouse, a boy who considered the world was against him.

'It was good of Alec to agree to me taking over the tenancy here,' Jim said now, pouring boiling water on the tea leaves in the fat brown teapot and placing it on the exact spot where old Mr Quick used to put it. 'One or two people have been kind to me. Ruby Brokenshaw says I'm admired for calling regularly on Mr Quick. Suddenly my estimation's gone up in the village. And what with the dear old soul leaving me his worldly goods and fifty-five-pound savings... I can't quite take it all in.'

'I'm so glad for you, Jim. A home of your own and the security of having a little bit put by, it's what you've always wanted. I hope you and Sara will sort out your differences.'

Jim made a grim face. 'She's hurt me, the way she's behaved. Well, she'll have the spare room for her new baby. I suppose she'll invite me over for Christmas and I suppose I'll go. The more I think about it, it was her way of protecting her new life. Eustace wouldn't hear of me working out my notice on the farm, he must have been glad to get rid of me. And now, thanks to Mr Quick, I can make a good start on my own little business, as a handyman.' Jim's enthusiasm was evident in the energy he used lifting a bag of biscuits out of the box. 'I can put my hand to anything; you know that. I've just bought a used van and I'm having my name printed on it. I shan't change anything in the cottage for a while. I can still picture Mr Quick sitting in his armchair there by the hearth. He'd have liked the idea of me living here. I'll look after his garden. And his hens and the budgie. I'll be getting Mr Quick a granite headstone; in the meantime I've made a wooden cross. The blacksmith's going to burn his name and the dates in the wood. Do you take sugar, Mrs Em?' Jim was suddenly shy and gave a boyish smile. 'I've never made you tea before.'

'No sugar, thank you, Jim.' She smiled back. 'Alec's very pleased for you. We have every faith in you to make us and old Mr Quick proud. We'll be happy to recommend you, it should bring you in some work. Have you got enough bed linen, that sort of thing? There's lots to spare at the farm. Just call in any time. Of course, we'll be grateful to have an extra hand in the fields for haymaking and harvesting. Goodness, Jim, you're already like a different person.'

'No longer a snotty-nosed workhouse brat, eh? Perhaps people will forget I ever came from there. You've brought ginger biscuits. I've missed Tilda's cooking.'

'I hope you're cooking for yourself.'

'I try.' He grinned. 'I might not have to for long. I've had a few hints from the maids round here, and a pie or two's been handed in. Now I've got my own little place, seems I'm marriage material.'

'You've been that for a long time.' Emilia paused. 'You call occasionally at Ford House.'

'So I do. To help out.'

'Any other reason?'

Jim took a moment to answer. 'Elena Rawley's hardly going to welcome any suggestion from me to step out.' Jim thought about his love life. He was content to visit a certain working girl in a backstreet in Truro two or three times a month. If he ever did feel like taking a wife it would be someone mild and respectable, someone who'd never make him feel small, never be unfaithful. A marriage in which he would be in charge of the lovemaking. 'I doubt if she'll ever get married. Will Alec be home in time for the village show next month? Miss Rawley's getting anxious about the arrangements, I think.'

'Well, it's not so easy for her now she's got the Annear children to consider.' Emilia didn't want to mention yet again that she had no idea when Alec would be home. She was asked that by someone new nearly every day, and Will and Tom were fretting to see their father, demanding that they be allowed to spend the next weekend at Roskerne with him. Alec was friendlier over the telephone but quieter than usual and vague. She drank her tea and left Jim to his new life.

–

A short time later Jim was on his way to Ford House, to ask if he could borrow the typewriter. He would explain about his new venture. 'I want to put up some notices,' he planned to say. 'Make it look professional. I'll hand them out round the villages and get some pinned up in Truro.' He couldn't type, of course, and he was hopeless at spelling, but no doubt the generous young lady would offer to do it for him, and he'd insist on paying her for the service. He could see the first sheet of paper now. *Jim Killigrew Esq. Handyman. Speciality Drystone Walls. No job too small. Wynne Cottage. Hennaford.* Or should that be *James Killigrew. General Builder*? He wanted to create the right impression.

'Uncle Jim! Uncle Jim!'

While the children made a mad exodus outside to the man who had taken over as father figure to them, Elena watched from the parlour window, her insides in knots. She was about to write a letter to the authorities explaining that it wasn't possible for her to keep Alan and Martha. Her income wouldn't stretch that far. One disaster, say with the roof or something, and things would be really stretched. It would be different if she could afford a full-time nanny. It was important to her that she helped lots of people, served the whole village. She was behind with the arrangements for the local horticultural show for the first time and it troubled her. It was strange to be putting all her energies into just two people, and the children needed a lot of attention in their present anxious state. Yesterday Alan had asked if he could have his own room when he got older and she hadn't answered. Fear and suspicion had marked his little fair face and he had taken Martha away to curl up together in a corner. She hoped Jim would take them rambling in the woods. He had a settling effect on them and she would get the chance to think about what promises she'd make to them to ease their passage into an orphanage.

Jim sent the children to play in the back garden, promising to join them soon for a game of tig, when he would chase them and catch them and whirl them about in endless tizzy-wizzys. The children would scream in delight and beg him for more. Elena met him at the back kitchen door, where Jim always knocked. He took it for granted he'd be offered tea but he'd drink it outside. In no way would he compromise the young lady, earning her disrespect. In the pursuit of juicy morsels to spread round, the gossips would think nothing of destroying her reputation, no matter how highly they had thought of her previously.

'What's the matter?' he said at once.

'The matter?' Elena shrank back on the doorstep, a guilty flush climbing her neck. 'Nothing. Why?'

'You look all upset. Got problems? Something I can fix for you?'

'No! No, nothing like that.' Elena tried to force a smile but one wouldn't come.

His lifelong cynicism, his wary expectation that fate would have yet another kick in the face for him, made Jim receptive to others' moods. 'It's something to do with the kids, isn't it? They're both well. What is it? Has a relative come forward and you're grieved you're going to have to give 'em up?'

Elena didn't answer. Her throat was choked dry. Jim was the one person she was dreading having to explain her intentions to. So many times he had said he admired the way she had taken the children in.

Jim was reading her thoughts. There could be only one reason why Elena Rawley was looking like a roasted turkey. She was throwing the children out! It was a double blow because she was the last person he'd expected to serve her own selfish needs. He stamped over the threshold and Elena retreated into the kitchen, to the far side of the room. She knew Jim could bellow when he was angry and she didn't want Alan and Martha to overhear a scene. 'You're not keeping them, are you? Why on earth not? Do you realize what you'd be doing to them?'

'I... I, it's difficult.'

'I don't understand. How could it be difficult?' Jim went closer and closer to her, until she was scrunched up in front of the dresser. He knew the terrible sense of rejection Alan and Martha were in for, the terror of the unknown, the dreadful possibility of them being split up and taken into different homes, or one adopted while the other was left to rot in a cold institution, and he was boiling mad. 'The kids need a home and you've got plenty of room. Too much trouble for you, I suppose. Bloody nuisances. Or don't they fit the bill for you? Yeah, who wants a pair of common brats living in such a grand house?'

'It's nothing like that, I swear!' Elena cried. 'I simply haven't the money to support them.'

'Support them.' Jim said the words gravely. 'And which way would you suppose Alan and Martha want to be brought up? Private education? Fancy dancing lessons? Mixing with fine people?'

'I wasn't brought up like that, Jim.' Elena wished she could tear her sight away from his accusing eyes.

'All they want is a roof over their heads, for goodness sake! Food in their bellies and to know someone cares. Most importantly they need to know they can always stay together.' Jim reached out with his hands, hovering them over her shoulders. She looked nervous and, thank God, in the wrong. 'Think again, Elena, I beg you. You'd never forgive yourself if anything bad happened to either of them.'

Elena's mind was a mess of confusion. Everything Jim had said was right. She couldn't reject the children. Their lives might be ruined for ever. She had taken them in. It wasn't right or Christian to fob them off now. Tears glittered along her eyelashes.

Jim said, 'You believe the Lord provides a way out of all our problems, don't you?'

She didn't have to think about it. 'Yes,' she whispered, swallowing hard.

'Good. Then look for that provision.'

'I… I will. Yes, I will. I promise.' Her legs felt wobbly. She had to move away from him, his righteousness and his powerful masculinity. 'W-would you like a cup of tea now? I could really do with one!'

Jim stepped back and she rushed past him to the hob. 'So you'll tell the kids they can stay for good? They need to know that.'

Spooning tea leaves into the pot, she said, 'Of course.'

At those words her spirit soared. She was doing the right thing. It was meant. Why hadn't she seen it before? She had been given a new ministry. Foster mother. And she would work as hard as she knew how to make Alan and Martha feel wanted and secure. As for her other works, there were others in the village, like the Harvey women and the rector's and schoolmaster's wives, who could arrange the annual events. It occurred to her that she'd have plenty of spare time to help them when the children started school. And if the village school was good enough for the squire's children until they were eleven, it was good enough for hers. *Her children*. She had never thought to become a mother – now the thought was fantastic.

She felt a rush of love for Alan and Martha and hurried to the window to look outside. They were huddled together on the swing Jim had made for them, looking doleful. She turned to her advisor.

He was smiling at her. She smiled back with ease. 'Would you excuse me for a moment, Jim?' Then she ran outside to tell Alan and Martha the news.

Chapter Eleven

Ben was wandering down a Paris street. He'd completed all the business he intended to in choosing new wines and an order of some fine table vintages was to be shipped over to England, to arrive at Truro docks within the week.

What to do now? He was in no mood for shows, clubs or casinos and had spent too many lonely evenings at his hotel. During the day, after leaving the sweeping vineyards, he had stayed in the countryside and gazed across peasant farms. He had taken advantage of the hospitality offered him at two small farms. Both farmers had been blessed with brawny young sons and he had left feeling isolated and cheated. He was bored. Fed up. Lonely. As bleak as he possibly could be. He wished Emilia was with him. He'd enjoy showing her the sights. More so, he would enjoy her company. So very much.

He should telephone Brooke and say he was coming home. He'd do so at once. No, he wouldn't. It was disturbing how he had hardly missed her and Faye, how he had lingered here in a foreign country. The French had an eternal love affair with wine – they said it had a soul. Ben wished he felt that way about something or someone. He had thought he would stay in love with Emilia for ever, and then the same thing with Brooke. But he had thrown away what he might have had with his first love and now his feelings for Brooke were drifting away. But he was longing to see Emilia again. While thoughts of Brooke gave him a sour taste in his mouth, like bad vinegary wine, thoughts of Emilia reminded him of how a Sauterne would unfold slowly and lovingly in the mouth. He had made love to Emilia only once. How could he have caused that rift and forsaken that wonderful pleasure again? She had always had so much to give, and now she was a mature woman: so much more passion! So he would go back soon. There could be something exquisite waiting for him there. Tris had mentioned that Emilia and Alec were having problems. She might like to talk to him about them. She might lean on him. Allow him to get closer to her. Fall in love with him again. He wanted that. More than anything. He'd give up everything he had for Em.

Some men, tourists, pulled up in a cab and got out, laughing. They sauntered into a fine building. A brothel. Here in France, brothels were something of a valued institution, a key part of the Gallic psyche. They were clean and well run – many, like the one he was soon to pass by on dreary legs, were, apparently, opulent inside, with custom-made furniture. Their clientele, men and women, included famous writers, artists, film stars and politicians, and they would arrive openly. It was said the prostitutes, if one became a regular, offered tenderness as well as their usual services. Ben was sure it was only an illusion, but he was carnally frustrated, and he had an unbearable yearning to be the centre of attention to someone, even if only for a short time. It was several months since he had made love with full passion and reaped total satisfaction. To go inside the brothel was tempting. But there was Brooke. Although his business associate Dougie Blend was 'a bit of a lad' and often pressed his spare women on him, Ben had never thought to be unfaithful to Brooke. Until now. Except with Emilia, but he didn't see loving with her as some sordid affair. The thing was, Brooke was failing in her wife's duty. An hour or two in the brothel would be for sex only. It wouldn't mean anything. What Brooke didn't know wouldn't hurt her. But there was also Emilia. He'd be unfaithful to her too. But as much as he wanted her, needed her, Emilia wasn't here. He was a virile young man. He had needs. And right now he needed a little uncomplicated company.

He fought with himself another five minutes, then he entered the house of pleasure.

–

Tristan Harvey found Emilia tending her rose beds, but he didn't speak to her straight away, taking time first to savour the exquisite sights and scents. Her dedication, her skill at pruning and keeping disease and pests at bay, and protecting the roses from the disposition of the weather, resulted in bushes and shrubs in formal outlays and random arrangements, in the ground and pots and containers, in mixed colours or colours of the same. And climbers and ramblers crawling along arches, walls and pergolas. Most were presently in bud, some of colour beyond imagination, pink, scarlet, honey, gold, cerise, amber, lilac, yellow, off-white and peach; in soft shades and bright and flamboyant and tinged and iridescent. A secluded corner was dedicated to the memory of Jenna in gently blossoming miniatures of mimosa and cream. Tristan drew in the scents, sniffing individual blooms, taking in whole bushes, knowing some scents wouldn't be apparent until the evening. He indulged himself, picking out, as well as the warm or strong perfume of rose, hints of musk, lemon, spice, myrrh, aniseed, honey, citronella and many more. Some roses had no discernible scent at all but gave a feast to the eyes. He went on treating himself, and Emilia, absorbed in deadheading a rambler, had no idea he was there.

'Hello, Em. A truly wonderful, impressive display again. They all look winners, as usual.'

Tris! This is a nice surprise. Is Alec with you? And the family?'

'Just Alec. I've brought him home. I wasn't happy about the way he was sitting for hours just staring at the same empty spot on the lawn. Sometimes it was as if he was looking for something, other times as if he was actually seeing something. And he was talking to someone. It got to be quite unnerving. He's even taken photos of the lawn and there's nothing unusual on it. I must say it's ruffled me, Em. I think you should make him see the doctor.'

Emilia frowned. Anxiety chewed like a handful of worms in her stomach. What on earth was the matter with Alec? 'I'll ask the doctor to call. Alec won't go to the surgery. Is he indoors? Has he spoken to Lottie?'

'He said he was going straight to his darkroom. He stopped long enough to admire the repairs Tom's made to Lottie's pram.'

'I hope she wasn't rude to him. She's been so hurt by his remoteness.'

'Oh, he gave her one of the brooches she liked. She seemed happy with it.'

'Well, that's something. I hope the doctor can make sense of what's going through Alec's mind. What he needs is a proper holiday. Brooke suggested it to me. I'll see if I can get him away. Just the two of us.'

Tristan thoughtfully stroked each side of his lean jaw. 'It's a good idea, Em, but I'd counsel that what he needs most at the moment is to get back into his usual routine.'

'Mrs Em! Second post's come,' Tilda called cheerily, heading down the garden. 'There's a letter for 'ee, from London.'

'Must be from Perry Bosweld,' Tris said, smiling. He liked the former army surgeon.

'Probably,' Emilia replied, keeping her feelings in check as she had trained herself to do. It was always horribly difficult. 'Thanks, Tilda.'

'Coming in for some of my elderberry wine, Cap'n Harvey?' the jolly, freckle-faced, ginger-haired housekeeper asked. She was nearing sixty years but with her gleaming red cheeks and straight posture looked much younger. A fixture of the Harvey household since the Great War, she was content to serve the family, insisting, despite Emilia's offer that she need not wear a uniform, to keep to her ankle-length grey dress and brilliant-white starched apron and frilled cap. She was a warm presence from the past and gave a comforting sense of continuity.

'I won't say no to that,' Tristan said. He'd take some of the delicacy to Alec. He had no intention of allowing him to shut himself away in a dark, isolated atmosphere.

'I'll join you in a minute,' Emilia said. 'I'll just tidy up here.'

If Alec could hide himself away the instant he came home then she would linger here and read Perry's letter. It was addressed just to her. He did that sometimes, knowing Alec never even glanced at the mail.

Dear Em. There was a wonderful leap in her heart. Perry had called her Em but had until now written to her as Emilia.

I was sorry to learn in the letter you enclosed in Libby's birthday card that Alec is still suffering from the result of his accident. I do hope his broken leg is well and truly on the mend and he has regained his spirit. I take it he has been somewhat depressed. Libby had a good birthday. She came up from school for the weekend, declaring she was too old for parties, so I took her out to dinner at the Savoy. She's quite a young lady now. Selina sent her a telegram from Donegal; she's taken a temporary post there in general practice. I wish you well with your roses this year. I'm sure they're very beautiful. I must say I'm rather proud of mine again. It's become quite a passion. One I'll never give up. I'd be interested to learn how you get on at the village show. Best of luck.

Thank you for the lovely snap you sent of Lottie. She is just like her mother.

I'll close now. With best wishes, as always.

Perry.

Emilia had put the photograph of Lottie, taken of her bottle-feeding an orphaned lamb in the kitchen and grinning up at the camera, as a sudden thought before sealing the birthday card in its envelope. She had wanted Perry to see her precious little girl, to send him something personal. Alec had taken the photograph but had not commented on it. She wanted someone outside the family to pay a compliment to her daughter, to see her loveliness, and Perry had, and he had included a word of love and affection for her too.

She leaned forward and sniffed a perfect golden rose. It smelled like heaven. She was in heaven. Perry had always signed his full name before, formal and correct. The mention of roses and the passion he had referred to were a secret message of love to her. She couldn't go to him, but that vague hope she kept in her heart increased a hundred-fold. She re-read the letter twice, kissed it, then put it back in its envelope. She placed it inside her chemise. In a little while she'd slip upstairs to her bedroom and hide it on the top shelf of her wardrobe, in a box where she kept her childhood pictures and scraps of schoolwork, which she kept locked, hiding the tiny key behind a boring old book in the sitting room.

Then she'd take a sip of elderberry wine with Tristan. With Alec too if he could be bothered to join them. She hoped he did not.

Chapter Twelve

Jonny Harvey came home for the first week of the summer vacation from university, but only to humour his father. As soon as he could get away he'd zoom up to London, where a group of his fellow students would be having a whale of a time, but not before visiting his Uncle Alec, who had raised him while his father was fighting in the trenches, and with whom he had a special bond.

Adele had talked him into taking her down on the beach. The tide was coming in fast, splashing into the depressions left around a scattering of low, weather-sculpted slate rocks, making fascinating little pools. Adele gazed longingly at them. 'Forget it,' Jonny said in the superior, sometimes rude voice he had acquired during this, his first term away. 'We're not staying long.'

Jonny had refused to allow her to bring her bucket and spade and shrimping net. Adele thrust her hands in the little gathered pockets of her plain white dress and glared up at his grumpy, handsome dark face. It was established now that he was even better looking than Uncle Ben, but she, an ordinary scrap of a girl, whose hair refused to mould trimly on her scalp, resented it. She resented her big brother showing so little interest in her. Even Will sometimes scrapped playfully with Lottie. 'Why do you hate it here? Why do you hate me? You don't talk to Vera Rose like she's a nuisance to you. And you shouldn't smoke. A man on the wireless said it's bad for you.'

'I don't hate it here. I just want to spend some time with people my own age. Go to parties, that sort of thing. And of course I don't hate you, although you are a bit of a nuisance at times. As for Vera Rose, she is my age, we have more in common. Don't sulk, Adele. Look, when we go to Father's shop later today I'll take you into the nearest ice-cream kiosk and buy you the most enormous cone. And if I want to smoke, it's none of your business. Most people do nowadays.'

'Vera Rose says she's going to smoke. All the film stars do. It's sophist— whatever the word is. I suppose I might smoke too one day. Jonny –' Adele hopped in front of him, spattering the pale golden sand over his bare feet – 'take me to Ford Farm when you go to stay overnight. Please!'

He bent low and said into her face, 'Certainly not.'

'Ohh! I hate you. I want to see Uncle Alec.' She folded her arms and walked on slightly in front of him, watching her little feet drag through the warm sand.

'You've had him here practically all to yourself for ages.'

'I want to see Aunty Em and play with Lottie. And Faye.'

Jonny sighed. 'I expect Father and Aunt Winnie will go to Hennaford for the flower and vegetable show. It's coming up soon. You can go then.'

'Uncle Alec says I should grow my hair long.'

'Why?'

'He says all little girls should have long hair. He doesn't like the short styles.'

'What a strange thing for him to say. Oh, look, there's another little girl just come round those rocks. She's waving to you. Go off and play with her. But we can't stay long or we shall be cut off and I'll be in trouble if I have to climb with you up the cliff.' More than a bit of a daredevil, Jonny had climbed the cliff in many places, many times, but here the cliff was earthy in parts and easily crumbled. Roskerne was a short stretch away. He reckoned he could allow his sister fifteen minutes. The newcomers had, presumably, scrambled down at the other end of the beach via a reasonably easy climb.

'It's Christine! Christine Shaw. She's staying at the hotel for the summer with her nanny. They often come to this beach. Miss Johnson can't be far away. We play together a lot.'

'Good. Run off then. I'll watch. Keep away from the water and come at once when I call you.' While Adele shot off to her friend, Jonny parked himself on a rock well back at the foot of the cliff. He was glad to be rid of his half-sister's constant chatter. She was sweet enough but the eleven years between them was too large a gap for closeness. He shut his eyes and turned his face up to the gently burning sun. Life was pretty good. His studies for his physics degree were on target – his wealth of intelligence saw to that. And he was wise enough to avoid getting continually and stupidly drunk, as a few of the fellows did. There were women in the colleges and locally who were entertaining and obliging. Some couldn't see why they shouldn't have free and easy sex on equal terms with men, and nor could he. He had much to look forward to, finally his chosen career in the Royal Air Force as a flyer. It wouldn't hurt to spend some time with his family before tootling off to his pals for some fun and games.

'Christine, dear, if you want to paddle, come to me and I'll hitch up your dress.' Jonny had been hoping to avoid the nanny – probably some plain and stuffy old maid type. The soft, harmonious quality of the educated female voice made him snap his eyes open and look down near the shore. A young woman, side-on to his gaze, perhaps about twenty-five, was calling to the girl playing with Adele. The nanny didn't notice him, and puffing lazily on his cigarette he took her all in. A nice filmy dress, a pretty sun hat and sandals. A lovely trim figure, long shapely arms which were pleasingly bare. Not tall, not short, willowy and blonde, and oh, so soft and feminine. Her hair was unfashionably long, lying just below her shoulders, stirring beguilingly in the gentle, warm breeze. He tossed the cigarette down. 'Mmm. I'll take a closer look at this.'

The nanny was occupied in hitching up the skirts of both girls so they could paddle in the pools. 'Just a few minutes now. Watch out for the splashes as the breakers come in.'

'Hello. Is that your little girl playing with my sister?' he said, as if he didn't know the truth.

'Oh!' She had not heard his approach. 'Oh, I mean, I beg your pardon. No. I'm her nanny. I'm pleased Adele has someone with her. I was getting quite concerned.'

'Jonathan Harvey. Jonny.' The woman straightened up, leaving the girls to scamper off. He offered his hand, smiling a smile of practised charm. 'Pleased to make your acquaintance, Miss…?'

'Johnson. Angeline Johnson.' She took his hand. 'Adele has spoken of you often. You're something of a hero to her, you know.'

'We adore each other. Your accent's not local. Are you down on holiday?'

'We're spending the summer here. Christine's parents are away in Monte Carlo.'

'May I ask if you're staying at the Watergate Bay Hotel? I often have dinner there. Adele has obviously played with Christine before, so you must know we live at Roskerne, just a little way along above the beach.'

'I saw you in the restaurant last night, with your parents. I have spoken to Mr and Mrs Harvey on an earlier occasion.' Angeline Johnson looked at her charge. 'They have kindly invited Christine to play at Roskerne.'

'Then you must come soon, today if you like. Poor little Adele is starved of company her own age. The tide will shortly forbid any more play here.' Jonny was wondering why he hadn't noticed this delectable young woman last night. She was soothingly pretty, with an interesting, sagacious expression. 'My father and stepmother stood me a very nice rare steak last night. I'm presently down from Oxford.'

'May I ask what you're studying?' She returned her soft gaze to him. She wasn't afraid to look him in the eye, therefore she was not shy. He was glad about that. He'd have to be careful not to give her any old flannel, she wasn't the type to buy it, and she wasn't the sort to treat like that anyway, someone just to look for sex with. He told her of his ambitions. Angeline Johnson added, 'I'd have liked to have gone to university.'

'Why didn't you?'

A wave rode up over the lower rocks where the girls were playing, splashed up in peaks and showered them with spray and they shrieked with laughter. Angeline Johnson laughed too. 'Another three minutes, girls.' Back to Jonny. 'I simply had no means to.'

'I'm sorry. That must have been a blow.' A blow because this fascinating, obviously clever young woman would never reach her full potential. He wanted to ask her what she had wanted to study and lots of other questions too, but in more relaxed circumstances. 'Would you care to walk back to Roskerne with Adele and I? We could dry the girls off and they could enjoy an afternoon in the garden. We could have lunch on the terrace. There will just be the four of us and my cousin Vera Rose.' He'd soon send his cousin packing.

The nanny took no time in replying. 'Christine has been pestering me to take up Mrs Harvey's invitation. Yes. Thank you, Jonny. We'd both like that.'

Chapter Thirteen

'You'd love it in Paris, Em.'

'So you keep saying, Ben.' Emilia frowned in concentration while making the final adjustment to her exhibit of roses in the flower tent. The village horticultural show was held behind the chapel, on land that had once belonged to the defunct Tremore Estate and was now owned by Ben.

'They're beautiful. There should be a rose named after you.'

Em looked over her shoulder at him. 'That's a nice thing to say.'

'You're very much like a perfect rose in full bloom. Beautifully mature, exquisitely shaped, magnificent.'

She missed the huskiness in his voice and thought he was teasing her. 'And thorny?'

'Mmm, you're a little prickly now and again. I wouldn't go as far as thorny. Your sharp edges are just another appealing part of you. You're lovely, Em. I'll always think so.' He got closer and sniffed her. She chose rich rose scents but she also smelled of womanhood and promise. 'And you always smell good.'

'I do?'

The desire in his eyes was also lost on her. Ben was desperate to get her to notice him, to feel for him as in the old days. 'Doesn't Alec say nice things about you?'

Emilia didn't answer. She attended to her display, formed in a dramatic circle and titled 'Sunset Crown'. Ben edged even closer, saw her mouth tighten. He was pleased. 'Where is he? I haven't seen him yet?'

'He's not coming.'

Ben gave an exaggerated lift of his eyebrows and sounded a little indignant. 'Why on earth not? He never misses a village event. Besides, he's the squire. People expect him to be here.'

'He says he doesn't feel like it.' Emilia's tone was dismissive.

'I wouldn't have thought he'd miss you picking up a trophy, even though it's inevitable.' Ben pressed a hand on her arm. 'Alec's being very difficult these days. Have you had a quarrel?'

'Yes, over Lottie's hair, of all things.' Emilia was simmering in anger over the whole silly situation.

'I want her hair to be left to grow long,' he had said yesterday in the den, where she had been seeing to the farm books.

'What are you talking about?' She had laid down her pen, keeping her seat, *his seat*, behind the desk.

'Lottie. I want her to look more like a little girl than some scruffy tomboy. And she should take dancing lessons with Faye.'

'Lottie doesn't want to take up ballet. She'd hate it. And long hair would be too restrictive for her. She'd hate it too. She likes to be active, Alec.'

'It's my wish, Emilia.' He'd come to the other side of the desk, pressed his hands down on it and leaned towards her, a looming figure. 'Don't take her to the hairdresser's again this year.'

'Alec.' She had pushed back the chair and stared up at him. 'I'll do nothing that will cause Lottie discomfort.'

'She's my daughter too,' he had returned, heated, aggrieved.

'I'm her mother. I will see to things like that for Lottie.' Emilia's expression had displayed inflexibility. The subject was closed.

Alec had contracted his eyes in a way she had never seen him do before. 'I insist! And I want her to dress in prettier, daintier clothes. I'll ask her if she's changed her mind about the dancing lessons.'

Emilia got up and went round the desk to him. Alec faced her squarely. 'You can insist all you like. Lottie stays exactly as she is.'

'I've never ordered you to obey me, Emilia, but I will not back down on this.'

'Nor will I.' She had said the words slowly and decisively.

'Allow a pair of scissors near the girl's hair and there will be hell to pay.' His voice had grown cold.

Emilia's temper had risen. 'No, Alec. There will be hell to pay if you try to make me do anything that will upset Lottie. I don't know why you're making these ridiculous demands but they aren't for her sake, are they? Watch yourself. You're not the only one who can make threats.'

In that instant Lottie came running into the den with Bertie and Hope, two of the farm's Jack Russells. 'Get those dogs out of here!' Alec hissed at her.

'The dogs can stay, my love, if you promise to sit quietly with them while Mummy finishes her work here,' Emilia said firmly. It was the first time she had overridden Alec in this way, clearly taking Lottie's side against him. Smirking,

Lottie went to her and slipped her hand inside hers, then raised her chin defiantly at her father.

Alec glared at her, then turned his full sight on Emilia. 'So this is how it's going to be, is it?'

'Yes. It's not me who's being unreasonable.'

He'd gazed icily, accusingly, at Emilia for some time and she'd felt the rift deepening between them. She knew she had been wrong to take sides against him in Lottie's hearing – it wasn't going to endear Lottie to him – but it was Alec who had put the distance between himself and Lottie. With a stern, critical sigh he'd stalked out of the den, banging the door after him.

'Lottie's hair?' Ben exclaimed. 'That's a strange idea for a father to take an interest in. It's up to a mother to see to that sort of thing.'

'Did I hear you say Alec isn't coming?' Brooke joined them, making a point of not standing too close to Ben. He had talked enthusiastically about his French trip, had smothered her and Faye with presents, but had done nothing more to her physically than peck her cheek. If she looked at him and caught his eye, he'd glance away. Although his voice was caring and friendly, his body language was cool, and sometimes she fancied there was an element of sarcasm in the things he said and did. He behaved as a loving, interested father to Faye – up to a point. He had no excuse, like Alec, who was unwell, to treat his daughter as second best.

'He's in a mood,' Emilia replied, having no care to show she was angry with Alec. He had reached the limits of her tolerance over his unreasonable notions about Lottie. Now he was ignoring Lottie and she was feeling hurt and rejected. She was presently with Tom and Faye but she was not enjoying the occasion as she normally would have done.

'Alec's always in some sort of mood,' Ben said, happy to drive a deeper wedge between his brother and former fiancée. 'He's getting weird.'

'He is not!' Brooke said sharply.

'He's tiresome and morose,' Ben persisted. He didn't mind if he was upsetting Brooke. His return from Paris had found her unchanged – she had greeted him in the drive as if he was a visitor rather than her husband – and his patience was wearing thin. 'He hasn't left the farm or done any work on it since he came home from Tris's.'

'You're being unfair, Ben,' Brooke carried on crossly. 'Alec's still suffering the trauma of the accident. His leg was quite badly broken and he thought he was going to die. Something like that's bound to be unnerving for a long time.'

Emilia was in no mood to intervene and let them continue arguing.

'You don't know him like we do,' Ben grunted.

'Perhaps it's the only way he can cope,' Brooke argued. 'He needs to see the doctor.'

'He flatly refuses to see him. When the doctor turned up at the farm at Em's request, Alec threatened to set the dogs on him.'

'Well, that shows how disturbed he is. You should show Alec some understanding.'

'If you're so concerned why don't you go over to the farm and try to cheer him up,' Ben delivered it as a challenge. With his wife out of the way he'd have Em to himself.

Brooke glanced at Emilia to see how she felt about this. Emilia's face was stern, almost uncaring. 'Perhaps I will. I've looked at all the exhibits. If Alec could be made to come out of his shell a little it would do everyone some good. Good luck at the judging, Em.' She left.

Ben gazed at Emilia. 'Don't worry. I'm here.'

Emilia looked through the crowds for Lottie, couldn't see her and she left her roses to go to her.

Lottie had wandered off to the chapel social room, which was joined to the chapel. She was hot and teasy and was seeking her grandmother, who was helping with the refreshments, for a glass of orange juice and a cuddle. By the door was a tall, black-haired man. He came forward, a strong limp in his right leg, which seemed very stiff and straight. His clothes were brighter than what men usually wore and he carried a jaunty hat. Lottie was old enough to know this man was extremely good looking.

'Hello.' His voice was cheerful and rang pleasantly. 'Would you happen to be Miss Charlotte Harvey? Lottie Harvey?'

Lottie pursed her lips. 'How do you know me?'

'I know your mother. She sent me a photograph of you.'

Lottie was a quick thinker. 'Are you——?'

'I rather think I am. Is your mother in the flower tent?'

'She was a moment ago. Does she know you're coming?'

'No.' He smiled, and it was such a lovely smile that Lottie found herself smiling back. 'I want to surprise her. I'll go along and find her then.'

Emilia was told where to find her daughter. She hurried past the tents and stalls, the ice-cream van, the seated brass band, the gypsy fortune teller's caravan, greeting people quickly as she went. She was aware of Ben following her, then someone hailed him and drew him aside in urgent conversation. Ben was always much in demand as the wealthiest occupant and second largest employer in the village.

She rounded the last tent. The social room came into view and she was at the top of a short gravelled slope.

And there at the bottom was the man she loved so much.

–

Brooke looked everywhere for Alec in the house and farmyard and then the garden. She gasped in horror and panic when she reached the rose beds. Every rose planted in Jenna's memory was gone. Emilia would never leave these precious roses this way, stripped and bare. It could only be Alec who was responsible. He needed to be found. He must have been half out of his mind to do this. Brooke ran back down the paths. The motor car and his horse were here, so Alec had left on foot. Then she knew where he'd be and her anxiety for him increased.

She found him, a silent figure with his head bowed, in the churchyard by the Harvey plot. And there was Jenna's little grave, completely covered with her mother's tribute roses, a scene of poignant, matchless beauty. 'Alec, what have you done?'

Without looking up, he said in a voice choked with grief and some anger, 'Everyone goes on doing what they normally do and behave as if she never existed. They've all forgotten her. My little girl will never go to the show. Look fabulous, don't they? It's what Jenna deserves.'

'No one's forgotten her, Alec.' Brooke used gentle, soothing tones. 'You know they haven't. Especially Emilia. She's going to bring her exhibit, her very best roses, here after the show. What's she going to think about this?'

'If she loves Jenna as much as she loves Lottie she won't mind. Will she?'

Although Brooke tried to draw him out, Alec would say no more. She went round the grave to him and linked her arm through his. 'Are you going to stay here until Emilia arrives?'

He shook his head.

'What then?'

For a long time he didn't move or speak. Then he disengaged Brooke's arm and took her hand and led her away. 'Where are we going?' she asked.

'I don't know,' he replied.

–

Emilia couldn't speak. She couldn't move. The world had stopped existing. She was in another dimension, a beautiful place, where there was just she and Perry. Warm shivers of delight spread through her; she was engulfed in golden waves of ecstasy. The love she had for Perry and the love he had for her passed across the small distance between them and united them. She wasn't aware of it but her eyes were wide and filling with tears of love, and her hands left her sides and reached out to him.

With little difficulty, just a pronounced swing to his right side, Perry climbed the slope towards her, his gorgeous smile shining from his depthless blue eyes. When he was close enough he took her hands and whispered, 'Darling Em. My dearest own darling Em.'

And now her words came flooding out. 'Perry! How? Why? I… it's so good to see you! It's so good.'

Some people, including by their excited voices Jim Killigrew and the Annear children, came up behind her, and

Elena Rawley came out of the social room, obviously to meet them, with a tray of refreshments. Perry gently, reluctantly, relinquished his hold, and said for the newcomers' benefit, 'Mrs Harvey, Emilia, it's good to be back in these parts.'

'It's good to see you,' she repeated, wondering if she was giving away her true feelings to the onlookers, who were sure to be gawping, wondering, like she herself was, why he was suddenly here. Surely her eyes were shining like stars? Surely they could hear her heart dancing in a new and excited rhythm? And see her hope, and her love for this man. At that moment she didn't care if they did.

'May I escort you somewhere? Perhaps to see the flower exhibits,' Perry said, formal and polite, but smiling in an intimate way.

They received many curious looks and one or two gasps of astonishment as the show-goers saw the handsome young man who had come among them again, walking at the side of the squire's wife. Emilia ignored them. 'Perry, why have you come? Not that I'm not utterly delighted to see you but there must be a reason. Is something wrong?'

'Nothing's wrong. Reggie Rule has gone to Switzerland to study for a few months. He offered me the use of his house at Highertown. I couldn't refuse, Em. I had to see you.'

'But Reggie's already been away for a month and he's gone away before. You didn't come down then. Has something changed?'

'Everything is the same for me. I've been miserable and lonely without you. I've missed you every hour of every day. I've concentrated on my work and with bringing up Libby. She's somewhere here, by the way. Forgive her if she's a little bit rude. She's just thrown a strop. She didn't want to come down to Cornwall but the housekeeper's got shingles and needs to rest. When can we be alone, Em?'

'How can we be with Libby staying with you?'

'She's to spend some time with Reggie's niece. And I was thinking about our secret place on the moors. Libby's vowed this is to be her only visit to Hennaford. She took the way Selina was treated here very badly. Of course, she was too young to know why and she can never be told.'

Ben had got away from the owner of the local nursery, who had boringly chatted on about his vegetable produce and claimed jealously that if it wasn't for Mrs Harvey's roses he'd be certain to win first prize with his. Ben lifted his brows when he saw who was monopolizing Emilia outside the flower tent. He went over to them. He thought Perry Bosweld a fine chap, unfairly shackled during his stay in Hennaford with a game-playing tart of a sister – Ben had been a victim of her tormenting, seductive ways when she had flirted with him and then brushed him off.

'Perry Bosweld! This is a welcome surprise. We didn't think we'd ever see you again in this neck of the woods, did we, Em?'

Emilia just smiled to herself, deliriously happy, dampening down the need to hold Perry's hand.

'Ben Harvey.' The two men shook hands, a dark and handsome pair, owning the confidence of young, well-off gentlemen. 'Well, Ben, this county of my birth has been calling to me to return for some time, you know. It's too beautiful to stay away from indefinitely. I might even come back and settle for good one day soon.' He smiled down at Emilia.

'Well, you are more of a sea and country sort than a town dweller. Isn't he, Em?'

'I totally agree with you, Ben,' Emilia said, careful to keep the enthusiasm out of her voice. Perry's arrival and him living close by again would cause terrible difficulties, not least discovery of their affair, which no doubt would resume, but she hated the thought of him being so far away at a distance. She wanted him near to her all the time. Gazing at him she realized how much she had missed him, that her life had been more than half empty.

'I overheard someone mentioning that Alec is missing the show this year,' Perry said, his eyes firmly on Emilia. She knew he was seeking a deeper explanation than perhaps that Alec was unwell.

'Alec's taking a long time to recuperate from an accident,' Ben said. 'Of course, you wouldn't know he'd suffered a broken leg. The plaster's been off a few days now but he doesn't make much effort to get about.'

Only to the churchyard, Emilia thought sadly. She'd stake her life he was there now. She bit her bottom lip, her heart going out to him. Here she was, happy to be with the man she loved more than Alec, and Alec was alone and miserable.

'He seems to have gone a bit loopy,' Ben said.

Emilia's emotions were in confusion and she didn't add anything to Ben's comment, but suddenly she was afraid that it was true.

Jonny was wandering around the show on his own, catching the eye of the single girls, putting a sparkle in the eye of women of all ages and status. He was happy to allow villagers to chat to him and question him about his life at university, but his mind was elsewhere, and not where he'd intended to be right now, in London. He broke away for a cigarette, not wanting his clean-living father to give him a lecture. He slipped behind the candyfloss stall. A girl was standing at a distance with her back to him but he took no notice of her.

He was deep in thought about Angeline Johnson. She was the reason he was still at home. As young as he was, he thought he knew all about women, but the nanny was different. Different to anyone he'd met, different to anything he'd expected. He couldn't say why. She just was. He'd have learned more about her if the girl she was responsible for wasn't such an attention seeker. Angeline doted on Christine and was happy to give in to her demands and to constantly set up games and distractions for her.

Lunch on that first day, after he and Angeline and the two girls had strolled along the beach and up to Roskerne, had been a delight. While the girls had played on the lawn, he and Angeline had sat on the terrace and sipped white wine and talked and talked. They'd mulled over the rising unemployment figures in this year of 1931, the hunger and poverty and the inevitable gloom that was settling over the country. Angeline had been stirred to passion over the situation – she had a strong social conscience – and all at once Jonny had admitted he had spent a carefree, privileged life, that everything had come easily to him, and he had ended up feeling almost guilty about it. 'If I could think of a way for you to get a place at university, I would,' he had said sincerely.

'I'm happy enough caring for Christine. She's a big part of my life now.' Angeline had looked fondly at the girl. There was no mistaking her devotion.

'But she'll grow up. Won't you feel you've missed out?'

'No. Never. I'm a fatalist, Jonny. What's meant to be, will be.'

They had laughed about the minor earthquake that had recently shook most of the country and the Scottish highlands, when tables had shot across rooms and timbers had creaked, and some had thought it was the Second Coming of Christ and had got down on their knees and prayed. They had talked of a local murder, a rare occurrence, both chilling and thrilling. And Angeline had talked of how she had wanted to be a scientist but how her parents' untimely deaths in a road accident many years ago had left her in the care of an aunt who was kindly but had a meagre income.

He had seen her, with Christine and Adele, twice since then. He knew he mustn't hurry her, but he would ask her to have dinner soon. 'Come to me,' he whispered now to her lovely image in his mind.

Libby Bosweld scowled down every inch of the one-acre field, squashing pink and white clover under her foot. She hated it here. She hated Hennaford and everyone in it. She didn't mind too much about coming down to Cornwall. Some of the girls at school had been down, staying in prestigious hotels. Their talk – not directly to her, for she was not a popular classmate – had reminded her of the wonderful beaches and the delights of the two contrasting coastlines, the north one untamed and rugged, the south warm and splendidly mild, and the moors evocative of *Wuthering Heights* and Jane Eyre; indeed it was the wild, mesmerizing Cornish moors that had inspired the Brontë sisters, rather than the vaster moors of Yorkshire. And there was a beguiling sense of history and spirituality in this bottommost county, both subjects that Libby took refuge in: past ages and the supernatural. Perhaps she would pluck up courage and speak to the girls. What Libby was miffed about was her father insisting that they come here where her adored aunt had been so inexplicably and unfairly ostracized. At least, because she was presently not in her father's company, although people were curious about her because she was a stranger, no one recognized her. She tended to keep away from him when he socialized, knowing people compared his outstanding good looks with her plainness. Even her top-quality fashions failed to make her any sort of a beauty. She was highly sensitive about it.

Smelling cigarette smoke, she glanced behind. And saw a young man who was as equally handsome as her father. He was unconscious of her, his thoughts far away, and she stared and stared at him, absorbing his careless movements, his dark, dark eyes, the perfect symmetry of his face and broad body. At fourteen years old, Libby Bosweld fell in love for the first time. He tossed down the end of his cigarette and, with his eyes lowered, stubbed it out and turned and went back into the gathering.

Something new stirred inside Libby and drove her to follow him. She had to know who he was, but when she got round the candyfloss stall he had disappeared. She was so disappointed she sought her father to demand they return at once to Truro.

She heard her father's voice inside the flower tent. She went in. He was standing beside Mrs Emilia Harvey and was congratulating her over the silver trophy and first-prize card sitting in front of an exhibit of the most exquisite roses. Roses. Every card Mrs Harvey sent to London had roses on it. Her father grew roses and belonged to a rose growers' society. He talked endlessly about roses. He had paintings of roses. He drew pictures of roses. A friend of his had asked him to choose a second name for his daughter; it had been Rose. Every card he sent to Corwall had roses on it. Roses, roses, roses. And Emilia Harvey loved them too.

So that was it! Why her father had dragged her back to Hennaford. It was obvious what had gone on between him and the Harvey woman all those years ago. He was here to start up their affair again.

Emilia got the chilly feeling of hostile eyes boring into her back. She glanced round and, with a stab of unease, met the fierce expression stamped on the unattractive young face.

Chapter Fourteen

Flames shot up the kitchen wall in Ford House. Pegging up dolls' clothes in the garden with Martha, Elena was alerted to the danger by the smell of smoke. 'Martha! Run to the tree house and stay up there with Alan. Whatever you do, don't come down until I tell you both that it's safe! Go on, darling. Run!'

Martha hared off on her little toddling legs, screaming all the way.

Her heart thrashing in panic, Elena dashed into the house. She saw at once that the fire was her fault. A tea towel she had hung over the drying line under the high wooden overmantel had slipped off and had caught alight because she had forgotten to close the door of the grate. The overmantel was ablaze and cracking with the heat and if she didn't act quickly the flames would soon stretch across to the curtains.

She raced to the back kitchen and filled a large enamel bowl with water, ran back into the kitchen and threw the water into the seat of the fire. It doused out a lot of the flames, making steam bubble and hiss on top of the range. There were two saucepans of peeled vegetables in water on the table and she threw them both at the remaining, still determined flames, then she emptied a pot of cold tea. Finally, she grabbed an apron and beat out the last of the blaze.

Shaking, coughing, her eyes stinging from the smoke, she retreated to the back kitchen door to survey the damage. She wanted to cry at what she saw but couldn't give way to tears or it would frighten Alan and Martha. The overmantel was a charred ruin. The wall around it was scorched black, the plaster cracked. Worst of all, there was smoke damage to the room and the back kitchen, and because she tended to leave doors ajar the passage and stairway and every room in the house would have suffered the same. She'd have to decorate throughout the entire house and wash every curtain and cushion and all the bed linen. The house wasn't fit to live in and it would cost a fortune and take a lot of time and trouble to put right.

Back outside, she called Alan and Martha down from the tree house. They were scared and reached for her. Kneeling down, she comforted them and found comfort herself by hugging their soft little bodies.

'Aunt Elena has been very silly and it's her fault there was a fire,' she explained, trying to keep control of her voice. 'We can't go back inside yet, I'm afraid, but at least none of us was hurt. That's the main thing.'

'Will we have to live in the tree house, Aunty 'Lena?' Alan asked, serious, still alarmed, but his eyes were glittering as if sensing an adventure.

'No, darling.' Elena managed a small laugh. 'There's nothing to worry about, but we need some help.' A lot of help if they were going to sleep at home tonight. And she knew just who to turn to.

–

Jim was at home that morning. He had just driven home his new means of transport, a ten-year-old, green-painted

Ford, formerly a baker's delivery van. It was well kept but the bodywork was a little untrue on the front right-hand side after repairs following a collision with a stone pillar, but Jim couldn't be prouder of it. He was filling it with his tools and placing a ladder on the roof rack. Parked in the village square, it had caused a rapid stir of interest and he'd received some requests for low-paid minor work and a lucrative job at the nursery. Gilbert Eathorne, who treated him almost as an equal now he was a local small-business man, had arranged for him to build a back porch. His business was up and running. He'd make more money from these first jobs in a week than he had used to do in two months. Eagerly, he read again the signwriting on the side of the van. *J. Killigrew Esq. General Builder. Hennaford. Near Truro.* He'd have to get a telephone installed. That would give something for people round here to talk about.

Absorbed in his achievement, it was a while before he heard the urgent voices calling his name. He swung round and stared, hardly comprehending what he saw.

'Jim! Jim! Thank God you're here. We need your help,' Elena cried. She was rushing towards him, Alan and Martha tugged along on each hand.

'What on earth…?' The children were clean and tidy, but not a pin was left in Elena's bun and her long hair hung down in tangles. Her face and arms were smudged with soot. He could smell it from where he stood, open-mouthed, eyes widened. Her skirt and blouse were blackened and the skirt had twisted to the side. The laces of one of her stout brown shoes had come undone. She looked vulnerable and very pretty. Jim stared a while longer, then ran to her and the children. He thanked God there were no nosy parkers about to exclaim over them or to get in the way or interfere.

'Come inside.' He ushered the little family, his friend and honorary niece and nephew, into his home.

'Don't go worrying,' he told Elena as she sat at his tiny kitchen table. She was hugging a mug of sweet tea on the faded oilcloth, anxiety marking her pale refined features, and she was shaking every now and then. 'I'll put Gilbert Eathorne and the others off for a few days. Yours is an emergency and they won't mind; too bad if they do. Your insurance will pay for what needs to be done.'

Elena brightened. 'Oh yes, I'd forgotten about that.' Then she was stricken. 'Oh no! I've been so busy with the children I've forgotten to go into Truro and pay the premiums.'

'Will we get into trouble, Aunty 'Lena? ' Alan said from where he was standing up on a hard-backed chair, with a cheeping Martha, amusing themselves with Arthur, old Mr Quick's ugly old blue budgie. Alan wasn't disturbed. He had learned that his Uncle Jim was always available to successfully put anything right.

'No, Alan,' Elena replied, wanting to bury her face in her hands and sob. 'But everything is going to be very difficult for a while.'

Jim gave the children a feeder of fresh birdseed to put into old Arthur's cage. Then he went to Elena and crouched beside her. 'Everything's going to be all right. I've just told you so, haven't I?'

'Yes, but—'

'No buts.'

'But Jim,' she tried not to wail. The tears gathering behind her eyes began to slide down her drawn cheeks. 'I can't really afford to pay for the repairs and decorating. I wanted everything to be perfect for the children.'

'Their life with you is perfect.' Jim reached for her trembling hands and wrapped his big, warm, rough ones around them. 'Elena, listen to me. I've already made contact with others in the building trade. I can get hold of cheap supplies and I'm not going to charge you for the work I'll do. Except for a mug of tea and the occasional meal. How does that sound? Better? The Lord provides, doesn't he? It's time you sat back and allowed others to help you for a change.'

For the first time she was able to gaze back into his strong eyes. 'Thank you, Jim.' She paused, then, 'I don't quite know what I'd do without you.'

'That's what I wanted to hear.' He smiled. 'Now, drink your tea. Then I'll take you and the kids back home in the van.'

Alan and Martha whooped in excitement.

–

Emilia was getting ready to go out. She rarely applied makeup, but she was highlighting her clear brown eyes with a little kohl and using a dark pink lipstick. She paid special attention to her hair, brushing it until it fell in thick, glossy waves.

'Where are you off to, darling?' Alec asked in an agreeable voice as he came into the bedroom.

'Truro. Shopping.'

'With Brooke? She's just arrived, looking well turned out.'

'No. I thought it would be nice to have a little time to myself. My mother will fetch Lottie from school.'

'Good for you,' Alec said, reaching her where she sat at her dressing table. He lowered his nose to the back of her neck and took a long sniff. 'You smell good.' He didn't add that the perfume was of country roses, those flowers were not a favoured subject right now. Emilia had said nothing in anger about the shock discovery at the desecration of Jenna's rose bed, saying their daughter was welcome to the flowers, but she was cross with Alec for still refusing to consult the doctor.

'There's nothing wrong with me,' he had declared stubbornly. After she had left her winning exhibit amid all the other roses on Jenna's grave she had gone home and had hauled him out of his darkroom.

'How can you say that? You're not behaving rationally any more, Alec. You're always tired, you're getting constant headaches. You hardly speak to anyone any more. Please, I'm worried out of my mind for you. Go to the doctor.'

'I'd get better if you'd stop nagging me!'

'Oh, so you admit you need to get better. Alec, see sense, please. At least get something to ease the pain, aspirin isn't working, or anything else you've tried. I've been wondering if you fractured your skull or injured your neck in the accident and this is what's causing the problem. Please arrange to have some X-rays.'

Suddenly he had seemed in the grip of a tremor and had leaned back against the darkroom door. A queer glazing took over his eyes.

'Alec!' She shook his arm.

He seemed to have slipped into a trance. It had been some seconds before he'd focused on her again. He didn't seem to have any strength and his voice emerged weakly and a little breathlessly: 'I'm all right, Emilia, honestly. I'm just not sleeping, that's all. Look, stop worrying about me. I just need to pull myself together. I promise I will. Now let me get back before my photos are ruined.'

Emilia was still working out whether she should be reassured or even more worried about his assertions. His 'little turn' was certainly something not to take comfort in. Her mother had suggested that men sometimes got 'a bit funny at a certain age', but even if that was true it would be another ten years before Alec reached that time in his life. Emilia had taken refuge in thoughts of Perry, and her arranged assignation with him today.

Usually Alec would have dropped a kiss on her, and Emilia would have smiled up at him, or stroked his hand or sighed in appreciation. She put her hairbrush down and clipped on pearl cluster earrings. She got up and lifted up her handbag from the bed and checked she had a hanky, her purse and perfume.

Alec watched her. Emilia looked particularly lovely and appetizing when she was aloof and dignified. He had kept his distance from her since the day of the horticultural show but now he wanted to be with her. To lay his hands on her, pull off her stylish Louis-heeled shoes and lay her down on their huge Victorian bed and mess up her hair and clothes. He was still sore over her stance about Lottie's appearance and fed up with her harping on about seeing the doctor, but he couldn't help himself and went to her. He gently wound his arms in under her cardigan and brought her wonderful familiar body in intimately close to his. 'You look absolutely appealing, darling. Beautiful. Your very best.'

Emilia turned her face away from the coming kiss. 'Alec, I have to go. I want to catch the midday bus.'

'Stay,' he crooned, nuzzling her neck. 'Take the car or let me drive you into town later. You don't want to ride on that boneshaker, surely?'

Emilia didn't want to take the motor car. Alec had never changed his old Ford Coupe. There was a risk it would be recognized if parked near a certain house at Highertown, a tiny hamlet on the outskirts of Truro, where Perry was staying. She pushed Alec away before he could attempt another kiss. 'The bus will do.'

Alec tugged her back into his embrace. 'Darling, it's been a long time—'

'That's your fault.' She yanked his hands off her. 'You're the one who's been behaving coldly. It's no good choosing to go to bed when I'm ready to go out. Aren't I allowed a little time to myself? And have you forgotten Brooke's downstairs? Let go of me, Alec. I've just enough time to say hello to her and walk to the village.'

'Cold, am I? I'm not the only one.' He stepped way back. 'I haven't looked to make love because you're so unforgiving about what I did to your blasted roses.'

'I'm not angry with you about the roses. They looked beautiful on Jenna's grave. I'm worried about why you did it. Why can't I get that through to you?' She glanced at the photograph Brooke had taken of him at Roskerne. It showed him gaunt and smiling softly, searchingly. She liked this image of him, it was full of his kindness and hinted of his former strength. She had made a pale-blue satin frame for it, trimmed it with spiralling dark-blue and purple silk rosebuds and placed it in a prominent position on the mantelpiece.

Grieved that he seemed to be fading away and was determined to do nothing about it, she looked at him.

He rubbed his brow, as if he hadn't heard her last words. 'I'd forgotten about Brooke.'

'I'm going, Alec.' Emilia made for the door but turned back. Alec had gone quiet. Abnormally quiet. Bouts of which were getting more frequent. He went to the window overlooking the lawn and stared down at it. 'Why do you keep doing that? What are you hoping to see?'

He kept his back to her. 'You wouldn't understand or care.'

'I do care and I'm sure I'd understand if you'd only take the trouble to tell me. Can we talk when I get back?'

'Go, Emilia. I want to be alone.'

'Fine. Have it your own way then.' She swept open the bedroom door. 'Be sure you're nice to Lottie if your paths happen to cross when she comes home from school.'

Emilia didn't get as far as the village. Smelling the thickly smoke-laden air coming from the direction of Ford House and then meeting Jim and Elena in his van on the way there, she stayed and did the only thing she could do. Miss her longed- for meeting with Perry and offer to help clean up some of the mess.

–

Brooke entered the bedroom shortly after Emilia left. 'Alec, are you coming down for coffee?'

'What?' Alec stayed at the window. 'Oh, Brooke. I'm sorry. Forgive me. Where's my mother-in-law? Tilda? Linda, the dairymaid? Was there no one to offer you hospitality?'

'We were going to have coffee together. Remember?'

'Oh… yes.' He ground his fingers into his temples. 'I'm sorry, I've got a severe headache. It makes me forget what I'm supposed to do.' Suddenly he put both hands on the window glass. 'Come back. Don't leave me!'

'That wasn't me you were talking to, was it? Who, Alec? Who do you see?'

He turned to her. 'You believe I see someone?'

'Yes, I do.'

'Do you think I'm going mad? Or senile? My grand-mother went senile.'

'I believe you've had a bad disturbance and now you're seeing someone. But you don't mind, because it's someone very special to you. By the way you've been behaving, I would make a guess that it's Jenna. If you're pleased, then I'm pleased for you.'

Alec came towards her. 'I'm so glad you understand, Brooke. I see my little girl often. As she would be now. Beautiful and dainty and she dances for me. And smiles. She smiles so wonderfully, just for me. I'm waiting for her to call me Daddy. I'm longing for that to happen.'

'She will, Alec. When the time is right.' Brooke's heart was filled with compassion for him. By right, she should tell Emilia what he'd said, but she knew it was a secret. She was the only one to have realized in the past that Emilia and Perry Bosweld had fallen in love. In view of his return and Emilia's obvious continuing love for him, Brooke considered this new understanding to be a secret that should remain between her and Alec. He wasn't mad, just confused. One day soon he'd see the doctor. For now, he believed he was seeing Jenna and it was giving him peace. He deserved that.

Alec felt, as he often did nowadays, that he couldn't breathe. 'Come for a walk with me, Brooke?'

'Into the woods where we went before?'

'Yes. I want to sit by the stream and let the running water soothe my head.'

'OK. I'd like to keep you company.'

They left the house by the back stairs, walked down the back garden and passed through the small iron gate into the adjoining field. Not speaking, content to have sympathetic companionship, they strolled down the valley, which graded down through reams of golden buttercups, and entered the woods at the bottom. Then they followed the wide, twisty stream until they reached a quiet, sheltered spot. They sat side by side under a beech tree, and allowed their minds to drift.

Brooke glanced at Alec. He was massaging his brow, grimacing in pain. 'Let me do that for you,' she whispered. She raised herself on her knees and caressed his brow, feeling the terrible tension in him. He closed his eyes. Eventually he sighed in relief and sagged forward, resting his head against her shoulder. Brooke put one arm round him and stroked his hair. 'Better?'

He nodded. 'Mmm.' He raised his head, opened his eyes and found hers were on the same level. Neither looked away but kept on looking at the other. Then it happened. Their faces grew closer. And closer. And their lips met. And softness and care and gentleness turned into passion and a sort of desperate need.

Alec rose and helped her up, and led her into a copse of tangled undergrowth where they wrapped themselves in each other's arms and made love. They took their time discovering each other. Kissing, touching, exploring, experiencing. It was as if he had never known the feel, the composition, the intricacies, the beauty of a woman's body, the depths of a woman's love before, and she had not known this in a man. They joined and connected in a way that was unique to them, not wanting the wonder, the joy, the brilliance of it to stop.

Chapter Fifteen

Perry had accepted an invitation of Ben's to dinner and he had brought a sulky Libby with him.

'Why have I got to be dragged along to this?' she complained on the doorstep after getting out of her father's Daimler. She took an instant dislike to Tremore House. Its origins obviously went back over a century but it had been mercilessly gutted and modernized. Knowing something about the big-headed Ben Harvey, she presumed the inside would be unfeelingly furnished with pretentious contemporary rubbish and absurd foreign pieces that its owner considered chic. There would definitely be no sense of the past or the mystical, which she could have taken refuge in.

'Because you're a little too young to leave on your own at night,' Perry explained once again, trying to keep patient. At times Libby could be as difficult and selfish as her mother but, thankfully, or at least Perry hoped, not as conniving or malicious. He doted so much on Libby it had not occurred to him that she did not inherit Selina's occasional compassionate streak; Selina had stopped the village's intolerance to its war-injured imbecile and she had been very good to Emilia over the loss of baby Jenna. 'I hope you're going to behave, Libby. Promise me you will.'

The last thing he wanted was for Libby to be here. Emilia and Alec were invited, along with Tristan, Winifred and Jonny Harvey. Hopefully Vera Rose Stockley, who had taken Libby out for walks during their brief residence in Hennaford, would come too and keep Libby occupied. He was desperate to see Emilia alone, to explain his decision to come to her after enduring so many years alone. So far, juggling everything and everyone out of the way so they could be alone had failed. There had been the Rawley fire, and the next planned meeting, in their secret meeting place on the moors, where they had first declared their love and made love, had been abandoned because Libby had got into a strop and refused to spend the day with Reggie Rule's niece. Libby did not make friends easily, she had a way of offending people. Perry knew she had little confidence and it was her way of defending herself, and he ached inside for her because he couldn't get her to see she was her own worst enemy. It was beginning to look as if he'd have to find yet another school for her. Selina was anxious for her to get the best education possible and to go on to university, but Perry was wondering if he shouldn't teach Libby himself during her remaining school years. Her marks were poor anyway – she hadn't settled in one school long enough to gain from its curriculum. He felt wretched and guilty about his daughter's misery, he should have made sure she had a more family-orientated life in which she would have felt secure. Last night, he had telephoned Mrs Nicholson to enquire if she was well enough for him to send Libby up on the next train – at least Libby could amuse herself by visiting the museums and art galleries and church buildings, the thing she enjoyed most, but his housekeeper was now suffering from a chest infection.

If only tonight he could get a few minutes alone with Emilia and share a quick proper kiss with her. 'Libby, darling, promise me?' he entreated again.

'I will if I can have that dress I saw in Treneal's yesterday,' she said, looking up under her dull brows.

'The one that's much too grown-up for you?'

Libby huffed and folded her arms. Her father owed her much more than a stupid expensive dress. He should be protecting her from the beastly girls who were making her life hell at school. They called her Lacking Libby. Because, according to their small minds, she lacked beauty, grace and style, and was hopeless on the hockey field and at singing and dancing. When her father turned up for a school play they had acted as if shocked that such a 'dreamboat' could produce her, 'the most ugly duckling that ever there was'. No one wanted to sit next to her in class, share their tuck with her, even borrow the stylish clothes her indulgent father let her have. Often she was ignored altogether. Recently they had started tugging on her hair, saying no girl should have such horrid plain hair, and that she probably wasn't really a female at all. Her breasts hadn't started to develop yet and she was taunted about this in the changing room at every gym and physical training session. The last day of term, she had even been sent a poison pen letter, threatening that if she brought her hideous, dull presence back to the school in September she'd be the subject of more physical bullying.

Perry sighed at the sight of Libby, rigid and silent and unco-operative. He had never given in to a bribe to gain her obedience before but he was worried that she might spoil the evening and then he wouldn't be expected to show his face in any Harvey dwelling again. If he was denied the chance of being with Emilia he'd fall apart with frustration.

'Oh, very well, but you'll have to let me agree when and where you may wear it. And don't think you can get your own way like this again, young lady. Now, do I have your promise?'

'Yes, Daddy. I promise I won't do anything to make you feel uncomfortable.' Libby crossed her fingers. She really wanted the dress, of a bias cut with a narrow rolled hem and a low neckline, but if she got the chance to rattle some of the rotten Harveys, one in particular whom she wouldn't be surprised to find would have a rose on her somewhere, then she would do so, in revenge for her Aunt Selina, who spoke of the family with hurt and hostility.

The rest of the dinner guests had already arrived. All except two were drinking cocktails outside in the garden. Brooke was playing a plonkety-plonk jazz tune on the piano in the drawing room while glancing often at a silent, immobile Alec, who was close by and appeared to be listening with his eyes shut. She knew better. He had a particular expression. He was in another place, recalling Jenna dancing for him. He saw her more often now, most often on the bank of the stream. He was so sure that Jenna would come to him every day that he no longer searched for her and frantically tried to hold on to her. Brooke was glad it gave him comfort, but she was becoming increasingly worried about him. She was now the closest person to Alec. No one minded the numerous times they spent talking for they didn't go off anywhere alone. After the time they had made love, Alec had said, 'It was wonderful being with you, Brooke, but we had better make this the only time. If Ben found out, he'd kill me. I mean he really would. We've had past estrangements and even now I'm always wary of him. And

I couldn't be unfaithful to Emilia again. I love her so very much.'

'I agree, Alec. I'm afraid Ben will always be jealous of you, that's why he has this hard edge to him, the desire to always better you. You've got something he wants but can never have. The Harvey birthright. He wishes it was him who was the squire.'

'Squire? What rubbish. I hate being called that. Few people actually did until Ben gained Tremore and people needed a way to differentiate between us. A long time ago, while I was raising Ben, he and I were close. I accept that's gone for ever. He hates the fact that I wanted Emilia, that she turned to me when he lost control over the loss of his sight. Ben has no need to be jealous of me. I never took Emilia away from him. He never really had her. She loves me, I know she does.' His voice had grown plaintive, weary and full of regret, making Brooke sit up in his arms and gaze at him. 'But for some time, for years now, I've known that for some reason I haven't had her full devotion.'

A guilty flush had risen up inside Brooke and she'd settled down where their eyes couldn't meet. How she wished she didn't know about Emilia's other love. 'Alec, I know she gives a lot of her time to Lottie, but who can blame her after losing Jenna?'

'Losing Jenna changed us both. I understand why Emilia puts Lottie ahead of me, I'm not jealous of that. But there's something else. I think about it a lot. One day I might unravel the mystery.'

I pray to God you never do, Brooke had thought, almost in a panic. Even though he'd just been unfaithful himself, the pain of knowing that Emilia loved another man more than him would destroy Alec.

Out on the terrace, which was drenched in warm, peaceful evening sunlight and laid out with royal-blue, white-edged, canvas furniture, Winifred remarked to Emilia, 'Alec's paler and he's lost weight but seems a little more relaxed.'

'I'm grateful to Brooke. She's got a way with him,' Emilia said, glancing at her watch and hoping Perry would arrive soon. 'She accepts Alec as he is and I've learned to do the same, so I've given up badgering him to see the doctor. He still pays Lottie little attention but he's not so impatient with her now.'

'I'm sure he'll snap out of it altogether eventually,' Tristan said in jolly tones, but he was lying. There was something wrong with Alec, very wrong. Mrs Rowse had told him that Alec was dropping things and had even walked into a wall.

'We're having trout and guinea fowl tonight. His favourites,' Ben said. 'Building up, that's what he needs. Don't you agree, Em?' He slipped an arm, deceptively matey-like, round her shoulders.

'I'll have to think about what I can tempt him with,' she replied. Alec was fond of plain, old-fashioned lamb stew. *Perry, where are you?*

'How's Elena Rawley's fire repairs coming along, Em? It was jolly bad luck,' Tristan asked.

'Yes. She's such a pleasant little soul. What a shame something like that should happen to her,' Winnie said. 'It's wonderful, isn't it? What she's doing for those two orphans.'

'It's amazing how fast Jim's making everything good again,' Emilia said. 'He can paint, put up wallpaper, see to the electrics and goodness knows what else. He's very talented. I feel proud of him.'

'Elena Rawley must be mad spending so much time in his company. People are beginning to talk,' Ben threw scorn on the discussion.

'Only nasty-minded people. Like you, Ben.' Emilia was vexed. 'Jim is good to the children. They look up to him. He's made a success of his life and it's time you acknowledged it.'

Ben felt any ground he might have made with Emilia slipping away from him. He rubbed her back. 'I suppose you're right. Oh, very well, I admit Killigrew has some worthwhile strings to his bow.'

'I'm shaken, Uncle Ben, hearing that coming from you. I must say I've always liked Jim,' Jonny said. He had just helped himself to another dry martini to relieve the boredom. He was looking forward to the excellent wines his uncle would lay on at the meal table – they would make this evening bearable. What a pity he couldn't have brought Angeline along, but young Christine was welding herself to her with ever stronger force. Jonny was so besotted with the nanny that he hadn't recognized that it was his eagerness with Angeline that was making Christine cling to her. He took himself off to join Alec, worried too about his favourite uncle.

Now Jonny had decided against going up to London, Emilia wished he'd ask to stay at the farm for a few days, but Tristan had told her about his infatuation with some young woman he'd met on the beach. The special rapport Alec and Jonny shared might draw Alec out a little. She was pleased when they appeared, drinks in hand, chatting, and strolled off down the lawn.

'Jonny mentioned bows just now,' Tristan said. 'That reminds me of the archery champion who is back in these parts. Perry's invited tonight, isn't he?'

'Can't wait to see him again,' Vera Rose said from her upholstered garden chair, where she had been sipping lemonade and listening to all the conversation. 'He's simply the most best-looking man on earth. I hope he's to be seated next me at the table, Uncle Ben.'

'He's far too old for you, darling.' Tristan was all paternal over the stepdaughter he loved dearly. She had never spoken of men before.

'But Jonny's interested in an older woman.' Vera Rose affected a wanton smile.

'Now look here, there's an age gap of at least fifteen years between you and Perry Bosweld!' Tristan was burning with indignation. 'You're not to flirt with him, do you understand, Vee? You'd make a fool of yourself and I don't think he's that sort of chap. You'd embarrass him.'

All the others were laughing, and when Winifred said, 'Oh Tris, can't you see she's teasing you?' Tristan was laughing too. 'And if the dear girl was interested in Perry she'd be all fumbles and blushes. I agree he's a devastatingly handsome man.' Winnie aimed a coquettish expression at Emilia. 'Don't you think so, Em? I admit I've taken pleasure in taking a second look at him.'

Emilia liked this, it would give her an excuse to gaze at Perry without anyone thinking it odd. 'Yes, Winnie. Perry is a very attractive man.'

Vera Rose was still smiling, but hurt was clamping the edges of her heart. She had no interest in any man but Jonny. She was in love with him, had been so for years, but it was unlikely he'd ever see her in a romantic sense. She was his cousin and stepsister and he saw her as nothing more.

'Wish I'd never invited the fellow now,' Ben laughed, squeezing Emilia's shoulder. 'On the other hand, if he can entertain you ladies by simply just being here, then us chaps can slip off to the snooker room. I forgot to tell you, everyone, he's running a little late because he's having to bring along that dull little daughter of his. Obviously, she takes after her mother.'

The piano fell silent and moments later Brooke came out of the French windows. 'Ben, everyone, our last guests have arrived.'

Emilia's soul and spirit lifted and with them her whole bearing the instant she saw Perry. His eyes homed in on her. Both found it an effort not to rush to the other's side.

Brooke saw the yearning interchange, the signs of mutual love and burning affection. She played the perfect hostess but never had she been more anxious to get an evening over with. She had made love with Alec, in truth she'd very much like to do so again, so she couldn't stand in moral judgement over Emilia's feelings for Perry. She felt sorry for them. She knew how easy it was to give in to an attraction, and the feelings between these two lovers ran far deeper than that. Should she warn Emilia, or Perry? Their love shone out of every last bit of them. What if someone else noticed it? If Ben did, he would surely cause trouble – the Harvey good name meant everything to him, and he would be jealous and furious of another man loving and wanting, and having intimacy with Emilia. Brooke sighed out her tension inwardly. If only she didn't know. And now she studied her husband. He was dancing attention on Emilia. Oh God! Oh no! He still wanted her. He probably hadn't fallen back in love with her, but it was as plain as the sun sinking gently in the sky that he desired to re-ignite the passion he and Emilia had once shared.

I could hate you for this, Ben. Why must you always live in the past? I'm not enough for you. Well, I don't want you any more. When this night was over Brooke resolved she would have to consider if she and Faye had a future here. Whatever her decision, she'd do nothing until Alec was well again.

Libby was glaring at the paving slabs. When it was her turn to be introduced she kept her head down, until she heard a young, strong male voice. Something made her look up. 'Pleased to meet you, Miss Bosweld,' that male voice said, inevitably socially polite. Its owner turned his head away almost at once to speak to someone else, but not before Libby saw who owned it.

Her knees swished into jelly, her cheeks burned. It was him! The youth she'd seen at the village show. He was a Harvey. Any revenge against the family was forgotten. He was here, the man she loved. He was just the sort she had dreamed of meeting, had prayed earnestly for. In her imaginings she would meet 'the one' when she wasn't looking for him. He would just be there. And Jonny Harvey was. If she could only get him to notice her, if she could scheme to get a photograph taken with him, hopefully with his arm round her, then she could show it off to the horrid, tormenting girls at school and boast that she had spent the holiday in love and being loved. She'd go up in their estimation then. They might even make her one of them. Someone important. Someone with a life. But how did a plain girl like herself get a handsome buck like Jonny Harvey to give her some of his precious attention? She had no idea. She sent up an arrow prayer that he would be asked to take her into the dining room.

Ben presided at the top of the table, filling glasses with an aromatic Château Latour and promising his guests a splendid pudding wine and finally liqueurs to make their palates sing! He served Libby wine diluted with water. As often as he could, he drew Emilia into talk that echoed the fun they had enjoyed as children, making a point of expounding how close they had been. The odd glance at his wife down the other end of the snow-white cloth revealed her fussing over Alec and encouraging him to eat as if he were a child. It suited Ben that she did not look up at him once.

Emilia was placed at Ben's right, and to her joy next to Perry. They touched hands briefly and made this their only deliberate warm loving contact for now. However, in the course of the meal they relished the accidental rubbing of shoulders and knees.

Libby was placed opposite Emilia, and in her desperation to impress Jonny, when she wasn't gazing at him and hanging on to his every word, she smiled at Emilia and her father, even though they were inappropriately in love – Mrs Harvey was wearing a gold brooch designed as a rosebud. Libby thought she understood matters of the heart now and was prepared to overlook the indiscretion. Dredging through her memories, she recalled that Mrs Harvey had been very kind to her. And she was lovely, it was no wonder her father loved her, and there was that old phrase, something Libby had now taken on board – you can't help who you fall in love with. Libby put doe eyes back on Jonny and prayed he didn't see her as an uninviting adolescent.

Extracting herself from Ben's persistent reminiscences, Emilia noticed where the girl's hopes were pinned, and feeling sorry over her gawkish attempts to butt into Jonny's conversation with Alec about his studies she tried to draw Jonny's attention to Libby. Even a small smile from Jonny, steeped with his natural crushing charm, would delight a gangling young creature like Libby for weeks.

'Libby wants to study history at university one day, Jonny,' Emilia said. Perry had written this in a letter.

'Oh, really?' Jonny smiled a dazzling smile at the girl from his end of the table. What a boring little thing Perry's daughter was; a throwback to a Bosweld who had married for money. Oh well, it wouldn't hurt to talk to her, but only for a few moments. Uncle Alec was quite animated when conversing but he was already wandering back to his own small world. 'What's your favourite era?'

'Um.' Libby went scarlet to the roots of her tawny, curly hair but she could just about think clearly under his fabulous gaze. 'The eighteenth century. The age of enlightenment. It was a very romantic time.'

'It was in Cornwall. The heyday of the smugglers. There's a smuggler's cove near Rosekerne.' Jonny made to look away.

'I'd very much like to see it!' Libby squeaked to regain his consideration. Then she wanted to die on the chair. She had made an idiot of herself.

Then, joy of joy, his stepmother was saying, 'You must pay us a visit, Libby. You and your father. What do you say, Perry? You've never been to Roskerne or seen Tris's shop. You'd be welcome to stay overnight. That way Libby could take advantage of the beach and explore the coast.'

'I'm afraid I've arranged for the delivery of some plants for Reggie's neglected garden tomorrow morning and a round of golf with Ernest, his father, in the afternoon,' Perry said, watching his daughter's face fall as if in anguish. 'Sorry, darling. We could go the day after.'

Kind-hearted Winifred saw Libby's distress. She thought that perhaps the girl was rather missing out tied to her father all the time and might welcome some freedom. 'Well, if your father agrees, Libby, you're welcome to come and stay with us for a while. In fact, you could travel back with us tonight. We're not staying late. I can find you everything you'll need until your father brings your things along.'

Vera Rose suddenly piped up, 'That's a very good idea, Mummy. Do come, Libby. Do say she can, Mr Bosweld.' Vera Rose saw this as the very thing that might hinder Jonny's growing association with the enigmatic nanny – a woman who Vera Rose felt had something to hide. There was something elusive and secretive about Angeline Johnson. Libby was clearly infatuated with Jonny. She'd probably follow him about like a faithful puppy, hang on to his every word, and that would help cut Angeline Johnson out, hopefully. And if Jonny became upset over it he might turn to his oldest confidante, Vera Rose herself, and she'd take the opportunity to turn the comforting hug she'd give into something else. Who's the saddest? she asked herself. Me or poor Libby Bosweld? 'It will be an exciting experience for Libby. After all, one can hardly come to Cornwall and not go beaching,' Vera Rose said, her smile offering the girl friendship.

Perry glanced at Emilia. She glanced at him. Here was the perfect opportunity for him to be in the house at Highertown alone. He said, 'It's a very kind invitation, Winnie. Thank you.'

'Thanks, Daddy.' Libby felt she could die with happiness. 'Thank you, Mrs Harvey. I'd simply love to come.'

'I wonder if you all wouldn't mind excusing me,' Alec suddenly interrupted. 'I'm getting such a headache.'

'Oh, darling!' Emilia was disappointed the evening was to be brought to an abrupt end, but she shot to her feet and went round the table to him. His face was twisted with pain and drained of colour. 'I'll drive you home. Just look at you. You're seeing the doctor, I won't let you argue your way out of it any more.'

'No, no, darling.' Alec's protest included him gently pushing her away. 'I can manage to drive. Then I'll take a walk to clear my head. Perhaps Perry can drive you back. He can go on to Truro via the back lanes.'

'I'll run Em safely home,' Ben interjected forcefully.

'I'd be glad to give Emilia a lift,' Perry said, his tone commanding. 'Are you sure you're going to be all right, Alec?'

'Yes. My apologies,' Alec said, as he went with Brooke to the door. 'Please, all of you, don't let the evening be ruined on my account.'

—

Two and a half hours later, Emilia and Perry were following the route Alec had taken. 'Alone at last,' he said, taking one hand off the steering wheel to hold her hand then returning it quickly. It was necessary to make a careful passage through the narrow, bendy lanes. 'I wish there was somewhere where I could pull in for a while.'

'It's just after eleven o'clock. Alec could be anywhere but everyone else should be in bed. No one will think it odd if I invite you inside for a cup of cocoa.'

He drove over the ford. 'I know it's wrong of me to take advantage of Alec being unwell but I can't help myself. I love you, Em. Darling Em. I love you so very much.'

She pressed her face against his arm. 'I love you, Perry. I'll never stop loving you. Why did you come? Why now?'

'It's quite simple really. It was the way you worded your last two letters. It told me things had changed for you. I'd decided I'd always stay away unless there was a chance, one small chance for us. There's a rift between you and Alec, isn't there? I'm not wrong, am I? Not living in foolish hope? Something's come between you. But witnessing Alec tonight, the way he was, it's obvious he's ill. If it's the cause of your troubles, then perhaps I should do the decent thing and go home.'

'No! I mean perhaps you should, but I don't want you to go. It's not what I should be doing but I won't let you go. I can't, Perry. Not now I've seen you again.' Perry brought the motor car smoothly to a halt in the farm's front drive. 'Come inside. You mustn't go yet.'

'I didn't intend to, darling Em.'

When they got to the front door they were alarmed to hear Lottie screaming in terror. Emilia raced up the stairs to her room. 'It's all right, sweetheart, Mummy's coming!' She met Tom running along the landing to Lottie, and Will standing groggily in his bedroom doorway. She pulled Tom aside so she could plunge first through Lottie's doorway. The room was in darkness. Emilia switched on the bedroom light and ran to her bawling daughter.

Lottie was sitting up, choking on her sobs. Emilia wrapped her up tight in her arms. 'Mummy's here, my love. It's all over. Don't worry.' Emilia stared round the room. 'Where's your nightlight?'

'D–Daddy came in. He took it away,' Lottie wailed.

Dolly and Edwin Rowse came in from their quarters in the older part of the house. 'What on earth's the matter with the dear maid?' they said together.

'Alec took away her nightlight,' Emilia said grimly, in fury. 'He's got some explaining to do.'

Chapter Sixteen

Elena was hurrying home from the village with a basket overflowing with groceries. She was going to bake a cake. She was an able cake maker. For years she had baked sponges and fancies for village socials, sometimes entering something in the shows and fêtes but never winning a prize. This cake she wanted to be special. It was for Jim's birthday. He had been going to spend the day working on Gilbert Eathorne's back porch and then take a quiet drink tonight in the Ploughshare. Then Alan and Martha had invited him to tea, saying he should have a cake.

Jim, who had been finishing off the last of the wallpapering in the hall, had laughed and said, 'Don't be daft. Only kids do that sort of thing.' Kids from rich families. The only fuss he had ever received on his birthday was when living with the Harveys and Mrs Em had laid on a special meal for him, and his twin. Sara was now nearing the end of her pregnancy, and although she had visited him in his new home and wished him well in his business, their old closeness was gone for ever. The last time he had seen her was weeks ago and she had not mentioned their birthday. It was unimportant to her, like he was.

'Aunty 'Lena, is that true?' Alan had asked her.

'Sometimes children and adults celebrate their birthdays, Alan,' she had replied, already planning to make Jim a cake and deliver it, with the children, to his cottage, as an extra thank you for all the hard work he had done for her. 'Come along, children. We mustn't stay here watching and getting in Jim's way.'

'I heard about a girl having a party once,' Alan prattled on. 'It's ages till mine or Martha's birthday. Can't we do Jim a party? Here? Just a little one? Please, Aunty 'Lena?'

Elena had got flustered and Jim had come to her rescue. 'Your Aunty Elena doesn't need any more work. No more fussing now. I don't bother with birthdays. Can't think why I mentioned it.'

'That's sad,' Alan had sighed as if in sorrow, copying Elena's reaction on hearing that Mr Harvey, up at the big farm, was unwell, and how he was seeing a doctor at the hospital and might have a serious illness.

'Yes, it is.' Elena's charitable side had been fully touched. She owed Jim so much. Making him a birthday cake was no work at all. She'd be glad to. And where else could he eat it except here? There would be no joy for him in having no one to share it with in Wynne Cottage. So it had been arranged.

Ambling along the lane in the shelter of the high hedgerows, a shabby straw sun hat protecting her from the burning rays of the sun, she planned salmon and cucumber sandwiches, sausage rolls and fruit trifle. She'd make lemonade punch and they'd drink a toast to dear Jim. *Dear Jim?* What had made her think of him like that? Her heart fluttered and a tiny blush crested her pale brow. Well, he was dear. A dear friend.

'Morning, Miss Rawley.'

Elena's eyes had been aimed at the dusty ground and she looked up at Myrna Eathorne, from the shop. 'Good morning, Mrs Eathorne. It's a lovely day.'

'Certainly is.' Mrs Eathorne was a comfy-plump, jolly sort. She eyed Elena's basket. 'Just missed 'ee in the shop, I see. I've just been along to Druzel Farm. Wally came to me in the early hours with word that young Sara had suddenly gone into labour. Well, I always help out at a time like this, there being no other woman on the farm. Midwife practically didn't get her coat off when the maid delivered another boy. A little over two weeks early he was, but as healthy as they come. That's two boys and two maids for Wally now. He'll be proud as punch when he comes in from the fields. And born on Sara's twenty-eighth birthday in the middle of a good haymaking. Some rejoicing there this day.'

'That's wonderful news. I'm sure Jim will be pleased and relieved over the safe delivery. It's another nephew for him.'

'True enough, but 'tis some other children he's quite taken with now.' Mrs Eathorne pushed out her chubby lips and gave a meaningful expression. 'All finished now, is it? The work he's been doing for you in the house? Or have you got something else planned for him? I'm sure he won't mind. I'm sure he likes the company.'

Elena retreated into vagueness. 'He has become fond of Alan and Martha.'

There was a devilish light, of the kindly sort, twinkling out of Myrna Eathorne's gaily wrinkled eyes. 'Now I weren't talking about they.'

'I don't know what you mean.' Elena was squirming. She knew exactly what the woman meant. Untoward remarks were circulating about the amount of time Jim was spending at Ford House. There had been whispers loud enough for her to hear in chapel. Maisie had reported that she was being pumped for information.

The mixed reviews were, 'No wonder she's got no time for the social committee now.'

'Hope she knows what she's doing. He could drag her down.'

'Can't blame her really, I suppose. He's a manly bloke. I wouldn't mind having him all to myself.'

'She'd better watch out. Jim Killigrew's a man, and well, men can't help themselves, can they?'

There was nothing Myrna Eathorne could say that Elena hadn't heard before. She had been torn over whether to ignore the gossips or to ask Jim to work in the house only when she was out. But that would have been impolite. Insulting. And unnecessary. Jim larked about with Alan and Martha but he was always respectful where she herself was concerned. Elena was getting cross. Mrs Eathorne had better be careful. She might receive an unprecedented vitriolic mouthful in return, and that would give the gossips something else to talk about!

'Look, m'dear.' Mrs Eathorne became soft and motherly. 'All I'm saying is that if there's an attraction growing between you and Jim, well, where's the harm in that? He's proved he's hard-working and trustworthy. He's as good to those kiddies as if he were their father. You never mind what the narrow-minded are saying. If you've got the chance of a little happiness then you grab it with both hands. Goodness knows there's enough misery in this world of ours. I reckon Ford Farm's in for a large dose of it. A gloom's settled over the place. There's great sorrow ahead and no mistake. 'Tis going to affect each and every one of us. Gipsy Idella told me so herself only last week when her clan passed through the village.'

Elena was stunned into silence by all this information. Mrs Eathorne patted her hand and walked on to the village, saying, 'You know where I am if you need a bit of discreet advice, m'dear.'

–

The recipe book was sitting in her hands and had been for some time. Elena had planned to look for a more exciting recipe than the usual Victoria sponge, but the words before her might as well have been written in a foreign language. Having received a sort of bald permission to think of Jim not only in romantic terms but to actually pursue him, she didn't know what to do. Yes, she did. She must tell Jim there would be no tea party, that people were gossiping, that her reputation, and his, were being compromised, and it must stop. From now on he must only see the children... where? There was no other place but here or his home where he could see them. And she couldn't deny Alan and Martha and Jim their special relationship. She didn't want to. Why should she? Jim had made the children happy. Having him here had made her... happy.

Alan was at school and Martha was napping with her new kitten on a scrap of eiderdown on the deep window seat. There was a contented smile on Martha's sweet little face. She couldn't destroy that. And why should she?

'Never mind what you lot think!' Elena told the absent gossips. 'Things will stay as they are.' Jim was an uncle to the children. And to she herself, he was... she wouldn't think about that now. It made the nerves in her tummy swarm and her heart jump about. *Get on with the cake. Or you'll let everyone down.*

She had plenty of time to bake something special. She must get back to the recipe book. Concentrate. Jim wouldn't be here until six o'clock.

Well, he wasn't supposed to be. But he was here now, tapping on the back kitchen door and coming inside.

Elena was stuck to the chair. The strength went out of her hands and she let the cookery book thump down on the table. She didn't even blink and was just aware that the sudden noise had not caused Martha to stir.

Jim was about to speak, to mention that he had some lumber in the van and... he forgot what he intended to do with it here. 'Elena? What's the matter? You look as if you've seen a ghost.'

'What? I... I. Jim! I mean, Jim. I was thinking about you. And... and then here you are.' As if suddenly recovering from a shock she was up on her feet and heading for the kettle. 'You, um, shouldn't be here.' The words fell in a rush out of her mouth. 'No, I didn't mean that. I mean, I mean, yes, I was about to make your cake. You shouldn't see it yet. The children want it to be a surprise. Not that it's finished yet. I haven't even started it. Look, I, look, you sit down. I'll make you some tea.'

Jim came up behind her. Close to her. Elena was trembling from head to foot. 'I think I should be making some tea for you.'

'I couldn't let you do that.' She swallowed the lump that was nearly choking her, and kept her eyes on the copper kettle, trying to make sense of her convex reflection in it. She must really look just like that at the moment. Strange and distorted.

To Jim, she looked lovely. He could smell the sweetness of her. He saw that nearly all the pins had fallen out of her bun. Her hair was just about spilled all over her shoulders. Without hesitating he pulled out those last pins.

She didn't object. She didn't object to anything he did or said: there had never been an occasion when they had got in each other's way, or been irritated, or done anything against the other's comfort. Jim was so comfortable to be with. She realized now that she had looked forward to each of his visits.

Elena was comfortable to be with. And she was peaceful. And warm. And kind. And wonderfully innocent. And feminine. And perfect. Perfect for him.

Martha woke up. Rubbed her eyes, saw her aunt and uncle together and thought there was nothing unusual about it. 'I'm going outside with Daisy.'

'You do that, sweetheart,' Jim said softly, without moving.

Elena turned round and smiled at the little girl. Her voice was as soft as thistledown. 'Remember to keep your sun hat on, darling.'

Martha left the kitchen. Elena glanced into Jim's eyes and gazed down, her face a soft pink, then she looked up at him again.

'Shall we stay here?' he whispered.

She nodded.

The last tress of her hair fell down and he used the back of a finger to gently brush it away from her face. Then he lightly took hold of her and pulled her slowly towards him until her face was resting against his chest. She wrapped her arms around him and sank into his strength. He placed a kiss on the top of her head and closed his eyes, happy to begin an unhurried, perfect romance.

Chapter Seventeen

Emilia was in the infirmary at Truro, waiting for Alec in the corridor outside the clinic of the consultant he was seeing. There were seats, but she couldn't keep still and paced the echoing floor of the corridor, almost unaware of the strong disinfectant smell and the human traffic passing up and down: brisk, efficient-looking nurses, porters carrying stores, a gaily whistling cleaner, long-faced relatives going up to the wards. Then she saw a patient, a small boy with his mother, and the fear in his little drawn face and the anxiety in hers.

She was as anxious for Alec as the mother was for her son, but seemingly Alec had no fear in him. After all the tests and examinations and X-rays he had undergone in the last few days, he had asked that he be alone with the consultant, as calmly as if intending to go the Red Lion Hotel here in town for lunch.

'I'll be all right, darling,' he'd said, while getting ready to leave home that morning, casually winding a tie around his neck. But he'd looked pale and gaunt in his second-best suit. 'I'm sorry I've been a worry to you. I should have agreed to seek medical advice long before. But I'm feeling fine now. Getting better every day. I promise I'll start eating properly. I'll soon regain my weight, you'll see.'

'But darling, you're still getting terrible headaches.' She had put on a two-piece, fitted, belted suit and T-bar shoes, and brought him a pair of well-polished brogues. He sat on a chair to put them on. He fumbled with the laces and Emilia tied them for him.

'Thanks, darling.' He rubbed at the back of his neck. 'Look, all that's the matter is just a bit of tension here. Well, I did take quite a thump when I fell off the ladder that day. I'm sure it's what's been causing the pain. I really must stand up straighter and ease everything with a bit of exercise.' He put his hands on her waist and squeezed, smiling into her eyes. It was the first time he'd touched her affectionately for ages. 'I'll have to get you to massage my neck and shoulders.'

'I'd love to.' She stepped closer to him, winding her arms round his waist, and he did the same to her. They'd stayed like that for some minutes, his head on the side of hers. Content and quietly together. And Emilia knew that whatever the consultant might say, she couldn't bear to lose Alec. As they slipped out of the embrace her mind was flooded with thoughts of Perry and her heart was weighed down in sorrow. It was a torment to love two men.

At the bottom of the stairs Dolly and Edwin Rowse, Tilda and Lottie were lined up to see Alec off. Alec made a joke of it, then as he got to the door he backtracked and picked Lottie up. He kissed both her cheeks. She stared at him from amazed, suspicious eyes. He'd said, 'Daddy will bring you back something nice from town.'

At last the door of the clinic opened and Alec appeared, shaking the medic's hand. 'Ready, darling?' Alec said cheerily. 'Off we go then.'

'What did he say? Mr Wilson?' She walked in sidesteps so she could see his face. He merely tucked her arm in his and led the way out of the bleak, grey stone infirmary.

'Alec, please.'

He took a long, deep breath and leaned his head back so he could take in the summer sky of deep blue and softly rounded white clouds. 'Everything's going to be all right, Emilia. I said so, didn't I? Mr Wilson's advised that because I'm presently so tired and sometimes feel light-headed that I shouldn't drive or operate the farm machinery.'

'But you will get better? The headaches will stop?'

'Oh, yes, darling. Eventually.' He lowered his head and kissed her lips. 'I do love you. You know that, don't you?'

'Of course I do.' She hugged him, her body sagging in relief. 'I love you. I've been so afraid for you. Is it all something to do with the accident?'

'All inevitable in the circumstances, that's what Mr Wilson said. Look, darling, would you mind looking round the shops or something? I'd like to buy that storybook Lottie wants. *Jack's African Adventure*, isn't it? Then I thought I'd meet the boys from school. Treat them to eats at Opie's. Is that all right? No need to pick us up in the car. We'll catch the five-fifty bus home.'

He seemed positive and happy, and Emilia was pleased to agree with him. They kissed goodbye and she watched him stride down the steep Infirmary Hill and turn into Charles Street. His head was up and he had his hands nonchalantly in his trouser pockets. She got into the car, parked on the hill, and with more relief surging through her she stayed a moment with her face in her hands. Then she drove the short journey to Highertown, leaving the car a discreet distance from Perry's temporary home.

Perry answered her knock on the door. 'Darling Em! What a lovely surprise. I've just come inside from the back garden, I've been putting in bedding plants. You're smiling. I take it Alec's going to be fine?'

She was instantly in Perry's arms. 'He's going to get better. He seems so different now. Oh, Perry, it's been so awful.'

He held her tight, crushed her to him. 'I know.' Perry was genuinely pleased that Alec had no terrible disease, and as a medic his mind had gone over several terrifying possibilities. His feelings over the last few days had been torn. Alec was the only one standing in the way of him and Em being together. If it had proved that Alec was in for something terrible then that would be fate, there would be nothing anyone could do about it, and after a suitable time he could have claimed the woman he loved so much. But he didn't wish Alec dead or struck down by some debilitating condition which would mean it would be easier for him to see Em. It had been a horrible wait for the results of the tests. He and Em had succeeded in spending some time alone but they had not made love. It would have been a tasteless, almost a ghoulish thing to do.

Now Em was kissing him differently, demandingly, filling him with desire. 'Let's go upstairs,' he said.

He was able to climb stairs as easily as someone with two good legs. In the large, sun-filled double bedroom he was using, he held her at arm's length. 'Let me look at you, really look at you.' He gazed at her and he studied her, every tiny part of her, imprinting her in his mind and on his heart, for he knew he would soon have to withdraw from her life again or he might tear her apart. All the while she kept her eyes fixed on him, adoring him. He touched her hair tenderly with his fingertips, then every approach and angle of her face, and her smooth, soft throat. He traced his hands gently, searchingly, along her shoulders, down over her arms, her wrists, finally grasping her hands, imprisoning them in his. 'You're so beautiful, Em. It seems centuries since we were here like this and almost every moment of my life without you has seemed wasted.'

'Don't say that, Perry.' She caressed his gorgeous face. 'You've had all those years with Libby.'

He glanced up at the ceiling, disquiet in his expression.

'What is it, Perry?'

'You've had too much to worry about over Alec, so I haven't mentioned this before. Somehow, darling, I think I've failed Libby. Of course, she's had no good maternal influence in her life but I don't think that what I've done has been enough. She's so unhappy. She's morose and difficult for the best part of the time and seems incapable of making friends. She hasn't any of the sort of steel and ambition that drives Selina, and Selina continually pushes her to be a high achiever. Even in her last letter Selina asked about exams. It puts Libby under pressure. The only things that interest Libby are the things she can do alone. I fear for her future.'

'Oh, Perry, I'm sorry you've been going through this. But I think you may have been worrying yourself unnecessarily. I was talking to Tristan over the telephone yesterday and he said that Libby seems perfectly happy trotting about after Jonny, and he's finding it rather amusing. She's spending lots of time with Vera Rose discussing girl stuff and giggling. Vera Rose will help her to grow up and gain confidence. Everyone is impressed at how well she can swim – that must be making Libby feel happy. I'm sure all Libby needs is some fun. And she's made friends now. That will help her to feel special. You've taken her things to Roskerne. You've phoned her since then. Did she seem happy?'

'Now I'm thinking about it, yes, she did. But I don't think she'll feel the same way when we return to London.' He went on in a tone of desolation. 'Em, I'd love to move back here but our feelings for each other would soon be discovered. It would destroy everyone we care for.'

Emilia gathered him against herself. 'Don't be miserable, Perry, darling. Let's not think about that now.' She didn't want to face up to him going away from her again.

'I'm sorry, Em. We should be making the most of this time together.'

He kissed her neck in delicate tiny kisses, making her shiver at each delicious contact. She kissed him in the same way, all over the area where his skin was exposed by his open shirt. They seared each other's lips with loving, insistent kisses.

She loved his warm, sensitive hands, and pulled them from around her and kissed each of his palms, placing firm, slow kisses down to his wrists and then up and down every finger. 'I've missed you so much, Perry. I've missed being with you. I've missed your touch and want it so much.' She kissed his lips, one at a time, tasting him; so wonderful again. 'I love your mouth. I love your body. I want you so much, all of you.'

'You have me, my dear, sweet, darling Em,' he said, taking her to the bed. 'All of me, now and for always.'

–

The young people at Roskerne had taken deckchairs, towels, play things and a picnic down to the beach. With them were Angeline Johnson and Christine Shaw. The tide was on its way out and there were hours in which to relax and have fun. The sun was high, a magnificent golden globe, the air was hot and fresh and almost comatose. It was the sort of day to laze in, the sort that if enjoyed would be remembered for years, perhaps a lifetime.

Libby was wearing sunglasses and a pink, ruched bathing suit, bought at an exclusive West End fashion store in London, and an expensive cotton sun hat. She had never felt more confident. Vera Rose had said she looked lovely. So Jonny would think so too – it was bliss to be anywhere near him. Vera Rose had been kind to her during the last few days. Arranging her hair differently with waving combs. Spraying her with scent, even her favourite *Flowers of Spring*, given to her by Jonny. Lending her frocks; they were only a little too big and old for her. Mrs Harvey had showered her with thoughtfulness and had said she would be a lovely young woman one day, that she was lovely now. When Libby looked into her dressing-table mirror she found herself smiling back. She didn't see her reflection as lovely, but it wasn't one she quickly hid from any longer. There was the fairy tale about an ugly ducking who turned into a beautiful swan. For Mrs Harvey to pay such a compliment she must see that she was destined to be a swan.

Libby had stunned the household last evening when she had appeared wearing the dress bartered for over her good behaviour at Ben Harvey's dinner party. She had pushed ankle socks into her brassiere and thought she had made herself a very fine bosom. Jonny must have thought so. He had stared at her, then, unusually for him, he had blushed and busied himself with his napkin. He had noticed her! From being all jolly and sometimes superior with her, as he was with little Adele, he saw her now as a blossoming woman. Unfortunately, Angeline Johnson had been there, having got a member of staff at the hotel to check on the brat under her care, and the condescending cow had smirked at her. The nanny was jealous because she wanted Jonny all to herself. She was at Roskerne and on the beach a lot, always whispering to him in corners, distracting Jonny's attention from her, making him turn his back on her. Getting Jonny to walk her and Christine back to the hotel.

Libby was hopeful she'd get Jonny alone for a while in the sea. The little girls preferred to splash about in the rock pools, Angeline Johnson only ever dipped her toes in the water, and Vera Rose was inclined to laze and sunbathe in beach pyjamas. Libby pushed her deckchair nearer to Jonny's, and listened in on the three older ones' conversation.

'I had a postcard from Louisa today,' Vera Rose said. 'She's touring the South of France with her aunt, but she mentioned she might be back before the end of the hols.'

'That would be nice. Louisa's a childhood friend of ours, from Truro,' Jonny explained to Angeline, unaware he was referring to his half-sister. 'Haven't seen her for ages.' He didn't understand why but he had a special rapport with Louisa Hetherton-Andrews, whose surname was taken from the now-dead brother and widowed sister who had adopted her. 'She never comes here though. Father doesn't approve of her for some reason and she senses it. It's strange. My Uncle Alec, Aunty Em and Uncle Ben adore her. She's an adorable girl.' He wished he hadn't added that last sentence. Angeline might think there was more to his feelings than friendship, but Angeline just smiled. She wasn't the jealous type. While she relaxed in her deckchair, Angeline was writing a letter. She was always writing to Christine's parents. She telephoned them a lot too. She was a conscientious nanny and Christine was obviously an adored child. It hit Jonny then that Angeline really loved Christine, and although she was friendly with him she didn't seem to be looking for anything closer, not even a holiday romance. He wanted her badly. He had never gone this long without sex before and he was getting fearfully frustrated. Libby, the bloody little pest, kept pressing up against him, flirting with him in her daft childish way, and it didn't help. She'd been persistent all morning and he'd got the awful urge to push her out of the way and grab Angeline's hand and suggest they leave the little girls in Vera Rose's care and go for a walk along the beach. The tide was way out and the little smuggler's cove, with its deep cave, was accessible. It was a perfect place for making love, one he'd used before.

Libby didn't like the sound of this Louisa. The affectionate way Jonny had spoken of her just now meant that if this girl suddenly turned up here, she'd stand no chance with him. Women adored Jonny. The nanny had paused in her correspondence and was smiling at him. A glance at Vera Rose, and Libby saw that she too was smitten with him. Libby's new-found self-belief made her determined she wasn't about to be forgotten.

She took some sun cream out of her beach bag. 'Will you rub some of this on my back, Jonny?' She knew there couldn't be much physical contact with Jonny, not at her young age, but she felt the very first stirring of desire and, carried along on the strength of it, she pulled the straps of her swimsuit down.

'Libby, no!' Vera Rose struggled out of her seat. 'I'll do that for you.'

Libby saw Vera Rose's look of horror. She saw it too on Angeline Johnson's face and, so she thought, disgust. And that same horrified expression was in Jonny's eyes, plus anger. Libby's face and neck was drenched in red. She wanted to die on the spot. She had suggested something inappropriate, and dirty. The girls at school were right. She was a misfit and a freak. She couldn't stand the accusation, the revulsion she saw on these people's faces. Breaking into wailing sobs, she dropped the sun cream and ran away down to the shore.

'What was that all about?' Jonny thumped his forehead. He had been embarrassed at the girl's request but didn't know what was the matter with the silly little goose. Then, 'Oh bugger...' The girl had formed a crush on him. Why, oh, why had his aunt invited the horrid little creature to Roskerne? It had taken all his patience to tolerate her. Libby Bosweld was gauche and pathetic. She pushed herself forward into everything with irritating enthusiasm. She got in the way of everything he wanted to do. Worse still, she was jealous of any attention he gave to Vera Rose and Angeline. The girl had insufferably referred to Angeline as a servant. It was time the little madam was sent packing back to her father. Perry Bosweld was a good-looking, thoroughly nice chap. How on earth had he produced such a plain bore? Jonny wouldn't consider bedding her even if she were a few years older.

Vera Rose sighed heavily. Watching Libby buzzing about Jonny, trying to flirt with him and now make a terrible, embarrassing hash of it had been a painful experience. It was something she should have stopped. She should have realized that Libby's feelings were getting out of control. At least she could have pointed out to her that Jonny had eyes for no one else but Angeline. Now what should she do? Go after Libby or leave her alone for a while? Libby would be devastated. She had become aroused, had put this on display, the most dreaded thing a pubescent girl could do, and Libby had not had the slightest notion it was happening to her. One thing was certain, the poor thing mustn't come face to face with Jonny again. She'd have to go back to Truro without delay. How was she going to face anyone ever again? It was horrendous.

'I think I'd better take Christine back to the hotel,' Angeline said, stern disapproval in her voice.

'No! Wait,' Jonny pleaded. 'Vee and I will sort this out. At least we'll soon be rid of the wretched girl.'

Libby kept running. She saw her swimsuit as she thought Jonny saw it, a flat, strawberry-like overstated confection. She saw her lightly tanned skin as an ugly red. She was ugly. Jonny Harvey thought she was ugly and he hated her. And because of him she had disgraced herself in the most repugnant manner. Damn him! She wished she'd never set eyes on him. The smug swine, who had women falling at his feet. How she wished she could go back and rock his cosy world. Tell him that the wife of his precious Uncle Alec was having an affair with her father. That it had been going on for years. That it was the reason her family had been hounded out of Hennaford. Only it couldn't have been. The villagers liked and respected her father. So what had her Aunt Selina done to be reviled? Something vile and embarrassing and unforgiveable like she had just done? Oh, God, life just wasn't fair! She kept on sprinting towards the sea.

Angeline had packed hers and Christine's things and was about to go to collect her. Checking on what Libby was doing, she watched as she closed in on the shore. 'She won't go in the water, will she?'

'Don't say we're in for some more drama,' Jonny growled, furious that Angeline was leaving and had refused to allow him to walk back with her.

Libby reached the first frothing wave and splashed straight into it.

'Libby! Come back!' Afraid now, Vera Rose called out between curved hands round her mouth. The roar of the ocean meant Libby wouldn't be able to hear her.

Libby was screaming to herself. She hated those she had left behind. She hated her father for bringing her here. She hated her Aunt Selina for deserting her to work in another country. She hated the girls at school. They said she'd never get married because no one would have her. She didn't want to be married now, to have to suffer those forbidden feelings again, feelings she'd had no right to have had at such a young age. She must be depraved. Those on the beach knew this. They'd tell others, tell her father. She could never face him again. She must never go back. She had nothing to go back for. Everyone would be glad to be rid of her.

And she hated herself. It was no wonder people couldn't stand to be near her. 'I hate this world!' she screamed and screamed. And she kept splashing into the waves.

'What's she doing?' Jonny started a run towards her. 'Libby! Libby! For goodness sake, come back!'

Vera Rose took Adele to Angeline. 'Take the girls up to the house. Tell my mother what's happened. I'll go after them.' She raced off in Jonny's tracks.

Angeline had trouble dragging the two girls away. They sensed the danger Libby was in, and like those unable to tear their eyes off an accident, they wanted to watch. Angeline couldn't help herself either. 'Oh my God,' she whispered.

Libby had waded out until she was out of her depth. The next roller lifted her off her feet and she disappeared.

Jonny was swimming frantically. The undertow was fierce. If he didn't grab hold of Libby in the next few seconds she'd be swept out to sea. Where the hell was she? She had learned to swim on other coastal holidays and should have known the dangers, but there was no sign of her, no raised hand or struggling body desperately trying to get back to shore.

Libby went with the waves. She didn't fight against them. Against what was coming. There was some pain, some discomfort, a rushing and a pulling and some strange sounds. Then only light.

Jonny felt the force of the water and knew if he didn't turn round this instant and make for the shore he'd be lost. Lost too. He thrust his head above the water and ran a hand down over his eyes for one more look. He thought he saw a dark head a long, long way out. He felt a great volume of water shifting him further away from the shore and he was filled with fear and panic. There was nothing for it but to turn and strike out for safety, and pray. How he prayed. He thrashed against the hands of the receding tide, but seemed to be getting nowhere. Salt water was in his mouth and it was blinding him. There was a horrid roar in his ears. He was drowning. As surely as Libby was. Or had drowned by now.

He was aware of pain, of his hair being wrenched almost out of his scalp. His lungs were bursting. He couldn't breathe. Death was coming.

To help her get the strength and momentum to drag him out of the water and not allow herself to lose her footing, Vera Rose screamed and screamed. She got the upper half of his body out on to the sand then frantically listened to his chest to hear if he was breathing. He wasn't.

'Jonny! Oh no! Oh my God.' She pushed him on to his front, turned his face to the side and started pumping his arms. He didn't respond. So she heaved him on to his back, and after clearing sand from his lips she put her mouth over his and started breathing into him. Moments passed like hours. She banged on his chest, crying, shrieking at him not to die. She breathed into him again and again. Then suddenly he coughed. She leaned back on her heels, watching as he retched up sea water. Then she helped him sit up. 'Thank God, Jonny, thank God!'

He gasped in huge pain-ridden lungfuls of air, then leaned against her breasts and tried to clear his vision out to sea. 'L–Libby?'

Vera Rose was crying the worst tears of her life. 'She's gone, Jonny. There was nothing you could do.'

'Oh no! What are we going to do, Vee? She was just a little girl. What am I going to do? It was all my fault. I didn't realize how she felt about me. She must have thought I was encouraging her. And then she must have felt so terrible.'

'It wasn't your fault, Jonny. You must never think that. Never!' There was vehemence in Vera Rose's cracked speech. 'It was Libby's choice. God above witnessed it. Libby, that poor little soul, just didn't want to live any more. I think even before what happened she must have been dreadfully unhappy. But that's the last thing we must tell Perry.'

'Perry? How the hell are we going to tell him? How are we going to explain?' Jonny made the gruelling effort to stand up. Panting, bowed over with his hands clutching his knees, he stared out across the vastness of the ocean, vainly hoping Libby might have somehow made it safely somewhere. She wasn't to be seen. She would have been swept a long distance away by now and was certainly dead.

Vera Rose was shaking her head in horror and disbelief. 'How could this have happened?'

Jonny clutched her hand. 'I can't think straight now. Come on. We must get to the house and hope Angeline hasn't told our parents everything.'

Chapter Eighteen

Two days had passed. In the den of Ford Farm Alec poured two large brandies, a second helping for himself and Perry. No words had passed between them for over an hour. None were necessary. They were connected by the soulless, gaunt appearance of fathers who had lost a child.

Feeling helpless, Emilia hovered outside the closed door in case she was needed. Her heart was rent in pieces over Perry's suffering.

'Leave them, Em.' Tristan placed a hand on her shoulder. His family had been left comfortless by the tragedy and he had brought them, and Perry, to the farm that morning.

'I wasn't going in, Tris.' Her eyes were filled with tears. 'It's so terrible. Perry hasn't said so, but he must be thinking that if he hadn't come down Libby would still be alive.' And guilt filled her to the roots of her soul. If Perry hadn't still been in love with her then the trip to Cornwall wouldn't have been made.

'Everyone's taking it hard, specially Jonny. Come and talk to him? He's blaming himself over what happened. He needs Alec, and he's feeling lost because Alec's with Perry.' The hurt at his son being closer to his brother was clear in Tristan's voice.

Perry needs me and I can't go to him! Emilia wanted to scream. She had not long left the house at Highertown when Tristan had arrived there with the appalling news. Tristan's account of the next thirty-six hours was harrowing, dreadful for Emilia to hear because she had ached to be there for Perry. He had gone into shock, unable to stand, barely capable of breathing for some minutes. She had wanted to be with him at Roskerne during the lifeboat search and the vigil on the cliffs for signs of Libby, but Lottie, frightened by the sudden death, had refused to be parted from her. The weather had changed to a mocking cold and wet and windy, and Perry had insisted on watching alone, shrugging off the raincoat Tristan had tried to put round him; refusing food and drink. When the authorities had called off the search it had been necessary to drag him away from the cliff and into the house. Winifred had called in her vicar and he had come and said prayers for Libby. Perry had listened soundlessly and had then asked for some of the weedy roses that grew in the garden. He had taken them down to the beach, asking to be shown the exact spot his daughter had gone into the sea, and after a second lonely vigil he had given up the roses to the hungry waves.

'I'll go to Jonny, but first I need to talk to you in confidence, Tris,' she said.

'Of course.'

They went outside into the yard and sat on the granite steps of the goat house. The spate of bad weather had cleared and summer was back on its balmy course. Emilia felt at odds with the radiant sun. She turned her back to it. 'Tris, Perry hasn't informed Selina yet. He doesn't know how to tell her. He feels that he's let her down. You see she is, she was, Libby's mother. Libby's real father was among a number of soldiers from an American unit during the war. To the world, Libby was Perry's and his late wife's.'

'I see. How many people know this, Em?'

'Just Alec and I. Should I find out where Selina is and send her a telegram? I thought I'd ring Perry's housekeeper and ask her for the address.'

'I think you should. She has the right to know and I'm sure Perry will be pleased that it's been done.'

Alec gazed out of the window. Jenna was there on the lawn. She waved to him. He waved back. Then he looked for Libby. She wasn't there. Should he tell Perry that one day she might appear somewhere for him?

'Is that Lottie out there?' Perry said, his voice dull and sluggish.

'Yes,' Alec lied.

'You have her and other children.'

'I have and they're a comfort to me. I know you're feeling as if it's the end of the world for you, Perry, but believe this,' Alec said, with warmth and sincerity. 'Something will happen one day to console you.'

'I can't believe that right now, but thanks for saying it, Alec,' Perry told the man whose wife he loved so much – without Em he wouldn't want to go on. 'I'd better stir myself. I want Jonny to know that I don't blame him at all. And even Winnie is feeling responsible because she was the one who invited Libby to Roskerne. I believe what the nanny of Adele's friend said, that Libby went too far out into the water. She was a foolish, headstrong girl. It was just a terrible accident.'

'It will mean a lot to Jonny. It hasn't helped, the nanny suddenly packing her bags and going off with the child in her charge. She was obviously afraid there'd be a fuss of some kind and she didn't want to be involved. Perry, what will you do now? Go back to London?'

'No, no.' Perry shook his head emphatically. 'I can't leave her. I can't leave Libby, she's out there somewhere. I'll stay where I am and when Reggie Rule returns home I'll rent something somewhere. I'm going to ask the rector here if I can put a memorial stone in the churchyard... bury Libby there if she's ever found. It's strange, but sometimes I have this feeling that she's happy, that she's free.'

'Believe it, Perry, she is. You mustn't be alone. I insist you stay here.'

Perry muttered, 'Thanks,' and hung his head. It was hardly decent of him to remain under the roof of the man he was cuckolding, but he couldn't bear to be without Emilia close by.

–

Brooke was in her bedroom, rifling through the pages of her diary. No matter how she tried she couldn't make the number of weeks that had recently passed any smaller. She had missed two monthlies. She was pregnant and the child could only be Alec's. She threw the diary in a drawer. 'My God, how did I manage to get in this fix?'

She sat on the bed, numb with panic. How was she going to explain this to Ben? The scant times they had made love since his return from Paris he had used protection. Those things weren't said to give total safety, but she knew in her heart, in her innermost being, that this baby was Alec's. There was only one thing she could do, tell Ben that the protection had failed. He'd be delighted she was pregnant.

And suddenly she was delighted. Somehow she knew this baby was going to go to full term and be happy and healthy, because it was Alec's baby. His understanding over how she felt about her two lost babies had made him a fit father for this one, which she was sure would be a boy. No one except herself would ever know the truth. She still loved Ben, although not as much as when they'd first met. She had considered leaving him, but not being the father of this child which he would raise as his son and heir would be just punishment for his self-centredness. Brooke was filled with happiness. She put her hands over her tummy and danced about the room.

She was brought up short at the window. There was a popping in her ears of the sort when something spooked her. A chill rode up her spine. Outside on the lawn was a girl. She was beautiful in a long white dress.

It could only be Jenna.

She raised her hand and blew Brooke a kiss.

Determined not to look away and find a second later that Jenna was gone, Brooke kept her eyes rooted on the vision. Jenna turned round and walked down the lawn and slowly and gradually she faded away.

Brooke went outside. She felt Jenna's presence all around her. She had come for a reason. Brooke put her hands together as if praying, and whispered, 'Jenna came to me because she knows I'm your friend, Alec. You lied about what the hospital told you. I thought you had.'

Chapter Nineteen

Three more days passed, and in the early hours of the morning a taxicab pulled up outside Ford Farm. Emilia, unable to sleep, tormented over Alec's continued lack of recovery and thinking of Perry, who was all too easily in reach along the corridor, saw the car's headlights and heard the crunch of its tyres on the gravel. She pattered downstairs before the house was disturbed.

Clicking on the hall light, she opened the front door. 'Hello?'

A suitcase had been deposited on the bottom step. A woman with a self-assured bearing was paying the cabbie. 'Thank you, keep the change.' The cabbie touched his cap to her and left. The caller strode up to the door. The instant Emilia saw who it was she clutched her negligee to her neck and shrank back to the stairs.

'Hello, Emilia. Aren't you going to invite me in?'

'Selina... of course, come in. We, I mean, Perry wasn't expecting you. You didn't answer the telegram.'

Selina Bosweld stepped over the threshold and dumped her suitcase down on the hall runner. Emilia was held unwillingly by her eyes, which had a magnetic quality and were the gorgeous colour of wild violets. 'Did you think I'd not come? With my own daughter dead? I'm sure you hoped I wouldn't. I went to Highertown first, banged up a neighbour of Reggie's and was told my brother is here. I'd be obliged if you'd bring him down to me. I take it if I get the chance to shut my eyes I can have the use of one of your sofas?'

Emilia wasn't afraid of anyone, but Selina Bosweld was a hard, predatory woman, given to baiting others and causing strife. Just before leaving Hennaford she had complicated matters by declaring to Emilia that she was in love with her. 'You can stay. I'll make up a bed. I'll fetch Perry. I'm very sorry about Libby, Selina.'

'Not as sorry as I am. Go into the kitchen, shall I? There won't be as much chance of disturbing your family in there.' The hawkishness Selina had about her came clearly to the fore as, without waiting for an answer, she stalked past Emilia. She pulled off her small felt hat and tossed it on the side table. Her thick tawny hair was cut short and shaped into the nape of her neck. Not feminine but it suited her.

'You're angry,' Emilia said to her back.

Selina whipped round and bore back down on her. 'I'm absolutely bloody furious! I gave my child over to my brother's care. I didn't expect her to be dead before she'd even ventured out into adult life.'

'Selina, please, keep your voice down. My little one, Lottie, has been very unsettled by Libby's passing and Alec isn't well.'

'Oh dear.' Selina's reply was steeped in sarcasm. 'You always have problems with your precious family, don't you, Emilia?' Selina gazed up and down Emilia in an intrusive way. Then she reached out and stroked Emilia's hair. 'You look very beautiful, by the way.'

Emilia grimaced and leaned her head away. 'I won't let you cause trouble, Selina. Perry doesn't deserve to be made to feel worse than he already does. And who are you to pass judgement? You were never a mother to Libby, and you've never gone out of your way to set her a good moral example.'

Reaching out, Selina grabbed a lower banister post and brought her body and face close in to Emilia. 'You're powerless to prevent me from doing anything I like. Be very careful how you treat me or I'll tell Alec just how close you are to my brother, the grieving father he's so generously offered hospitality to. All this must really suit you, having your lover under your roof. How many night-time excursions have you made to his room? Trips to the barn? I bet you comfort him all the time.'

'You're unscrupulous,' Emilia hissed. 'There should be nothing on your mind except grief for Libby.'

A sudden river of tears washed down Selina's strong face and dripped off her chin. 'I am grieving for Libby, more than you could ever know. I knew she was unhappy in London and that's why I moved far away to find something better for her. I was about to send for her. Her and Perry. They would have been happy in the countryside of Donegal. I'd planned a new start for us all. The very last of all the new starts we've had to make. But you and your revolting family have taken both of them away from me for ever. Libby's dead, drowned near your brother-in-law's property while in the care of his son. And Perry will never leave here now, you've seen to that. He must be dependent on you by now. I'll make you all suffer for this.'

'There's no need for us to quarrel, Selina.' Emilia was thinking, hoping, it was grief that was making the worst side of Selina so apparent. 'Or for you to make recriminations or talk of revenge. At a time like this people should seek support and comfort.'

With lightning speed Selina caught a length of Emilia's hair and twisted it around her finger. 'I'd be willing to forget all that I've just said if you're willing to give me comfort, Em. I suppose those who love you still call you Em?'

'Selina, what are you doing?' It was Perry coming awkwardly down the stairs in his dressing gown. Not bothering with his prosthetic, he was using the strength of his arms and good leg. 'How long have you been here?'

Selina moved back. 'Emilia and I were just consoling each other. I've just arrived. Perry darling –' she held out her arms to him and was crying again – 'hold me. I need you so much.'

Shortly afterwards Emilia went back upstairs, overwhelmingly disturbed by Selina's arrival and what she might do. She heard Selina's and Perry's voices and then both of them crying in the kitchen and it filled her with fear. There was no use hoping Selina had changed her mind about her threats. She was vindictive and she was clever. She could be cruel in subtle and callous ways. She didn't care about the feelings of others, the consequences of her heartless actions. Looking down at Lottie, fitfully asleep and clutching a teddy bear, Emilia feared for her precious child.

She went in to Alec. He was up and sitting on the couch. He had a glass of water in his hand and was taking painkillers. 'Do you know who's come?' she asked, joining him, putting her arms around him protectively. 'It's a shame it's disturbed your sleep.'

'I won't have that woman here for long,' Alec said, closing his eyes and leaning against her neck, trying to shut out the pain in his head. He hoped it wasn't apparent to Emilia that his left side was weak and not working properly. 'Not even for Perry's sake. Selina Bosweld's pure poison.'

'Don't worry. I won't let her stay. I'm sure Perry will move her on to Truro in the morning.' Voicing this made Emilia's heart plummet like a rock. Selina would torment Perry.

'It's a pity he'll have to go too. I'm sorry for Perry. I like him. You like him, don't you? A lot. I've noticed that.'

'You can't help liking someone like Perry,' she said carefully. 'Alec, you're shivering yet you're sweating. I think I should call the doctor.'

'I keep telling you, darling, there's no need. I'm just a bit run down.'

'It's more than that, surely? Alec, are you sure you've told me everything Mr Wilson said to you at the infirmary?'

'More or less.' He felt something brush his arm. He smelled a sweet, delicate scent. Jenna. She was getting nearer all the time. 'Darling, what I need is some good fresh air. As soon as it's light I'll slip out for a walk. Hold me till then?'

'Of course. Is there anything I can get you?'

He snuggled into her. 'I only want to feel your arms around me. Don't worry about Perry. He won't let that witch downstairs spoil things.'

'I hope so. Perry's the only one who can handle her, but with Libby gone...'

'He'll be happy again. I'm confident of that. Tell me you love me, angel. I need to hear you say it.'

Emilia kissed him and gathered him into herself possessively. Her thoughts, her emotions, only with him at that moment. 'I love you very much, Alec darling, and I always will.'

-

Under the warming touch of the early morning sun, Alec made his way to the bank of the stream at the bottom of Long Meadow. His fingers were aching because he had written a letter, something he hadn't attempted for years, and the pain in his head was at searing level, made worse by the effort and concentration it had taken to hold the pen and put down the right words. He could hardly see as he stumbled on and now his left side was almost useless.

He fell down under a towering oak tree. As he struggled to lean his back against the tough old bark, as he had done so many times before, to think, to plan and to cry out in hope, and to come to terms with his impending fate, he yelled out in agony as a wave of pain seemed to slice his head in half. It left him dizzy and panting for breath.

He tried to focus his sight. He searched for his reflection in the clear water of the chuckling stream but couldn't see a thing.

He was blind. Blind for good.

He had hoped fear wouldn't take hold of him. But it did. He was afraid. He knew what was coming, and although he had tried to prepare himself for it, he was afraid. And so utterly lonely. He had felt loneliness during huge chunks of his life. His cold, loveless upbringing had robbed him of the capability to give all of himself to anyone. He had never had the strength of Emilia, the goodness of Tristan, the intelligence and devil-may-care spirit of Jonny, able to give and take in complete honesty or disregard. His had been a limited life; his only regret to be parting from it so soon was to be leaving behind, to fend for themselves, his wife and sons. And his little daughter, God forgive him, whom he had been too afraid to love. He prayed Emilia would do as he'd entreated her to in his letter, to seek happiness and not to pine for him.

Pain and terrible weakness and a horrible strangeness overwhelmed him. 'Oh God.' His voice was no more than a whimper of a breath. 'I don't think I can do this alone.'

'It's all right, Daddy.'

Somehow from deep within he found the strength to speak. 'Jenna?'

There was a tinkling, merry laugh. 'Yes, it's me. I'm here, Daddy.'

'Where?'

'Look up. Open your eyes.'

Alec did as her sweet voice said. He could see her. He could see Jenna. His beloved daughter was a being of substance, bathed in a shining white light.

'Is it time?'

'Yes.' Smiling, she held out her hand to him. 'Come with me, Daddy.'

'Jenna, my angel.' For the first time he was able to smile deeply, openly, trustingly. He could see and speak perfectly now and there was no more pain or paralysis. 'I forgot for a moment that you would come for me.'

He got up and walked the short distance to Jenna and took her hand. Without looking back, they walked away together.

Chapter Twenty

'Perry, have you seen Alec?' Emilia asked, as he came down to breakfast.

'No, afraid not. What's wrong, Em? You're looking worried.'

'I am. He was so strange last night.'

Alec had asked for the lamp to be left on and he had clung to her all night, quiet while awake, murmuring he loved her while asleep, which was no more than a few minutes at a time. He'd seized her hand, reached for her, as if to reassure himself that she was still there. Hoping his strange manner meant only a need for affection and not the beginning of more strange behaviour, she had enjoyed their time together; a special time. During those long, silent hours she had suspended reality and felt that by having the two men she loved in the house she had everything she could possibly want. She forgot Libby, and Selina, and how she would soon have to face sending Perry away. Life would be impossible if he stayed close by. She could not risk Alec discovering hers and Perry's love and being hurt so much. Alec needed her and she would never desert him.

Finally, she had dreamed. Of Jenna. Of her tiny helpless baby as a beautiful little girl, sitting on the dairy steps. Emilia's heart had been caught with joy and she had gone to Jenna and gazed into her angel-like face. 'Hello! Jenna, you've grown so much. You're perfect.' Her daughter now had no physical and mental impairments. And she had such a gorgeous smile. She was fading away. Emilia reached out to keep her from leaving. 'Thank you for coming to me, sweetheart, for telling me you're well and happy.' She had woken feeling the same wonderful, awesome emotions as in her dream. Alec had gone and her arms had felt empty. She'd tell him about the dream as soon as he got back from his walk. He'd be delighted, perhaps it would be just the thing to hold some promise for him. But it was now long past the time she was expecting him home and she was very concerned.

Selina came through into the dining room. She had something in her hand. Emilia ignored her, sighing at her unwelcome presence. Because of this darn woman she was about to lose Perry living here, and she had treasured looking after him, to be able to console him over Libby. They had spent some time together re-establishing Jenna's remembrance rose bed; Perry planned to create one for Libby one day. And Alec liked him here. They shared a quiet drink together in the den each evening and Alec would emerge a little less weary. The boys got on with Perry; they had serious discussions about the Great War, and although Perry had been robbed of the deftness of hand that was required to be a surgeon he was skilled at building matchstick models, and had allowed them to monopolize him with board games. Dolly and Edwin and Tilda thought him an honourable, warm-hearted gentleman, blaming only his wanton sister for past events. They took pleasure in his unassuming presence and the genuine interest he showed in them. People from the village were of the same mind and many had called at the farm or written to him to pass on their condolences.

To Emilia's joy, the one who had taken to him most was Lottie. She sought his company, and Perry, understandably in the circumstances, sought hers. They had connected: it showed in their every word and action together. Yesterday Lottie had climbed up on to his knee with her *Jack's African Adventure* picture book and he had read every word to her, and they had talked about the pictures and made up a new adventure for the boy Jack. Then Lottie had pressed her head against his chest and slipped off to sleep. Perry had laid down the book and wrapped his arms around her and kissed her brow, tears sparkling along the lashes of his closed eyes. Emilia had not intruded on them but had silently joined Perry in his grief.

'I took the liberty of going into the den to make a private telephone call,' Selina said. 'Hope you don't mind. This envelope was propped against the desk lamp. The writing's very infantile, almost illegible, but it's addressed to you, Emilia, by your name, so it's not from one of your children.'

Frowning, Emilia took the envelope from Selina's well-shaped hand. 'Haven't a clue who this can be from.' She took out the slip of notepaper inside and went to the window to read it in better light. The letters were strangely looped and some were formed back to front and some words were crossed out, but gradually she pieced together the message. *Angel, you're not to grieve over me. I'll be all right. Make a new life for yourself. I'll love you for ever, the children too, Alec.*

'Alec!' She was gripped by panic, it seemed Alec was saying goodbye.

'What is it?' Perry asked, alarmed by her distress.

'I don't know! I've got to find Alec. At once. I think he's in danger.'

Selina took the note from her and read it aloud. 'Mmm. Don't like the sound of that. Perry told me last night about how badly Alec's been ailing. Where's he likely to be?'

'He went out for a walk. He said he needed some fresh air, but he's always wandering off.' Emilia was already heading for the door. 'I'll search for him and when I find him I'm going to get in touch with the consultant at the infirmary. I want to know exactly what's wrong with Alec, there's obviously something. Perry, will you call Ben and tell him to come over? And will you look after the children until I get back?'

'Of course, Em. I'll be waiting for you.' Perry was longing to go to her and lovingly support her. He was feeling unsettled since Selina's arrival, even though she had stated she did not blame him for Libby's death. They had planned to go on to Highertown after breakfast and wait there a few days in the hope of Libby's body being found. Perry hoped his sister would not be long in returning to her practice. She had asked him to go with her and had seemed to accept his refusal, but one never knew with Selina.

'I'll come with you, Emilia,' Selina said, with a half-formed smile. 'You may need a doctor. I'm sure we'll find Alec quickly. As I remember his usual haunts aren't far away. Perhaps… Emilia, don't get upset but perhaps you ought to take a look at the gun cabinet. Make sure everything's there.'

'How dare you!' Emilia just stopped herself from slapping Selina's face. 'Alec would never kill himself. This scrap of paper isn't a suicide note, it's…' She was at a loss. 'If you saw how he was last night…'

'Then I'm happy to take your word for it,' Selina replied calmly. This was different to her mean manner. Understanding and supportiveness underlined every bit of her.

'The note is probably a cry for help. Let's go and look for him.'

'I'll go by myself. Alec won't want to see you.'

'Em,' Perry said, laying gentle hands on her. 'I'd go with you but I don't travel very fast. I don't think you should go alone. Whatever's the matter, Alec doesn't believe himself to be well. Let Selina go with you. I'll try to get in touch with Mr Wilson.'

Reluctantly, she accepted Selina's company and led the way out of the house before the children realized there might be cause for alarm. She thought Alec was most likely in the churchyard, but as Long Meadow was on the way she took Selina there first.

'Slow down and take a deep breath,' Selina ordered after they'd hurried along the lane in the opposite direction to the village and had then climbed to the top of a lengthy sloping field that had long been stripped of its growth during haymaking. They had reached a stile – it towered over them and was made up of oddly aslant granite blocks and was incorporated into a hedge that was hectic with blackthorn bushes. 'If Alec needs help, you won't be any use to him completely wrung out, and if he's fine he won't want to see you all hot and bothered.'

Emilia paused with her foot on the first implausibly projecting step. A breather was a sensible idea. The stile took concentration to scale safely. 'You and Perry have talked about Alec. You're both medics. Have you any idea what's wrong with him?'

'Let's find him first, before we make wild guesses.' Selina studied her stricken expression. 'It can't be easy having Perry under the same roof as Alec. What are you hoping for?'

'What do you think?' Emilia snapped miserably. 'God knows I don't want any harm to come to Alec.'

'Whatever Alec's been suffering, he's always struck me as a strong man. I'm sure he knows what he's doing. Don't make him a victim of anything, Emilia. He'd hate that and it would end up destroying you.'

'What a complex creature you are, Selina Bosweld,' Emilia said, as she started a careful ascent of the stile, angling herself to avoid the barbarous thorns. 'You're a complete and utter bitch at times, yet you'll offer just the right thing at the right time.'

'Thanks.' Selina followed her in easy, liquid movements. 'After this I'd like us to talk, Emilia, Em. I'd like us to be friends.'

'Why? I thought you were angry with everyone. If Perry hadn't come here to see me Libby would still be safely in London.' Emilia jumped down the last step on the other side of the hedge. 'Don't you think I'm partly responsible for Libby's tragedy?'

'Perry can't help being in love with you. I take no issue with that because I feel the same way.' At Emilia's impatient glare, she added, with a raised hand, 'OK, you don't want to hear that. Yes, I sometimes feel angry with you, no one likes rejection. But I'll never blame you for what happened to Libby. Not you.' But she did blame others, particularly Jonny Harvey. She had threatened and frightened him once when he was ten years old. Consequently Tristan Harvey had publicly humiliated her. Ben Harvey had taken a superior stance over her. Jim Killigrew had jeered at her. Because of it the whole village had rejected her and it had made Libby miserable. If she could settle some scores while she was here, she'd do it, as ruthlessly as she knew how.

They were at the top of Long Meadow and Emilia gazed down to the stream. She laughed in relief. 'There he is, stretched out and deep in thought.'

Selina took a long look down at Alec. As Emilia made off for the descent she grabbed her. 'Perhaps I should go down to him alone.'

'Don't be silly. Alec doesn't like you. You're the last person he'd want to see.'

'I like your blunt tongue,' Selina said lightly, but she was careful to keep up with Emilia's quick steps.

'Alec! Alec!' Emilia called out when halfway down. She wished Selina would remain at a discreet distance so she could talk privately to him about the reason behind his words in his very first letter to her.

When they reached level ground, Selina stopped. She put a firm grasp on Emilia's arm. 'Emilia, I think you should stay here.'

Emilia pushed her hand off. She was under attack from niggles of alarm. 'Why? What on earth for? Alec!' He was leaning strangely. 'Alec, it's time to come home for breakfast.'

Selina again gripped her arm. 'We'll go to him slowly. Emilia…'

'Why?' She let Selina's hand stay. 'What are you trying to tell me?'

'Can you see that Alec has no colour? My dear, you're going to have to be very strong.'

In fear, Emilia tried to wrench herself away but Selina clung on to her. 'Slowly now.'

One slow step at a time they went, along the well-worn path that was bordered by thistles, buttercups, daisies and nettles, to the stream. To Alec. Emilia's eyes were rooted on him.

He was still.

So still.

Unnaturally still.

A numbing sense of unreality swept over her. She advanced on her husband in the care of a woman she loathed, but who right now she was clinging to for help, for support, for strength.

They reached Alec and as if in slow motion knelt down beside him.

'Alec,' Emilia said. 'Darling.' She touched his hand. It seemed frozen. With eyes as huge as a frightened child's she turned to Selina.

'I'm very sorry, Emilia. He's gone. By the look of him it was peaceful.'

Shock settled on Emilia. She felt she was suffocating in ice. 'He's...?'

'Dead. Yes, he is. Don't be afraid. He wasn't. Look at his calm expression.'

Last night, the letter, it all made sense now. What sort of sense she was too numb to say. 'He – he knew, didn't he? He knew he was going to die and he knew it would be today?'

'It seems he did.' Selina reached forward and closed Alec's eyes. 'Ben will come to find us. Would you like to stay with Alec until he comes? I'll step away, leave you together.'

'Yes.' Emilia's voice sounded far away, as if it didn't belong to her. 'I'd like to hold him.'

Taking Alec's head and shoulders into her arms, alone with him, with tears flooding from her eyes, she told him how much she loved him and always would. 'I'm sorry, darling. You were suffering, weren't you? Suffering a lot. You should have told me, but never mind. It's the way you wanted it and that's fine with me. The boys and Lottie are going to miss you so much. I'll take good care of them, I promise. Thank you for the letter. I'll treasure it always. What a wonderful man you were. I'll remind the children of it always. I dreamt of Jenna last night. I'll bury you beside her. It's what you would have wanted, isn't it? You and Jenna, together again at last.'

Chapter Twenty-One

Vera Rose climbed up into the attics at Roskerne. Jonny was there. It was one of his favourite places, amid clutter from the Stockley past. In his black suit and tie, he was leaning forward on an old sea chest, his elbows dug into his knees. Cigarette ends were piling up in the ashtray in the palm of one hand and a nearly empty bottle of vodka was dangling from the other.

He gulped down another mouthful of drink, drew in on the cigarette between his lips then exhaled noisily, screwing up his eyes against the smoke. 'If you've come to tick me off you can turn straight back round and bugger off.'

'I've come to join you. Can I have a cigarette? And a swig from the bottle?'

'No, you bloody well can't.' He swayed and it took an effort to check his balance.

Vera Rose parked herself on a low leather square stool, close up and facing him. This was how they had sat during childhood games, Jonny always the leader, on a higher par than her and any other playmate. 'I can't make you give me a cigarette or a drink but you can't stop me from damned well swearing.'

He allowed his stunning slate-grey eyes to focus on her. 'What do you want, Vee?'

'I just want to be with you. I know how close you were to Uncle Alec. Aren't you going to take off your suit? It will get grimy up here.'

'As if that matters! God, I hope I never have to go to another funeral for the rest of my life. That was the hardest thing I've ever had to do today. Aunty Em's face – she looked so lost, so small. And the boys. They can't take it in. Thank God Lottie's too young to understand. And to be there with Perry Bosweld – good of him to come, but oh Lord, so soon after Libby... And later, I saw Selina. She never spoke to me, she just stared as if she hated me, well, I can't blame her for that. Hell and damnation, Vee! Why are people dying all around us?' He took another gulp of vodka, swiping drips off his chin.

'Libby's death was an act of desperation. Perry made enquiries at her school, she was being shamelessly bullied. I don't expect she could face going back there. At least Perry and his sister have been spared the full reason of why Libby ran into the sea. It's something we must forget. And if it wasn't that, then something else was bound to have brought her life to an unbearable level. That poor girl might have attempted to take her life at any time. She's at peace now, I'm sure. And Jonny, listen to me, Uncle Alec's death was inevitable. He had a brain tumour. What you must cling to was how brave he was.'

'The world is worse off without him. I'm worse off without him. I thought he'd be there when I graduate, and at my passing-out parade after my RAF training. He won't be here for anything I do from now on. It's not bloody fair. He was only forty-one years old, for goodness sake!'

Vera Rose leaned closer to Jonny. 'Yes, but he did a lot with those years. He raised Uncle Ben single-handed.

He worked tirelessly through the war years with very little labour to keep food on the country's tables, and during that time he stopped you from being abducted – goodness knows where you would be otherwise, if your mother and her man friend had managed to get you away – and Uncle Alec was your security until Uncle Tris resigned from the army. Uncle Alec loved you as much as he did his own sons and he had the highest hopes for you. What you've got to do now is to honour his memory. It won't hurt to get hopelessly drunk today, but after this you must work hard to do everything that would have made him proud of you. I know it will be hard for you returning to university after all that's happened, but you've got to knuckle down when you go back up.'

Jonny put out a shaky hand and tugged on her hair. 'I wish I saw things as simply as you do, Vee. You're a lovely, uncomplicated girl.'

'You used to see things in easy terms, Jonny. Meeting Angeline Johnson has muddled you. Were you in love with her?'

'No, I shall never fall in love. Don't want to. I was attracted to the image I had of Angeline. It was a pretty shallow trick of hers, running out on us like that. I'll never trust another woman as long as I live. Do you know what? I've talked to the hotel manager. He believes Christine was actually Angeline's child, fathered by a married man. This chap phoned her every night; you remember how she always wanted to get back at a certain time. Well, you'd think it would be the mother to enquire about her child. Must be why Angeline fussed so much over the girl, there was an obvious strong bond. And come to think of it, did you ever hear Christine called her Miss Johnson? No!' Throwing back his head, Jonny finished off the vodka, then he allowed the bottle to drop and topple over on to the wooden floor. Drunk and morose and full of indignation, he let out an obscene phrase. 'Devious, that woman was. Played me for a fool. Wasn't interested in me at all. She chatted to you nearly as much as she did me but I never saw it. She just wanted some company for herself and Adele for Christine. I thought she liked me. She was a bloody tease. I didn't even get to...'

Vera Rose was pleased the nanny, after giving a statement to the police, had scampered out of the area the same day as the tragedy, but she was disappointed that it had made Jonny cynical about women and even more determined to keep a watch on his heart. She was wasting her time being in love with him, and now she supposed it was no more than infatuation that she'd felt, in the same way poor young Libby had. The trouble was that a clever, gorgeously handsome man, with a strong masculine body, who was not short on charm and charisma, bred hope and dreams that were almost impossible to resist. 'Get what, Jonny? Get to go to bed with her? Why is that sort of thing so important to you?' She already knew what his answer would be.

'I bloody well enjoy it,' Jonny squawked impatiently, as if answering something stupid. 'Now don't come out with all that guff about giving all of myself away, tender moments and emotional mishmash. Sex is sex. It's wonderful. And despite what the romantics and religious preach, I find casual encounters absolutely bloody fulfilling.'

'Angeline would have meant more to you than that though, wouldn't she?'

Jonny pressed against his pockets, searching for his cigarette case. 'Nah, not really. I don't think so. Who knows? Who cares? Might have been my first relationship, but it wouldn't have lasted. I'm too young to think about that sort of thing and I'm definitely not made for monogamy. If you ask me few people are. Too many married couples stay together simply because they think they have to or because they've nowhere else to go or they're too frightened to make the break. Sad situation, I say.'

'My mother is happily married to your father, they're in love. And so were Uncle Alec and Aunty Em.' Vera Rose thought it worthwhile to mention that there was another side to life than just selfish enjoyment, that commitment and loyalty should not merely be scoffed at.

Jonny made a throwaway gesture. 'My mother left my father and died giving birth to her lover's baby, remember? Uncle Alec had a bitch of a first wife, apparently. Uncle Ben and Aunt Brooke aren't happy at all, even though they're hoping this latest sprog will turn out to be a son and heir. Have you noticed their body language? There's enough married misery in our own family, Vee. You'll never convince me life-long togetherness is worth it.' With shaking fingers, Jonny lit another cigarette. He narrowed his eyes at his cousin-stepsister. 'Have you… ? No, don't answer that. You're a decent girl and I'm jolly glad you are. And if you're ever seduced, I'd be obliged to track the swine down and give him a thorough thrashing.'

'You've double values, Jonny, and you talk a lot of nonsense.' Vera Rose got up.

'W-where're you going?' He didn't want to be alone. To think about his uncle's last minutes. To wonder if he had been in unbearable pain, frightened, lonely. Had he felt deserted? Utterly forsaken?

'There's not much use in staying with you while you're like this. Try not to let Uncle Tris see you. Don't forget how upsetting all this has been for him too. I think you should sober up and go to the farm for a few days before heading back to your studies. Aunty Em needs all the practical help she can get. I'm going over to Truro myself at the end of the week. Louisa will be back. She phoned to say she was sorry that she and her Aunt Polly missed the funeral.'

'I'll look forward to seeing Louisa again. The old gang will be back together for a while. Stay here a bit longer, Vee.'

She was in no mood for more of his woes, or the boastful reminiscences he'd probably embark on at the mention of Louisa Hetherton-Andrews – his shy little thing from town, he called her – and he playfully teased her endlessly by calling her Lou-Lou, which she bore patiently. Louisa had a birthmark on her face, which she was sensitive about. Jonny had once thoughtlessly said she must play a witch in one of his games because she had the mark of the Devil. Louisa had been hurt and Jonny had apologized profusely and made it up to her by splashing out a month's pocket money on a Celtic cross pendant, which Louisa wore often. He still loved to tease her. Vera Rose saw Jonny for what he was then, a likeable, immature youth, sometimes selfish and irritating.

She stalked away, but Jonny shifted and she fell over his legs. He caught her and she instinctively flung her arms round his neck to get steady. 'Mmm, you smell nice,' Jonny murmured, holding her firmly, wrapping her in to himself. 'You always smell so nice and fresh and so you, Vee.'

'Do I? Let me go.'

'No, I need you to stay. Please.' Then he was crying. He needed to express his grief and she hugged him, allowing him to cry against her neck.

He sobbed and shook for some moments, then placed the side of his face against the side of hers. 'Thanks for that. I'm glad you came up.'

'Make Uncle Alec proud of you, Jonny,' she whispered, overcome with emotion herself.

'I will. I swear.' His arms were around her and he interlocked his fingers with hers, bringing her fast against him. 'You feel so soft, Vee.'

She knew she should break away, but now she was in Jonny's arms it was the most wonderful place to be. He moved his hands and clasped them round her in a different area of her body. They stayed like that, everything silent except for the sound of their deep breathing.

She moved until she was looking up at his chin, then she went a little further until she was gazing at his mouth – such a full, firm, sensuous mouth – and then she was looking straight into his eyes. Shameless, his eyes were, and uninhibited. The darkness in them seemed to have wicked flecks of gold. It made her want to be just like that, free and easy, not just good old sensible Vera Rose, the girl who had never given her mother a day's worry. And Jonny was beautiful. He could have just about any woman he wanted, but right now she had him all to herself. She settled down against him again, and although not moving, she smelled him and made herself familiar with his masculine shape. He was remarkable, seemingly unbreakable, strong and tough.

Jonny began to caress her back. It was good to hold a woman again. Even Vee. He loved the soft contours of the female body and Vee's was nicely curved. He was aware of her breasts against his chest, her arms draped over him, her long silky legs; one was bare up to the thigh where her skirt was bunched up. She sighed. Such an innocent sound yet wholly provocative. She stirred. And it stirred him in the way he liked best.

He knew he should relinquish her but he couldn't help himself. She felt so warm and alive. He pecked her forehead. He kissed her cheek. She didn't respond but she didn't pull away from him either. So he sought her lips. He tilted her chin and quickly found her mouth.

Vera Rose had enjoyed his earliest exploration and was hoping he would take it further. She raised her face with the motion of his hand and she closed her eyes for the first contact of their lips. He didn't disappoint her. Gentleness and expertise mingled on her lips. She had never been kissed this way before. There had only been a shy good-night kiss from a boy who had escorted her home from a dance, but this was different. And now he was adding passion. It was decadent, earth-shattering, intoxicating. Something unquenchable, something she didn't want to stop. She gripped his hair and moved her mouth under his, with his, against his, as if she had done this with him a thousand times.

Jonny put a hand over her heart. He felt it thumping. He felt the heat of her skin under her clothes. He slid his fingers down her body and placed his palm over her stomach. He massaged there. She didn't protest. He went on with his demanding kisses. Slowly, so slowly that she would hardly realize what he was doing, he pulled her blouse out of her skirt, then he slid his hand inside the blouse and up over her chemise until he hit the glorious bare skin up near her neck. He ran a feather-light touch down the column of her spine, and got the return he was hoping for, a little shiver, and another and another; she was enjoying his touch. He took his hand out from her clothes and used it to caress her face. She was flushed. Without knowing it, she had uncurled herself, responding to him, and he had greater access to her body.

'All right?' he whispered, pecking her forehead.

She nodded, incapable of speech at that moment, knowing only that he was breeding wonderful sensations in her and she should flee. But she wanted to stay like this with him for ever. He picked up her hand and kissed it; he was so tender and loving. He trailed a fingertip underneath her eye, down beside her nose, down over her lips, then her chin and throat. Kissing her mouth again, he played the backs of his fingers a little lower down than where he had gone before. He went lower and lower, turning his hand over and going on with the descent inside her chemise. She knew where his journey was heading and she should grasp his hand and tell him to stop. But she didn't. And his hand crept inside her brassiere and she leapt in a strange, fantastic bliss as his warm, rough flesh closed over her bare flesh. Her breasts were in perfect proportion with the rest of her figure and were firm and smooth, so she had no fears he wouldn't like what he'd found.

'You're beautiful here.' He shuddered in excitement. He withdrew his hand and ran it up in under her skirt. 'I want you, Vee,' he breathed over her mouth. 'I must have you.'

He let her go and led her to an ancient couch, one that bore the scorch marks of the disobedience of his earliest smoking habit. Vera Rose was trembling. Her whole self felt as if it was on fire. Faced with the reality of actually having sex, of letting a man use her most intimate and embarrassing part, specially Jonny, an insatiable womanizer, made her pull back from him. She was sure he had taken others girls to this piece of furniture, and there would certainly be others.

'Don't be scared,' he whispered, clamping his hands on her shoulders. She didn't move. All she could do was stare down at the marred, green-striped watered silk of the couch and feel she was about to be totally lost. Jonny nuzzled behind her ear and swayed against her body. 'It'll be all right, I promise. Your first time might as well be with me. I'll be gentle, understanding. I won't get you into trouble. I've got protection. You'll love it, Vee. Let yourself enjoy it. Women do these days, you know. And why not? Forget all that Victorian prudery, it's rubbish.'

But? She knew there were a hundred buts, yet none would come to her. She was too far gone in sensual need, so caught up in desire she had forgotten all her mother's advice and warnings about 'that side of life'. Jonny came round her and kissed her mouth and her response was immediate. She loved the feel of his lips, the taste of him. He ran his mouth down her neck, unbuttoning her blouse, kissing her cleavage. She knew it was a worthless question but she had to ask. 'Do you love me, Jonny?'

'Course I do,' he said, slipping off his jacket and tie and then getting on with undressing her. 'I'm not the marrying type and you'll always be the closest girl to me. Come on, relax. I know what I'm doing. Let me initiate you into the grown-up world.'

Vera Rose had one last moment of doubt, then she allowed him to do just that.

Chapter Twenty-Two

In Truro, Perry faced his sister across the breakfast table.

'You don't have to come with me every time I go to the farm. I'm sure you'd like to do some shopping or something.'

'Something, Perry?' Selina turned over a page of *The Times,* took a large bite of toast and marmalade, then settled her eyes on him as she munched.

Perry hated her eyes. They were rarely quiet and all too often, as now, the irises sparkled in mocking rays of beautiful violet and glints of cold silver. They hinted of the exotic and the barbaric. In the past she had been a caring, sympathetic nursing sister – she had devotedly nursed him back to health after half his leg had been blown off by a grenade – and he didn't doubt that now as a doctor she had the best of ways with her patients, but this one good side to her was definitely missing now.

The instant they had got here in Reggie Rule's house, on the evening of Alec's death, she had given him a hard look. Nothing more. But he had known he was on different ground with her now, that they were not united in grief over Libby in the way she had first shown.

He shrugged off her answer as if not really interested – Selina was on top form in her old cat and mouse games. 'Thought you might have liked a spot of lunch in town.'

'I've not a single friend hereabouts, have I, remember?' She returned to a report of how the country's gold reserves were dwindling alarmingly, and how it was being proposed that the salaries of the armed forces, teachers and policemen should be reduced. At one time Selina would have been concerned about the inevitable unrest this would cause. She had too much unrest curdling in her soul now to care. Swiping over the page, she added with a contemptuous grin, 'I said goodby to my reputation when I took too many lovers during my time at the infirmary.'

'It's hardly something to be proud of.' Perry pushed away the fried food she had cooked for him. He had no appetite. Selina made him feel sick. She had taken him away from Em's comfort, and it grieved him that he was not there all day long to comfort her when she needed him most, or her family, whom he was enormously fond of.

Selina poured herself another cup of tea and slowly stirred in sugar. With her elbows on the table, she held the cup to her lips, her sight again rooted on Perry. Perry knew she would not move or speak until he looked at her. Acid-ridden bubbles of apprehension rose in his gut. She was about to lash out about someone or something and he had no choice but to listen. The violet orbs scoured him. 'Nor is knocking off a married woman under her poor dying husband's roof. The good people of Hennaford, not to mention the surviving Harvey brothers and Emilia's children, would change their good opinion of you, and her, if they ever discovered the truth.'

'Is that a threat?' Of course it damned well was. Perry thought he would gag on the bile surging up in his throat. 'You know very well that nothing happened between Em and I while I was staying there. And I wouldn't have broken up her marriage. I've got more scruples than you, Selina. Is this about Dolly Rowse making you feel unwelcome? You should ignore her. She's old-fashioned. She remembers your affair with the relative of the rector's wife. Em seems happy to have you at the farm. You're forgetting that. I thought that the pair of you discovering Alec had given you and her a certain bond.' As if! But he'd hoped for calmer moods.

Not the sort of bond I want. 'Pifft! She tolerates me because she wants you there, and she won't let me near that youngest brat of hers.'

'Em's always been overprotective of Lottie. Selina, swear you won't cause any trouble for Em.'

'Oh, you know I never make that sort of oath, brother dear.' She reached for his plate. 'Not hungry? Never mind. I'm ravenous. In fact I'm just in the mood to take anything of yours that I fancy.'

'What the hell does that mean?'

Selina ate and smirked. Only Emilia knew of her other leaning.

Perry's disablement meant he couldn't get up quickly, but he scraped back his chair and left it rocking. He leaned across the table. 'Hurt me as much as you like if that's what you want, but I swear to you Selina, if you do anything, anything at all to harm Em, if you cause a rift between her and her family, I'll kill you. I will.'

A slight raise of her chin, a glacial look. 'You've grown away from me over the years, Perry, and I've grown to resent that. I've asked you to come to Donegal with me, but rather than be with your last living relative you've refused. You'd rather be anywhere than with me, wouldn't you? Well, I don't think I'll go back there anyway. There was just a lot of boring countryside and the other doctor was just a whisky-swigging old fart. He disapproved of everything I did. I'll stay a little longer in this wretched place to see if my daughter's body is found, then I'll leave here and I never want to see you again!'

'Fine by me. Over the years you've brought me a hell of a lot of trouble!'

Selina gathered in her brows. 'We don't quarrel very often but when we do we really let rip. I think we're revealing our true feelings. Perry, be sure you don't do anything to upset me in the next few days or I *will* tell the Harveys what a whoring little bitch their precious Em is. That she's your whoring little bitch.' The more she went on, the more Selina changed. The good symmetry of her body seemed to distort, her long graceful neck to shrink, her colour darkened from a healthy pink to blotchy red and then to the puce of a rotting corpse. Perry had to fight with himself not to reach out and throttle her to get her to shut up. 'She'd have to flee Hennaford like I did, in humiliation, a lifelong outcast, never to be forgiven. Oh, you and her could be together, but not as you've no doubt planned, as a cosy little set-up in her dead husband's farm in about a year's time. She could go away with you. Will probably be able to take her brat with her but not her sons, the farm belongs to them. And not with her parents' blessing and she'll hate that. All she'd have is a cripple, and a snivelling kid, who, because she was denied her security, would probably go exactly the same way as my Libby!'

'You despicable bitch! You're blaming everyone for Libby's tragedy except yourself. It was your immorality and nothing else that drove us out of Hennaford. You were the one who caused Libby all that pain, pain she never learned to deal with. You were nothing to her. She hardly saw you while you studied. If you were at my house you went out every evening seeking sexual conquests. And it could never be with anyone on mutual terms, you had to seduce someone innocent or happily settled, married or very young. You are an evil, corrupting she-devil!'

Selina laughed, a cruel, derisive cackle. 'But don't you see? Even if we had stayed in Hennaford all those years ago your affair with the squire's wife would've come to light eventually. The husband wasn't sick back then Alec Harvey had already suffered one selfish wife who'd made his life hell. He adored Emilia. He trusted her. He thought she was totally his. He'd have taken a shotgun to you, Perry. And Libby would have ended up an orphan with a scandal chasing her. Either way you look at it, both of us made a mess of Libby's life. And I shall punish myself for that for the rest of mine.' She glared at him, smiling almost madly. *I'll punish all the others responsible for Libby's misery, including you.*

Perry collapsed in a heap back on the chair. He could barely breathe and was very near total panic. 'Please, Selina, don't do anything terrible, I beg you. I can hardly cope with losing Libby. I couldn't go on without Em. Look, if it's what you want I'll go away with you, today. It's unlikely Libby will be found now. Let's pack right now and leave.'

Selina gazed at him with eyes devoid of feeling. She folded the newspaper and got up from the table. 'I'm not leaving Cornwall yet. Libby's death was not a tragic accident. Someone was negligent and I want to learn all the facts. Do you know, I think I *will* slip down into the town. I fancy a spot of window shopping, and who knows who I might meet? It's market day, so a lot of people from Hennaford will be about, villagers, farmers, perhaps a farmer's widow...'

She had gone too far with this last threat. His panic folded away. In a voice that was deadly calm, he said, 'Fine. I'll go over to the farm by myself. I've arranged to do some paperwork, to give Em more time with the children. I'll see you when I see you then.'

Suspicion was now the greater part of Selina. Perry was a fighter, as determined to cling on to something that he wanted badly as she was. The deep, abiding love he had for Emilia wasn't something he was just going to be prepared to have swept away from him. It meant he would protect her at all costs. She'd have to keep on her guard and be at her most cunning. 'Good, that's settled. I'll expect you back for supper.'

Perry damped down his fury and agitation while he waited for her to leave the house. He sat at Reggie Rule's desk, pretending to be busy by going through the drawers. In the bottom drawer was an oddly shaped lump covered in thick cloth. He lifted the cloth and found an officer's pistol. He had one just like it himself, up in London; his, like Reggie's, had been brought back from the front. When Selina banged her way out of the house – to make the point that she was superior to him – he picked up the pistol and gripped the hard, cold metal. It was several seconds before he put the weapon back in its place. He whispered, 'I won't let her hurt you, Em, darling. Not ever.'

He reached for the telephone to tell Emilia he was on his way, to hear her voice to help dispel the revolting darkness Selina had pierced into his soul. His heart leapt as the telephone rang sharply.

'Hello. Perry Bosweld speaking.'

The voice on the other end used apologetic, soothing, but official tones. 'Mr Bosweld. This is the coxswain of the

Newquay lifeboat. I'm very sorry to have to tell you this, but I also hope you'll find it something of a relief. We've been informed of a body washed ashore further up the coast in the Padstow area. We are reasonably confident it's your daughter.'

Chapter Twenty-Three

On the granite slabbed pavement of River Street, in Truro, a girl was pretending to be looking in the window of the sweet shop while, in fact, she was watching Jim Killigrew load his van with supplies from the adjoining ironmonger's shop.

If not so deep in thought about what time he'd finish his next assignment, erecting a shed and laying a concrete path at a house in Shortlanesend — and how soon after that he could see Elena, he'd have noticed the observer, a striking figure in a pale yellow, crêpe de Chine, puff-sleeved dress, the skirt slightly flared, and a chic but delicate hat of the same colour over her shiny fair hair, and white net gloves. A gold chain with a Celtic cross was around her pale throat. Her shoes of soft leather were flat, befitting her age, but she carried a small clutch bag with a gold clasp. Two shop assistants out for a breather during their lunch hour gazed at her with admiration and envy.

The girl kept up her covert scrutiny, trying to find the courage to speak to Jim, someone she had known for years, from the occasional time she had been taken for a picnic at Ford Farm and had played with Vera Rose Stockley, and had been teased by Jonny Harvey; both older than her by five years. She wished she had walked on past Jim now, or gone into the sweet shop, but it wasn't her nature to be rude, to ignore someone in a lesser position; she had been adopted and she pondered every day that her origins could be lower than that of the humblest person.

Jim placed a galvanized bucket and a pickaxe carefully into the back of the van; his vehicle was his pride and joy, too precious to be banged about. On his way back into the ironmonger's he saw the vision of blossoming feminine softness, a vision of sunshine to match the fine day. She was a pleasure to the eye, pure and fresh, and looked older than her age. She raised her hand immediately, a habit of hers, to conceal the half-crown-sized, ragged, dark-pink birthmark on her right cheek. 'Miss Louisa! Back from your travels then?' Jim never wore a hat but he wouldn't touch his forelock to anyone. Out of respect for this shy young lady he wiped his grubby hands down his shirt. He offered his hand, knowing Louisa Hetherton-Andrews would stop hiding her birthmark and gladly present hers.

Her voice was agreeably well-to-do. 'Aunt Polly and I arrived home yesterday. I think I must have seen nearly half of Europe by now.' She stepped up to his van, trailed her forefinger, an inch away, in front of his boldly printed name. 'I'm most impressed by this. May I say that I'm glad to see good fortune has smiled on you?'

'That's not all.' Jim beamed, his chest swelling with pride. 'I'm engaged to be married, to Miss Elena Rawley.'

'Miss Rawley? Really? I'm amazed. Well, congratulations. When's the wedding to take place?'

'Christmas Eve,' Jim was delighted to announce; the whole of Hennaford was amazed. 'We're adopting two orphaned children. Alan and Molly wanted us to have a Christmas wedding.'

'You're adopting two children? How very noble of you. Please accept my best wishes for the wedding and your future all together. I see I have to catch up on a lot of news in Hennaford, although I don't know many people there. I've heard the tragic news about Mr Harvey, of course. Aunt Polly is stricken, she and Mr Harvey had been close friends for a great many years. She's at our dressmaker's, ordering black. We're to go to the farm tomorrow.'

'Mrs Em will appreciate that. Jonny Harvey's staying there at the moment, helping with the harvesting. I worked at the farm myself yesterday.'

'You get along well with Jonny, don't you? He hero-worshipped Mr Harvey, but as I remember from the past, when he wasn't around, Jonny used to trot along after you.'

'He's a good sort.' Jim smiled as he recalled teaching Jonny to use a slingshot and Cornish wrestling.

Jim's smile made Louisa conscious that she had spent several minutes speaking alone to a young man in the street. The matrons of the town would disapprove, and if any of the girls at her exclusive school saw her she'd be teased endlessly. Louisa was popular and had many friends, but the presence of her birthmark made her prefer not to be the centre of attention. 'Well, I mustn't hold you up any longer, Jim. You must be very busy. And I must catch up with Aunt Polly. It's been nice seeing you. Goodbye.' She turned round and walked off towards St Nicholas Street.

Jim lit a smoke and stared after her until she had disappeared from sight behind a horse-drawn coal lorry. The girl was going to be eagerly sought after by the cream of the town's young toffs. It was a pity she was bothered about the birthmark, it did little to detract from her fair face.

'Glad to see you've an eye for a pretty girl, Jim, even one who's far too young for you. I could hardly believe my eyes when I read the wording on this van. Your own little business, eh? I'd never have thought you had it in you.'

The smile, the warmth left by his meeting with Louisa Hetherton-Andrews metamorphosed on Jim's face into a scowl of hatred. 'I've only got two words to say to you and the second one is "off"!'

Selina was prowling the city. She was in a filthy mood, having tried to sort out her thoughts quietly in the small, select, first-floor High Cross Restaurant that overlooked the splendid, three-spired, Edwardian-built cathedral. She had come here in former days when she had wanted to be alone, to the charmingly shadowy surroundings, where the lighting came from tall, tapering candles and fresh flowers were put out every day. A diner at a corner table, a businessman whom she knew to be Dougie Blend, a roguish associate of Ben Harvey's, had aimed a provocative smile, a smarmy smile at her. Blend, apparently, knew what he was doing in the bedroom department, but his sort – nattily suited, heavy-breathing, chunky-bodied, loud-mouthed and greasy – had never taken her fancy. Throughout her lunch of locally caught stuffed mackerel, Blend had continued to ogle her. She hadn't given him eye contact and was infuriated when he had waddled to her side, and said breathily, 'Pardon me, miss, but I believe we've had the pleasure of meeting before, a few years ago.'

'I don't think so.' Selina took a sip from her glass of white wine. 'Go away.'

Dougie Blend had shuffled nearer and bent to speak into her ear. 'We've never spoken directly but we've spent many pleasant evenings at the same establishments. I'd never forget someone with the beautiful colour of your eyes. Or someone's tastes. You enjoy men and lady friends.'

'Only when I choose to.' She had never given her real name in the places he had mentioned – she was relieved about that. Afraid he might make a scene – Dougie Blend was known as an unprincipled man who'd think nothing of embarrassing someone publicly – she had smiled directly at him. 'Perhaps I might choose to some other time, I'm rather busy today.'

'I'll live in hopes then,' he had replied jovially, revealing large, voracious teeth. He handed her his business card. 'Get in touch, old thing, any time.'

Draining her wine glass in one angry gulp, she had signalled the waiter for a refill. And to her added frustration, a woman next accosted her. An old woman, smartly attired, but her coat, hat, gloves and shoes were at least a decade old. 'I'm so sorry you've been bothered by that dreadful man. He thinks he can speak to anyone he likes just because he's an alderman. He disgusts me. I wish they didn't allow him in here.'

'I wish they didn't allow you in here either,' Selina muttered under her breath. She said aloud, 'If you'll excuse me. I'm about to go.'

The old woman seemed not to hear. 'This is a respectable place, it's… it's…'

Selina looked over the annoying stranger with a medical eye. She was blinking, as if her mind had suddenly shut itself off and was struggling to get restarted, and she was rocking on her feet. For a moment Selina thought she was showing signs of senility, then she realized she had taken a little too much to drink with her meal. The last thing Selina wanted was to carry out some sort of muddled conversation with this woman, but the compassionate side of her was stirred – and she hated it when this happened – the part of her that people reluctantly admired, which she saw as a quirk in her character. She got up and eased the woman down in the opposite chair and ordered coffee for her.

'How very kind of you. I'm Miss Gertrude Roberts,' the stranger said, some of her senses coming back to her. 'I'm a retired district nurse.'

'Oh, really?' Selina said. 'Do you live close by?'

'I've a little house up in Bosvigo Road. It's not far from here.'

'I know where that is. I think you're a little unwell, Miss Roberts. Drink your coffee and I'll put you in a cab and take you home.'

'Oh, you would? I can't thank you enough. I don't usually get like this.' Gertrude Roberts hiccoughed, and Selina was suspicious she got a little inebriated often.

'How many years were you a nurse?' Selina said. Conversation would keep Gertrude awake.

'For forty years.' There were tears in her eyes and Selina summed her up as desperately lonely now her life's work was at an end. 'I served the St Allen district: Zelah, and Marazanvose and Hennaford.'

'Hennaford? I used to know some people there.' Selina wondered if this would prove useful to her. 'Harvey, I think they were called.'

'Oh, there's been such sadness there. The squire, he was only a young man, died a few weeks ago, and before that he and his wife lost a two-week-old baby. And there was that business with the baby with the birthmark…'

The old woman was rambling, about to go back over every memory of every birth she had attended. Selina cut her off. 'Tell me about what you do now. Do you have a routine? But first let me ask the waiter to order us a cab.' She listened to Gertrude's prattlings for ten minutes, then escorted her home and saw her safely inside her front door and into an armchair to sleep away the afternoon.

'I can't thank you enough,' Gertrude had muttered as her eyes closed. 'You must call on me any time.'

'I don't think so,' Selina had murmured, locking Gertrude's door and posting the key back through the letterbox.

Wearing sunglasses and a headscarf tied film-star style so no one would recognize her, she left the row of ordinary terraced houses and made her way back down into the town, moving on to Kenwyn Street, and turning into Little Castle Street, where she could look up to the top of the steep Castle Street, where the livestock market was. She could hear the indistinct voice of the auctioneer and see a busy scene. It was unlikely Emilia was up there transacting business, her father usually saw to that. Selina was fuming about so much wasted time. And fuming with herself for not crushing Perry before leaving the house at Highertown. She turned right into River Street, and while passing along on the other side of the road from the County Museum, she had thought of an excellent punishment for him. Either he agreed to leave Cornwall and move somewhere overseas with her for good, or she'd let the world know about his affair with Emilia. It was the old story and one she relished with malice – if she couldn't have Emilia, then as sure as hell he couldn't either!

The thought of Perry pining away for Emilia made her smile. A vicious, feline smile. He'd go. Perry would do nothing to risk harm to his precious Em. As the days and weeks and years dragged on without her, perhaps he'd put a gun to his head. There wouldn't be anything else for him to do. He'd not take up with another woman, not even for carnal relief. He was pathetic – good and kind, honest and considerate – but pitiable. It would be a just punishment for Libby's death, and for having the only person in the world that she, herself, had ever loved or could ever love. Perry deserved the horrible lonely end coming to him.

Aiming to fix Perry into a new life, planning to make every decision for him from now, to control him entirely until there was only a shambles left of the man Emilia Harvey was in love with, she crossed the road to a gentleman's outfitter's to buy him some new clothes. Then she saw Jim Killigrew watching some sweet young thing.

The words on the van parked beside the pavement had hit her with surprise. It was hilarious. Well, bully for him! Jim Killigrew, the eighteen-year-old youth whom she had so ruthlessly seduced and tossed aside, had grown up and had his own little business. She had known nothing of this. She had not gone to Alec's funeral, not wanting to be spurned by the villagers, which would have upset Emilia – now she wished she had. Did she have a lot to make up for! A shadow as dark as midnight settled on her face. Jim Killigrew had made a success of himself. Success until now. This was where his luck would run out. He had laughed at her humiliation during a public event, the day Tristan Harvey had torn into her over terrifying his wretched son with the threat to castrate him. She'd had to run to get away from the jeers of the crowd and had fallen flat on her face. And Jim Killigrew had stood over her and laughed and crowed. For that she would bring his life crashing down. All she had to do was to find his present weakness.

Swearing profanely, Jim strode back into the iron-monger's. Selina waited. He came back out, hefting a heavy box under one arm, which he put into the back of his van in one effortless movement. Selina watched appreciatively. She knew his strength. Most men would have had to carry the box in both arms and then found it tricky to balance the box in one arm while opening the van door, then there would have been a grunt of relief when the box was relinquished. Not so with Jim. His robust form, his powerful muscles were a match for anything. Such stamina and a quick mind to learn he'd had as a youth. Now he was in his prime. A wholly fine sensual being. Selina wetted her lips with her tongue.

Jim closed the van door and made for the driver's seat.

Selina was beside it, her ungloved hand resting on the handle. 'Aren't you going to offer your sympathy over the loss of my niece?'

'I'm sorry for your brother. I've got nothing else to say to you.' Jim was finding it hard to keep his temper in check. How dare she try to take him for a fool again, playing one of her rotten games. She was immoral and evil, the total opposite of Elena. 'Get out of my way or I'll run you over in the street!'

Selina grinned, revealing her teeth. 'Oh, don't be like that, Jim.'

Jim was about to tear her hand off the handle when a motor car pulled up behind the van. It was Perry in the Daimler. He wound the window down. 'Selina! Leave off annoying Jim. Get in the car. There's been news.'

Chapter Twenty-Four

Was his spirit here? His essence? Some last tiny particle of him before he left the earth for ever? Would she see him in the corner of her eye, but when she turned her head to look he'd be gone? Would she smell the wonderful scent that was unique to him? People said that sort of thing happened.

'Alec?' She turned in each direction. 'Alec?'

The stream seemed to tinkle a little louder on its way, a joyful note. The warm breeze rustled lazily, peacefully through the overgrowth of long grasses and nettles. The leaves of the oak tree above crackled merrily under the strength of the sun. The sun danced sparkling patterns through the branches. 'Alec? Is any of this you?'

'He'll never leave you, Aunty Em.'

'Oh! Jonny. I never heard you.'

'It breaks my heart to see you looking so lost.'

'I—I was just thinking.' Emilia dried her tears. 'Here in Long Meadow, it was a good place to come to die. The best place for your uncle. I could bear it more if only he hadn't been alone.'

'I don't think he was alone.'

'You don't? How can you be sure?'

Jonny sat down in the exact spot where Alec had been found. He held out a hand to her. She joined him. 'Listen again. Close your eyes. Absorb the atmosphere.'

She did so. And heard the clear leaping water, the brushing of the leaves, the cattle lowing in the next field, the coo of a wood pigeon. 'Now does that feel as if he was lonely? Everything he knew was here. It was the place where he found peace. He left you in the house, Aunty Em, left you at the farm with the boys and Lottie because he knew you'd look after it and them.'

'Thank you. Thank you, Jonny. I'm seeing Ernest Rule, the solicitor, this afternoon for the reading of the will. Your father and Ben are coming with me. Would you like to come too? I think Alec would've wanted that.'

'I'd be honoured to be there.'

Emilia rested and thought about Alec, taking refuge here, relaxing here, taking photographs here. Yes, it had been a good place in which for him to die.

She thought about the words he had struggled to write in his letter. Such love he'd had and freely he had given it. And strength and courage to face his torment and end alone. She had known there had been something wrong with him but she had never allowed her thoughts to dwell on the worst thing. And when it had happened, the way Alec had chosen to go made it seem somehow poetic and beautiful. No harrowing bad memories. Just Alec with her one day and not the next. She thought about how differently Alec would have felt if he'd known about her and Perry. No doubt he would have followed the usual road of a cheated husband and taken his wrath out on Perry. He would have fought to keep her, she was certain of that, and she would never have left him and the boys, but all the love between her and Alec would have been gone for ever. It would have been her fault, and sometimes it made her grief, her loss, almost unbearable. He had told her to seek happiness. She felt she didn't have the right to do so. Her feelings were so numb that when Perry was at the farm she treated him only as a very close friend.

After another ten minutes Jonny suggested they return to the farm. 'You look very grave suddenly,' she said, as they made the climb up the valley.

'I hope you won't get too upset by this, Aunty Em,' Jonny said, catching her hand. 'I left the farmhouse just after you and there was a phone call. From Perry Bosweld. I'm afraid the poor chap's been asked to identify a body.'

'Oh, Perry,' Emilia wept. 'How terrible for him.' If only she could be with him. And a thought came into her mind that she should have felt sorry for but never would. If only it was Selina who had died and not Libby. If the body turned out to be Libby's, she hoped passionately that Selina would quickly take herself off again, for as surely as day followed night, the beastly woman would unforgiveably cause trouble somewhere.

—

'Jim! I thought you were working at Shortlanesend this afternoon.' Elena was surprised to have him suddenly appear in her kitchen.

'The customer asked me to start tomorrow instead.' Jim hugged her closer than usual. It was he who had postponed the job. Unsettled by his encounter with Selina Bosweld, he'd needed to see Elena.

Elena leaned back in his arms and studied him. He seemed to be in a heavy mood. 'Is everything all right?'

'Course it is.' He put a gentle kiss on her lips.

Moments later, Jim was settled at the table with a mug of tea. Elena fetched the cake tin. 'I've made these cheese scones specially for you.'

'You don't need to keep spoiling me.' He gave her an affectionate, grateful smile.

Elena always blushed prettily when he paid her a compliment. 'I like to.'

He rolled his eyes, adding a merry twinkle. 'Mind I don't start taking you too much for granted.'

'You wouldn't do that.'

'What makes you so sure?' He teased her gently.

'I know you.' She liked to be teased in this way. It took the place of more intense courting. Jim had not kissed her properly yet. She was glad of that. Apart from the children's company – they were now taking a nap – they spent many hours alone; anything might happen, and she had no idea how to deal with that side of life.

'Already?'

'Of course. I'm a good judge of character. Jim...' She became serious in a way that Jim called her biblical mood.

'What is it, sweetheart?' Jim became alert.

'I saw Mrs Rowse from the farm this afternoon. She told me that Libby Bosweld's body's been found.'

'Oh. That's sad.' Mention of the girl intensified his disgust over the meeting with Selina Bosweld. 'I saw her aunt in Truro today. God, I hate that woman.'

'Jim, please, language,' Elena tutted, 'and you shouldn't hate anyone.'

'Elena, you don't know what she's capable of.'

'Tell me. We shouldn't have secrets.'

He could never, ever, tell this gentle innocent woman, whom he had come to love in a peaceful sort of way, about the shameful association between him and Selina Bosweld. The memories he had were terrible; he still felt abused and humiliated. Elena probably took it for granted that he wasn't a virgin; she might not even have thought about it. She'd be horrified if she learned he had been seduced in the very room she slept in.

Jim took a gulp of tea and picked up a newspaper and hid behind it. Damn it, he shouldn't have mentioned the Bosweld woman. He longed for a cigarette, but he'd not been here long and had extinguished one on the back doorstep. Elena would raise her sweet enquiring brows if he went outside for another so soon. He believed that she had a direct line to God and was supernaturally protected, and he had this irrational fear that God might decide to put his thoughts into her mind. Protected... Jim suddenly had a very real fear. Selina Bosweld was vindictive and he had clashed with her this afternoon. He might have to be very careful for a while; it might be necessary to protect Elena and the kids, and his future with them. He clenched his fists. That bitch had just better not try anything or there could be another sudden end for the villagers to talk about.

–

Dolly Rowse drew in her lips and hurried past the sitting room into the farm kitchen. 'Emilia, you're not serious about allowing that woman to stay here? Surely not?'

'What else can I do, Mother?' Emilia stood back from the airing cupboard with fresh bed linen in her arms. 'She's just seen the body of her beloved niece. She's in a terrible state. Perry was right to bring her here. And what about him? He needs to have caring people around him. He'd never cope with Selina on his own. I could hardly send him away, could I?'

'I s'pose not,' Dolly bit her lip. 'But my dear, can you cope? You've only just become bereaved yourself.'

Emilia stared at her mother. It was rare for the doughty housewife to give her endearments and look at her with such treasured concern. 'I think so. Alec would have insisted that Perry stay. It's dreadful for him, he adored Libby.'

She would never forget the look of desolation on Perry's face as he'd led Selina into the farmhouse. 'Th-there was no mistake, Em. It... it was her swimsuit. I'm sorry...' He'd been barely able to get the words out. 'Selina's gone to pieces. I had to come here. I didn't know what else to do.'

Selina was clinging to him, sobbing worse than anyone Emilia had ever seen, hardly able to stay on her feet. Emilia had gone to them, reached for them both, although she had only wanted to hold Perry. The three had hung on to each other for some time. Emilia had felt Perry's tears wetting her hair. 'You did the right thing,' she whispered to him.

Selina had virtually collapsed and Emilia had helped Perry drag her into the sitting room, where she had been since, sobbing under a blanket, refusing to talk, or eat or drink.

Emilia said her mother, 'Perry's not close to Selina. In fact, so he told me, they had a dreadful falling out just before they drove up to Padstow. Hopefully she'll go away again very soon, and he'll have no one. I'll make up the beds for them.'

'That woman might be in a pit of grief right now, but I don't trust her. I don't like her. Nor does Jonny. He soon made himself scarce outside again when he saw she was here,' Dolly breathed noisily. 'As long as she's under this roof I'll be keeping a very close eye on her. I'm your mother, it's my place to see you're all right. You've put off the reading of the will. Told Ben and Tristan not to come. You'll have to see to that soon.'

'I know, Mother. I'll do it.'

Dolly held out her stout hands. 'Give that to me. I'll see to the beds. You look after your guests. And for goodness sake, Emilia…'

'What?'

Dolly shook her head. 'I know you won't want to hear this. There's something not quite right about Selina Bosweld. You be careful, that's all.'

Perry had slipped outside to the garden for a cigarette. He was sitting on a low stone wall.

Lottie crept up to him, her battered doll, Dulcie, in her arms. 'You've been crying? I heard you, and the lady. Why?'

He put the cigarette back in the case and cleared his throat. He didn't want to look at the little girl right now, to be reminded how Libby had once been, and he gazed above Lottie's head. 'Um, my daughter has… she's gone to heaven.'

'But she went up to heaven before my daddy did.' Lottie edged closer to him. 'Why're you upset again?'

Perry sniffed and swallowed hard. 'Well, um, you see, it will happen from time to time, me getting upset.'

'Think they're together? Your daughter and my daddy?'

'I don't know. Perhaps. I expect so.' Perry glanced down, avoided Lottie's worried, enquiring expression, and saw the doll. 'What happened to her? She's been through the wars.'

'Dulcie got hurt in the storm. It was my fault, I left her outside in her pram, then my daddy fell off the ladder. Do you think that's my fault too? He was always cross with me after that.' Perry heard the choke in her voice. He put his eyes fully on the girl and was horrified at the guilt and fear he saw in her. He swept Lottie up into his arms. 'Oh, no, darling! Your daddy's accident had nothing to do with you. It was the weather. And he loved you, he really did. Your daddy was a very poorly man, that's why he seemed a bit strange sometimes. I promise you it's the truth. You must never think that he didn't love you and care about you. He did, very much.'

Lottie settled against him quietly, and Perry found comfort in her trust.

Emilia went into the sitting room and sat down on the sofa that was across the room from where Selina was reclining. Selina had stopped crying and was staring into space. The sparkling violet hue of her eyes was gone and they were dull and red-edged. Emilia was wary of the other woman – she'd had no need to be pressed by her mother about that. Selina Bosweld had the power and the pitilessness to ruin the lives of everyone she loved. But Emilia, too, if it was necessary, could string someone along for her own sake, although in her case it was for protection and not malicious assault.

'Can I get you anything?' Emilia asked, with an under-standing sort of smile. 'How about a drop of brandy?'

Selina didn't seem to be listening. 'I bought that swimsuit for her. I wanted her to have a blue one, but she insisted on pink. I didn't argue. I always let Libby have her own way. I suppose I was making up for being a bad mother. I loved Libby very much but not in a maternal way. I could never have those feelings, but now... I had no idea what you must have gone through when you lost your baby. We have nothing in common, you and I, Emilia, but now we're two mothers united in grief.'

'Yes, we are. I'm so very sorry for you, Selina.'

'Are you really? Or are you only sorry for Perry, like all the others? If I was anyone else you'd be over here giving me a comforting hug, or is your aloofness because I've told you I've got feelings for you? You despise me, don't you, Emilia? And I think you're a little afraid of me.'

Emilia got up and moved over to her. 'I admit I'm afraid of what you might decide to do, Selina. But I swear that I do feel sorry for you. I can see how distraught you are. In your profession you live with death nearly every day, but this is the first time you've lost someone you had an emotional tie with. Your room will soon be ready. Perhaps you'd like to lie down.'

'I think I'd prefer to freshen up and take a walk down to the woods, sit by the stream, take advantage of the sunshine. I'm not going to mope. Besides, it will be better for Perry if I'm out of the way for a while. I'll come back for supper, if that's all right?'

'Of course. You'll be all right alone?'

It was new to Selina to have to fight to remain in control of herself or a situation. Emilia's unexpected kindness dealt her a massive blow to the heart. 'I'd love to have your company but I'm sure you'd rather stay here for Perry.'

'I can't leave Lottie. I'll see you later then.'

'I could take him away from you, you know.' At one time Selina would have said such a thing as a menacing threat, now it came out as a simple statement. 'Make it impossible for him to be with you.'

'I don't doubt that, Selina.' Emilia kept her voice steady and soft, her manner easy and pliable. She didn't want to think of a future without Perry – it wasn't right but she couldn't bear life any other way. 'Do you intend to try?'

Their eyes met, an unspoken pleading in each fraught gaze as they tried to guess what was really in the other's mind. 'We must talk again later,' Emilia said. 'Decisions will have to be made about Libby's funeral. If I can do anything to help...'

Dolly came into the room, breathing in the heavy, critical way she had when not happy about something. 'Miss Bosweld's room's ready. Would she like a cup of tea?' She never spoke directly to Selina unless she was forced to.

Selina was staring at Emilia. 'I just need... Tell Perry where I'm gone, will you?'

–

Jonny was down by the stream. With the Bosweld woman at the farmhouse he wasn't sure if he could bring himself to stay on. The terror she had struck in him so many years ago didn't worry him now, of course. She couldn't physically hurt him – he was far stronger than her and no longer intimidated by her sort. She was high on his list of those he despised, but he felt he was a contributor to Libby's death and should offer her his condolences. But how was the best way to approach her? It would be cowardly to say nothing at all.

He was preparing to light a cigarette.

'Can I have one of those?'

'Miss Bosweld!'

'Jonny Harvey.' Selina surveyed him without expression, the youth who had not taken enough care of her daughter. 'You haven't changed at all except in height and girth. Heard you were stunning to look at. You must be quite a ladykiller.'

Seeing her grief-ravaged face, Jonny was unable to prevent a guilty flush from climbing up his neck. He held out his packet of Woodbines. He lit both cigarettes from a box of matches. 'I, um...'

'Yes?'

'Well, I, um, wanted to say... about Libby.' Under her continuing direct gaze it was difficult to think what to say, let alone get the words out. 'Th-that I... oh God, I'm so sorry. It doesn't sound enough, but I don't suppose it ever will.'

'Tell me about them.'

'What?'

'Libby's last moments.'

Jonny took in an urgent draw of nicotine. His voice was in a panic. 'I couldn't reach her in time!'

'So she just went in for a swim? On her own?'

'Yes. We'd told her there would be no swimming that day, the tide was on its way out...' He swallowed hard on the lies. 'But she just ran on.'

'And you and the two women with you just watched her?'

'They were seeing to the children. I thought, I thought Libby would just paddle about on the shore. But she just kept walking into the waves. We shouted, we all shouted to her. I ran after her. I tried to bring her back in, I swear I did.' The fear and horror were taking hold of Jonny, he was near to tears. 'I tried to find her... but she was swept away... she disappeared... if I'd stayed in any longer I would've drowned myself. I have nightmares about it every night. Miss Bosweld, I'll never forgive myself for what happened to Libby.'

'Nor should you. And I'll never forgive you.'

For such hard words, all about her seemed calm. Horribly calm to Jonny. He'd have preferred it if she had ripped into him. 'I'm so sorry. I'm so very, very sorry.'

'I accept that you are,' Selina said. She glanced about at the sheltered belt. The banks of the stream here widened out and formed an area of pond. It was restful, beautiful. 'If I remember rightly, this was another of your uncle's favourite places. He was always going off to be alone, wasn't he?'

The last thing Jonny wanted was to stay here with her, especially to talk about his Uncle Alec, but he felt obliged to. 'Yes. He was a remarkable man.'

'I liked Alec. He didn't deserve the end he got.'

'No. He should have had at least another thirty years.' Jonny felt he'd made an insensitive blunder. 'I'm sorry, Libby was much younger than him...'

'Her death was quicker and unexpected, but I don't want to think about her fear and pain and panic. Now, a brain tumour, now that's a terrible way to die. And Alec knew what was coming to him.' Selina let her cigarette end fall into the water. She was close enough to Jonny to feel him tense. He didn't want to hear anything horrible about Alec's end, but he was going to. She wanted him to be beleaguered by gruesome thoughts to the end of his life, to never find solace in a place like this again. She was a doctor. He'd believe anything she said. She'd make Alec's last weeks on earth sound worse than the suffering in the trenches, and Jonny could add it to the nightmares he had about her daughter. 'He would have been seeing double, probably thought he was going mad. And the hallucinations would have been terrifying. Some people believe they're being eaten alive by maggots, or covered from head to foot by spiders; that sort of thing.'

Fear and regret for Alec took tight hold of Jonny. 'Uncle Alec had very bad headaches but he never said he saw things.'

'Well, he wouldn't, would he? He wouldn't have wanted to worry anyone. Well, mustn't get morbid. I guess he's at peace now.'

'He looked peaceful when you and Aunty Em found him. She said so.'

'Anyone would look peaceful having that sort of agony brought to an end. We should shut up. It won't do us any good to dwell on Libby's or Alec's distress. You won't tell Emilia what I've said, will you? It would upset her terribly.'

'No, of course. I won't say anything to anyone. Um, well, I'd better leave you in peace. I'm sure you'd like to be alone. And I ought to be getting back to work. I won't be any use to Aunty Em dawdling about here.'

Selina saw his dreadful discomfort at being with her, and his misery over her exaggerations and lies; it had seemed to her that Alec had accepted his fate and had welcomed his quiet end. 'Actually, I'd rather you stayed. Perry's taking solace with Lottie. Everyone else is busy. I don't want to be alone. And Ben's just turned up to help out. Shall we walk or sit? Let's walk. Deeper into the woods. I've happy memories of spending time in the woods when I lived at Ford House.'

She had great memories of open-air assignations with Jim. She knew men. Jonny Harvey wasn't an innocent, he was long past that glorious, sweet state, so she wouldn't have the pleasure of seducing him. But she was the last woman he'd want to romp with. How he was going to hate himself afterwards.

–

Emilia stood beside Ben in the threshing barn. Flecks of dust, made golden in the shafts of sunlight streaming in through the windows and cracks, floated in the air that smelled strongly of warm, earthy grain. 'What am I supposed to be looking at, Ben? It's been exhaustively swept clean for the new grain.'

'Just wanted you to check all was in order.'

'Thanks, but Jonny's already seen to that.'

'I want you to know, Em –' Ben dropped his arm round her shoulders, as if in a casual manner – 'that I'll always be available at any time you need me. You have the children to bring up and the farm to run. After the threshing there'll be the crushing and grinding, and so on. Life's going to be hard for you from now on.'

'It's kind of you, Ben, but I have my mother and Tilda, and my father, and we've been more or less running the farm on our own for several months now. Perry's made sure all the paperwork is up to date. But it's good to know I can call on you and Tris.' She touched his hand where it was draped near her neck.

He placed his hand over hers and kept it there. 'So much has happened to us both in the last few years. It was in here we had our first kiss.' Bringing that up was the reason why he'd coaxed her in here. 'You haven't forgotten, have you?'

'Um… no.' She turned to go. 'I'd better see to Lottie and the boys. They're all feeling so lost.'

Ben held on to her. It was what he wanted so much, to always have her in his arms. 'I can't believe Alec's left us all. Standing here like this has reminded me what a great debt I owed him. He was good to me after our parents died. I feel bad about how easily I forgot that.'

'Alec was good to everyone. But don't put him on a pedestal, Ben. Alec saw himself as an ordinary man, he'd hate to be revered like some plaster saint.'

Ben grinned. 'Yes, I suppose he could be a bit of an old misery and quite stubborn at times. I'm going to miss him.' He meant that, and as he realized just how much, tears grouped at the corners of his eyes.

'Don't cry, Ben,' Emilia whispered, strangled with emotion. 'You'll make me cry too, and sometimes I don't think I'll ever stop.' And she didn't want to fall down in grief right now, certainly not, for Perry's sake.

He rested his brow against hers and then he kissed her there, firmly, making his lips linger. He glanced down at her lips and ached to kiss her properly. 'We both loved him, and I'll always love you, Em.'

She broke from him, not knowing the full import of his last declaration. 'Alec would have been sorry to miss the birth of your baby. It's wonderful that Brooke's pregnancy is going so well.'

She left him. Ben pushed his hands into his trouser pockets. For so long he had wanted a son. Now he hoped the child would be a girl. Life with Brooke was still a strain. If she gave birth to a girl he'd work to send her away. She could go back to America for good, for all he cared. Then he could have Em. They could have a son together to inherit Tremore, and until Will inherited this farm, he would be squire of Hennaford. He'd have everything he could ever want.

Chapter Twenty-Five

Ben wanted to drive Emilia to Truro for the new appointment with the solicitor. Tristan offered too.

'I'm taking Alec's car,' she said, already on the way to the Ford Coupe. She cut a stately figure in a black suit, hat and gloves but seemed smaller, younger and appealingly vulnerable.

'I'll drive,' Ben said, jumping to guide her round to the front passenger seat.

She switched direction. 'I'll drive.'

Ben glanced at Tristan and lingered. 'But we'll look ridiculous being driven by a woman.'

Tristan didn't argue but he looked uncomfortable as he opened the driver's door for her.

'Too bad.' Her bearing grew and her tone was inarguably decisive. 'I can always go on my own or ask Brooke and Winnie to come with me.'

Ben shot round to the front passenger seat so he could sit next to her. 'Don't be daft. You women wouldn't understand a word of what's being said.'

'Steady on, Ben,' Tristan chided. 'Em's, ah… well, she's perfectly capable…'

'You two can keep quiet in Ernest's office. If there's anything I can't understand, I'll ask him.'

There was a gathering watching them from the front gate, Emilia's children and parents, Perry, Brooke and Winifred. At the last moment Jonny had declined to come with them and had gone to change his clothes and get back to work. Expecting to hear later in the day that he had inherited his father's properties, Will was standing straight and confident, slightly in front of the others. The air of superiority about him reminded Emilia of Ben's perpetual attitude. Ben and Will were instilled with a liberal measure of conceit. Lottie was between her grandmother and Perry, holding their hands. Emilia felt Perry's eyes on her, transmitting his love, but on this one occasion she couldn't look at him.

Parking near the top of Lemon Street, where Ernest Rule had his office, Emilia led the way inside.

The solicitor's demure, grey-clad, middle-aged secretary showed them into his office. Ernest Rule was not typical of his profession. The usual certificates and diplomas were displayed on the magnolia-painted walls, and there was the expected potted greenery and leather seating, but also there were many proudly framed photos of Ernest Rule with the rugby teams he had played for during his youth and prime, from his schooldays to Truro City to Cornwall. He had the build of his best love, and was still as muscular and powerful looking, despite nearing retirement age. He had a head of thick, tumbling white hair and a full white beard. Through business and socializing, he had been a close friend of Alec's, and he had not been ashamed to spill a few tears at his funeral.

He shook hands with Ben and Tristan. For Emilia, he added a kiss on her cheek. There was some small talk while they waited for the complimentary tray of tea and biscuits. 'This is a very sad occasion.' Ernest scratched his ear, a trifle overcome. 'There was no one I respected more than Alec. He unexpectedly came to see me shortly before he died. Emilia, you are in for a bit of a surprise.'

She had been dreading this day. It would make Alec's death final. Real. Sometimes she fancied he was about to come through the farmhouse kitchen door, or be about the yard, or in his den collecting together his photographic equipment. Or in bed beside her. She could swear there were moments she heard him breathing, or that he had put his arm over her. This morning she had found his wardrobe door ajar. It was likely that Tilda had put something of his away, but she wanted to believe it had been Alec who had been there. She was desperate that the proceedings here wouldn't make him more distant. How could Alec be just a memory? He had been hers and she his for so many years, and even when she had given her heart to Perry, she had never stopped loving him for a moment. His children, their children, were at the farm. His echo, their echoes, would always be there.

The company sat in the appropriate seats on either side of the desk. Ernest cleared his throat. 'Are you ready, Emilia?'

She nodded. In between Ben and Tristan, she felt as if she was shrinking, in some horrible dream. Her brothers-in-law reached for her hands but she kept them grasped together.

Ernest read the will. It didn't take long.

Emilia was so shocked she couldn't move or speak.

Tristan gazed down at the Wilton carpet.

Ben stayed quiet but fidgeted.

'Are you sure that's right? That it was what Alec wanted?' Emilia rammed her hanky to her eyes and flooded the cloth with tears of bewilderment and shame. She felt broken and disorientated and so full of remorse, for her love for Alec had in no way matched his for her.

'It was. Can I get you anything, Emilia?' Ernest asked in soft, slow words.

'He's left the farm to *me*? He's left *everything* to me?'

'It was Alec's very clear wish that he left everything to you, Emilia. He trusted you totally,' Ernest explained, glancing down at the document in his hands. 'As it states here, he's leaving it to you to best distribute anything of his to whom you see fit to have it.'

She felt as if she had been ripped in half. She couldn't bear to stay still and shot to her feet and flew to the window. She didn't see the domed Anglican St John's Church just across the street. Alec had done this almost certainly on the day he'd got his results at the infirmary. He knew he'd die soon and he had loved her so much he'd given her every last tiny bit of himself. Every memory of him, from the time as a schoolgirl when she had first become aware of him as the village squire, then his dairymaid and then his lover and then his wife, flashed through her mind. And standing behind every memory of him was Perry. She had been unfaithful to Alec. Alec had thought he'd had all her love and her total commitment and he had rewarded her for it. He had been ill, dying, in pain and distress, and she had lost her patience with him and put Lottie before him. And Perry. When he had got those test results and knew he was under an imminent death sentence she had gone to Perry and made love with him. There was a lot of Biblical and legal and slang names for a woman like herself, but first and foremost she was a betrayer.

'I don't deserve it! I don't want anything!'

The three men were on their way to her. Ben jostled to reach her first. He placed his hands on her rigid shoulders. 'If you're worried about Will's reaction, don't be. You can leave the property to him. You can give Tom and Lottie and anyone else anything you'd like.'

'It's what Alec wanted,' Tristan said gently. 'You'll cope, Em. You'll know what to do in a few days when you feel settled again. You'll go on as before. And you have us, we'll help you.'

'You've had a shock, Emilia. I'll get you some brandy,' Ernest said, retreating to the little drinks cabinet.

'But it changes everything!' Emilia cried, throwing back her head. Since Alec's death she had allowed herself a vague idea that after a year or two Perry and her would marry. They would help to run the farm until Will was twenty-one, then move to a house in the village and support him from there. Now she was trapped. She could never bring herself to marry Perry and have him at the farm as her husband, usurping Alec in his own bed. She had been strong, so strong since that morning she and Selina had gone to Long Meadow, everybody said so, and said they admired her for it, but now she was falling apart.

She came to on Ernest Rule's couch.

A voice said, 'Drink this, Em.'

'What?' She waved a hand in front of her face.

'Try to take a few sips. You fainted.' It was Tristan who was holding a glass of water near her lips. He'd felt it was time he took charge, not trusting Ben to have the sort of sensitivity required here. 'I've been expecting you to be overcome. You've rather too much on your plate, my darling. You've taken the Bosweld tragedy to heart as well, and I'm sorry about that. When we get back to the farm I'm going to suggest they move out. If they don't fancy going back to Reggie's house they're welcome to stay at Roskerne. Actually, it might help if they spent some time where Libby was lost, until her funeral. Em, you need to rest, to have peace and quiet for your own and the children's sakes.'

'Yes.' Her voice was weak and wrung out. 'Perry must go, and Selina.'

'I'll be relieved when that woman's left Cornwall for good,' Ben said harshly. He was lurking behind the couch, peeved it wasn't he giving Emilia comfort.

'That might not happen,' Tristan said. 'Libby's going to be buried in Hennaford churchyard. Selina might want to come back from time to time to pay her respects.'

'What?' Ben nearly exploded. 'When was this decided? It's hardly appropriate.'

'It's what Perry wanted,' Emilia said, regaining her full senses. She stayed slumped, utterly dejected.

'Why, for goodness sake?' Ben demanded. 'I thought the girl hated Hennaford.'

Ernest gave a small, forceful cough. 'I don't think here is the time and place to discuss that.'

'Do you want to go home now, Em?' Tristan gently removed her hat, knowing she hated wearing anything on her head, to give her a sense of freedom.

'No. No. I just want some fresh air.'

'Do you think you could manage a stroll down to the Red Lion?' Ben said. 'A drink and a light meal might help to fortify you.'

'No! I don't want to be indoors.'

'Where do you want to go, my love?' Ben reached a hand down and caressed her hair, his voice was full of tenderness. 'How about going somewhere quiet for a little while, somewhere where we went as children?'

'That's sounds like a good idea to me,' Ernest said. 'Best thing to ease your mind, Emilia.'

'Shall I drive us back, Em?' Tristan offered.

She nodded.

Ben was concerned for her, but he was jubilant. The situation was playing straight towards his ends. 'I don't think you should be alone, Em. Tris can tell the family that you need some time to think before you give them the news.'

–

'I'm fascinated about this trip you've got in mind, Brooke,' Winifred said. 'But will Ben approve of it in your condition? Aren't you worried? About, you know...?'

The sisters-in-law were strolling around the front garden of Ford Farm. They had come outside to get away from Selina. In no way was Selina behaving untowardly, mostly she was keeping to her room, but her presence in the house made the atmosphere bad.

'I've every confidence, Winnie, that I'll carry this baby to full term. The gynaecologist isn't totally happy about the journey but he says he can't think of a reason why anything should go wrong now I've completed my first trimester. I'm determined to take Faye to see the one-hundred-and-two-storey Empire State Building in New York City. It was only in the planning stage when we were there last year.'

'I'd quite like to see it myself, this tallest edifice in the world. Call such a thing a skyscraper, don't they? I still think you'll find it hard to convince Ben that you should go. You know how keen he is that this latest pregnancy doesn't end in tears.'

'Ben doesn't have full sway over me. I don't stop him going anywhere he chooses. I shall be glad to stay close to home when I have two children to care for. Don't worry, Winnie, I shall take things very easy. There's no way I'm going to risk harm to this precious child inside me.' She looked sideways and stared at the house, then turned towards the farmyard. Not long ago all this had belonged to her baby's father. 'I wonder how long they're going to be? Oh, no, here comes that ghastly woman.'

Selina was making her way across the lawn to them, her hands in the pockets of her loose trousers, which suited her so well, her tawny head slightly down. 'Tristan's back on his own and he's looking very grave.'

–

'Everything will fit in eventually, Em. Just give it time.' Ben stood beside her at the outer reaches of the woods. She was gazing up over the buttercup-strewn valley at the sprawling buildings that made up the farm and her home. She didn't speak, so he made another attempt to break through the gloomy silence she had fallen into since leaving Truro. 'You must simply accept Alec's loving gesture for what it was.'

'It means so much more than you could possibly know,' she said, the tightness in her throat making the words difficult to say.

'I'm sure it does. I wouldn't dream of leaving Tremore to Brooke if she gives me a son. Alec was unconventional in many ways and he loved you with all that he had in him. It makes him a far better man than me.'

'He was better than most people. And you could never understand what this means to me.'

'Try me. We always understood each other until that time we fell out over the accident to my eye. I want to help you, Em. I'd do anything for you, you know.'

'Thanks, Ben. I don't want to talk about it any more. I never will. I shouldn't have come here. My place is at home with the children.' She started up the valley, her stockings being pulled on thistles and rough grass, her high heels making the ascent clumsy. She could swear with frustration. By now, Tristan would have asked Perry and Selina to leave. What was Perry thinking? He'd now have to face his daughter's funeral at home with only the company of the insidious witch, his sister. She would have to explain to Perry why he must leave Alec's home. It was all going to be unbearable for them both.

She stumbled, her foot turning to the side, and she lost her balance and tumbled to the sloping ground. She sat down and cried, wept angry, bitter tears. Ben dropped down beside her and gathered her into his arms. He was the first man to have ever held her and she clung to his consoling familiarity, her head bowed against his chest.

He kissed her hair. 'Don't worry, Em darling. I'll make sure that everything will be all right from now on.'

Chapter Twenty-Six

A few days later, Selina made her way to Ford House. To see Jim Killigrew's ready-made family, the weak spot in his carefully assembled armour. Hearing about Jim's intended bride had been more surprising than discovering he had his own small business. To most, Elena Rawley was belittling herself by marrying Jim – many villagers and the Methodist friends of her father were openly against the association. Those worried over her future also thought Elena wasn't Jim's type of woman, but Selina knew that, after her experiences with Jim, the plain young virgin was just the sort of wife that would appeal to Jim – as well as the big house and money Elena had. The orphans? Well, they went with the package and he wouldn't mind that too much. Thankfully, the orphans did not appear to be about anywhere. She was to learn they were away, playing with the children of the daily help.

Elena was displeased to find who was knocking on her door but she was too charitable not to offer hospitality, and the Bosweld woman had just been to lay fresh flowers on her niece's grave. She was going to receive some more fiercely given well-meaning advice for allowing this scarlet woman to step over her threshold. But Selina Bosweld had said she had something important to say, so how could she send her away?

Selina sat down in the parlour and waited, with her handbag set demurely on her lap, until Elena carried in the tray of tea. 'I must say you've done wonders with the place. You and Jim. It was quite old-fashioned when my brother and I lived here. Your little kitchen fire was a blessing in disguise. I'm sure you believe that sort of thing anyway.'

'Yes, I do,' Elena said firmly. Having Jim in her life had given her confidence and she wasn't about to allow this woman to undermine her, as she had done way back, outside in the garden the day of their first meeting. 'Do you take milk and sugar, Miss— I'm sorry, Dr Bosweld?'

'Milk, yes – sugar, one lump.' Selina produced a slim silver cigarette case and co-ordinating lighter and raised her brows. 'Is one allowed to smoke in here?'

Elena knew she was being challenged and mocked. She placed her second-best china in front of Selina. Only genuine people, no matter of what standing, were treated to her Royal Doulton. 'Jim smokes outside.'

'Forgive me, I shouldn't have asked. People are more lackadaisical up in London, you see, and where I was in my last practice it didn't bother them too much. Jim was always a thoughtful boy. I knew him very well in former days. He came here often, to do little jobs for me. Anyway, you must allow me to congratulate you on your forthcoming nuptials. What's your dress going to be like? Do tell. I'm not likely to be here to spill the beans and ruin your big entrance as you float down the aisle.'

Elena was to wear her mother's wedding dress and veil, a subdued but beautiful Victorian satin and lace creation, but this woman was the last person she'd divulge that to. 'I haven't decided yet. There's been so much tragedy in the village, I haven't given my own happiness much thought.'

'Happy, are you? How fortunate. I hope it all works out for you. You and Jim are about to make some big changes, and sacrifices.' At the personal remarks, Elena's body stiffened. Selina wasn't surprised, but rather than the boring little mouse becoming confused and whimpering, there was a spark in her, and undoubtedly the urge to protect those she loved. So she was in love with Jim, and whether Jim felt the same way or not, he'd considered himself to be on to a good thing. The wrecking of their engagement would make a fitting revenge. He wouldn't be laughing this time when she took her last leave of this crummy village. Selina stretched her face to look serious. 'Well, I really ought to say why I've come here. It's quite simple, I wanted to thank you for attending my niece's funeral.'

'Not at all.' Elena didn't know what else to say. She had written to Mr Bosweld expressing her sympathy and had shaken his hand and muttered something appropriate after the burial. It had been the saddest funeral she had ever gone to. Many villagers had packed the front pews of the church, but it had been obvious most of them were only curious about why the tragic Elizabeth Bosweld's final resting place was to be here among their forebears, where she didn't really belong.

'I know what people are thinking,' Selina said, seizing her teacup. She was having trouble keeping her temper. Back at Highertown, after they had been – to Selina's mind – contemptuously kicked out of Ford Farm, she and Perry had quarrelled long and hard about his intentions for Libby's funeral.

'She wasn't happy anywhere for long,' he'd yelled bitterly. 'It's something I'll never forgive myself for, but at least she was happy living in Hennaford, where she'd got Casper, until you ruined it. I'm going to travel up and fetch the dog, and Mrs Nicholson too, if she'd like to join me, then come back to live in Cornwall where I can be close to Libby.'

'Then why not have her buried at sea? It makes more sense.'

'The sea's already had her once! And I don't want her in some public cemetery, so don't come up with that idea either. My mind's made up. Legally, I'm her father, I have the say and there's nothing you can do about it.'

'You might end up regretting your decision.' She'd eyed him with mocking coldness. 'It seems it's not entirely cast in gold that your precious Emilia is going to have you.'

'Em's just badly shaken by the facts of the will, that's all. It's bound to make it sink in to her that Alec's never coming back. It was Tristan's idea that we move out. We shouldn't have stayed there anyway, it was thoughtless of us.'

Selina had laughed her most deadly laugh. 'Don't you see? The fact that Emilia's not just passing through, as it were, at the farm before her son comes into it, means Alec is never going to go away. He's made the most romantic, loving and adoring gesture someone ever could, he's passed on his trust. She must be feeling as guilty as hell about you. It's over for the pair of you, Perry. Finished! Kaput! You'll never stop loving each other, but Alec's loyalty and devotion to her and her betrayal of him will always be there between you. She knows that already. She'll be the Widow Harvey for the rest of her life. And you'll be nothing. It's all such a hoot. Alec couldn't have got his revenge any better if he'd actually known that his little dairymaid wife had a lover, one he'd had sleeping under his roof at his own invitation.'

Pale and expressionless, Perry had listened to her stream of spite. When he spoke it was in a strangely quiet pitch. 'My biggest wish now is that you were dead.'

The echoes of those words were frozen inside her head because she knew he had really meant them.

Selina explained to Elena the reason for Libby being buried at Hennaford and by the time she had finished she was weeping genuine tears. Watching the small white coffin being lowered into the ground had fragmented her heart for ever.

Elena was moved by what she saw as real and lasting grief. 'I wish there was something I could do for you.'

'Actually, there is. I feel you're the only person I could ask to do this. Everyone else round here has, shall I say, a very low opinion of me, and I can hardly ask this of Emilia Harvey; she's her own grief to bear. When I go away I don't know if I'll ever come back. Would you, dear Miss Rawley, Elena, please place some flowers on Libby's grave for me from time to time? Perry will do so regularly, specially on her birthday and Christmas, of course, but I'd liked to be represented too. Next spring, would you pick some violets from the hedgerows? Libby loved wild violets.'

'And people would know they're from you because of the colour of your eyes,' Elena said. 'Of course I'll do that. I'd be glad to.'

'Thanks. You're such a good person. I suppose I'd better soon take my leave. You must be very busy.' Selina passed a brittle smile above her teacup. As she'd expected, Elena relaxed. Selina was grateful for her kindness but it irked her how badly the other woman wanted her to go. She studied her. Her sweet face had released some of its tension and her shoulders had dropped. She was appealing. What a delicious prize she would be. 'If you don't mind me saying so, that's a pretty frock you're wearing. I don't recall you showing your bare arms before, and you've no stockings under your sandals.'

Elena rubbed her arms and drew in her feet. Her guest had jumped into another mood and was tossing about personal comments. 'Actually, I am a little busy.'

Selina glanced at her watch. 'Well, I really must go. My next stop is Ford Farm. It's been nice talking to you, Elena. I wish you all the happiness for the future.'

For a future without Jim, Selina thought, with viciousness. Jim's plans to live in this big, fine house would be scuppered as soon as Elena began to relate her conversation this afternoon. Jim would assume she had been told all about how and when he had lost his virginity, and he would lose his temper, really let rip at the deliberate ill will aimed at him, and Elena, the dear, sweet little innocent, would be disturbed, and hopefully disgusted, and wonder if she could go through with the marriage. Better still, Jim would probably come after Selina herself and cause an almighty scene in which he would issue all manner of threats. The love and the trust that had formed under this roof would be destroyed.

Elena went upstairs to the front landing window and looked down as Selina pulled away in the Daimler. Passion didn't teem often through Elena's slight form but now she was spilling over with it, passion of the indignation and furious kind. So the risqué rumours that had circulated about Jim being involved with the promiscuous former nurse were true. She had been his mystery woman. Recalling how distraught he had been after the association had ended, it was plain that Selina Bosweld had cast him aside in her usual cruel manner. Did Selina Bosweld really think she cared about Jim's past? That he wasn't a virgin? That he had been seduced – ruthlessly seduced, no doubt. He hadn't deserved to be a victim of hers.

This was the only time in her life that Elena uttered a swear word. 'You bitch! You viper. I know your game, Selina Bosweld. You didn't fool me for one minute. I'll lay flowers on poor young Libby's grave, the niece you didn't really care about,' she promised. A Bible passage ran through her mind – *vengeance is mine, saith the Lord*. Then Elena made another promise. If the beastly woman even tried to cause any heartbreak to Jim and her new family, she might not wait for the Lord to act.

—

'Hello? This is Ford Farm.'

'Mrs Rowse, this is Perry Bosweld.' He held the receiver away from her bellow. 'May I please speak to Emilia?'

'Course you can. You'll have to hold the line though. She's out in the dairy. Just give me a minute.'

Dolly could walk briskly and she made her destination within the designated time. Emilia had recently been taking refuge in the dairy, as if she was clinging to former happier times. Head down, dour-faced, she was attending to the clotted cream production; the cream that had been separated from milk was scalding in a bain-marie. 'Leave that! Perry's on the phone for 'ee.'

'Tell him I'm busy,' Emilia replied in the flat tones she used nowadays. 'And that I'll ring back later.'

'I'll do no such thing. And you said that yesterday and you didn't do it. Come on! I know you've got a lot on your mind but the poor man's got a lot on his too. It might

237

be important. Anyway, it's basic good manners to speak to him.'

Emilia sighed at the intrusion – she wanted only to keep her mind numb. Speaking to Perry would be the hardest thing. Dolly read Emilia's sigh as annoyance, then saw it was helplessness. 'Now don't get upset, my love. Where's Linda? What's the use in having a dairymaid if you keep sending her off to do something else? Wipe your hands, I'll carry on here.'

Never had Perry felt more agitated and lost. He waited impatiently, praying Emilia would speak to him this time. He leapt when he heard her voice. His heart dipped to his feet. She sounded so weak, dull and hesitant. 'Hello, Perry. What do you want?'

'What do you think, Em? I want us to talk. I want to see you.'

'I—I can't. Not now.'

'Why not? What have I done? Look, I happen to know that Lottie's at Tremore House with her cousin today. You've got all your harvest cut and have all the help you need. What other excuse do you have? Em, darling, please don't do this! I don't understand. You're breaking my heart.'

The despair in his voice drove her very near to tears. 'I'm so sorry. The last thing that I want to do is to hurt you. Perry, it's so difficult.' She frowned. 'How did you know where Lottie is? Where are you?'

'In the village telephone box. Selina's got the motor. I've hired one. I'm going to drive to the churchyard. You and I being there won't be thought odd. I'll wait there for you.' He put the receiver down before she could object and increase the terrible sense of rejection she'd thrust upon him. He'd understood why Tristan Harvey had asked him and

Selina to leave the farm the day Alec's will had been read, but when Emilia had returned from her walk with Ben she had been strangely aloof, had hardly met his eyes, and it was as if the eight years in which they had been in love had never existed. Alec leaving her everything had disturbed and confused her so much.

Changing into her black funeral clothes, picking some lilies rather than roses from the garden, Emilia cycled slowly along the two miles of lanes to the church. Perry was sitting on the bench beside the weedy green path by the newer graves, not far from where Libby had been lain. Emilia saw that he had put pink roses there, a pretty posy to add to the wreaths; there were a lot of wreaths – the villagers had felt sorry for the girl lost so tragically. Perry struggled to get up. Emilia grimaced. He was using his walking stick, which meant he was in pain. He got like this when he was tense, finding his prosthetic demanding.

'I'm sorry,' she said. A week ago she would have hastened to him, to receive his love and comfort and give the same to him. Now she felt nothing for Perry. And not even just nothing for him. Sometimes she was finding it hard to relate to Will, Tom and Lottie, and this was adding to her bewilderment.

'Don't worry about it,' he replied, swallowing the hopeful smile he'd been about to form. Emilia was looking at him as if he was a stranger. At least she had come, it was something to cling to. 'We've both got a daughter buried here now.'

'And I've got a husband.' She faced the direction of the older graves, where the Harvey plot was. The lilies were laying over her arm and she looked down at them with intent.

'Is this what it's all about? Alec? You're feeling guilty about us?'

'Yes. But more than that, I feel terrible for letting him down. I'll never forgive myself. He's given me everything and I'd betrayed him.'

'I was afraid you'd say that.' Perry gripped her arm. 'I know I should do the decent thing and tell you to go to him, stay his grieving widow for ever, and say that I'll leave and never come back. But I can't! I'm not strong enough. Em. Please don't send me away.' He gave an ironic laugh. 'Selina's been plotting to break us up, she blames me for Libby's death and wants to punish me. Strange thing is, it's Alec's wish that's threatening to do it, and he didn't even intend to. I suppose it's a just retribution for both of us.'

He looked down at the ground. There was a long silence. Neither of them moved. He said, 'Do you want me to go away?'

Her voice was barely a whisper. 'I don't know.'

'At least you didn't say no immediately. Perhaps you just need some time. Dear God, I hope that's all you need. Everything's a mess. I shouldn't have come. Libby would still be alive. Nothing would have prevented Alec from dying, but you might have felt differently about us, yes, I'm sure you would have done. I feel terrible too for us being together while Alec was dying. But nothing can change that now.' He wanted to say a lot more. That if she rejected him for good he'd have nothing to live for because he could never love again. He said, 'I'll leave you now. I'll stay at Reggie's house for another two days, then I'll travel back up to London. I don't intend to keep the house, but I'll wait there for six months and hope you'll get in touch, and if not then I'll go. I shall come back here on the anniversary of

Libby's death next year. I shan't come to the farm. If you want to see me leave some roses for her.'

'I understand. Don't blame yourself over Libby. It was my fault. I was the one who changed the tone of our greeting cards. Goodbye, Perry. Take care.'

He hesitated but she remained silent. 'Goodbye, Em. Remember I shall never stop loving you.'

She heard his irregular steps trudging over the ground, travelling away from her. There was already a yawning distance between them. She walked off to deliver the lilies. With a start she heard the engine start up and the car Perry had hired move away. She whispered on the silent air, 'Whatever happens, I will always love you too.'

–

Selina found the farm lacking its new owner, but there were three visitors at the back door. Tristan Harvey and Vera Rose Stockley had arrived to see how things were, and the sweet young girl she had seen talking to Jim Killigrew in Truro had just stepped out of a taxicab. Selina was expecting a hostile reception for herself but she was unprepared for the reaction of Tristan to the girl.

'Miss Hetherton-Andrews.' His whole demeanour was stiff, his face dark and glowering. 'What on earth brings you here?'

Louisa was wearing a blouse and trousers and country shoes. She visibly tensed against the frostiness. She blustered, 'I've come to see if I can help out and to see Jonny before he goes up again. If that's all right. Aunt Polly is collecting me later.'

'Course it is.' Dolly Rowse came outside to usher everyone in for tea. She eyed Selina charily. 'Most people are welcome here.'

'I don't want a drink, thank you.' Selina smiled warmly at Dolly as if she hadn't just received a rebuff. Then she turned her lovely eyes on the girl. Tristan calling her by name had made her aware of who she was. She had a birthmark on her face. The old district nurse had prattled on about someone with a birthmark. Tristan obviously didn't like the girl. He wasn't the sort to have some weird country superstition about people with birthmarks, so what was this all about? 'I'm fascinated to meet you, Miss Hetherton-Andrews. I'm Dr Selina Bosweld.'

'Oh! You're… ? Oh, I'm sorry.' Louisa was a little unnerved. She had met many obnoxious grasping types on her various travels, and apparently this woman was one, with an added malicious streak. 'What I meant to say is, please accept my condolences over your recent loss, Dr Bosweld.'

'Thank you. Well, as Emilia isn't here I think I'll run along. Goodbye all.' She took a sneaky glance back and saw Dolly scowling after her, and Tristan scowling at Louisa Hetherton-Andrews.

She had no intention of going immediately and lingered to light a cigarette. It amused her how the others quickly trooped inside to take advantage of Dolly Rowse's never empty teapot, making the point they were glad to be rid of her company. Was Jonny Harvey in the fields or somewhere in the yards? She left the flagstones and strode over the dusty cobbles, keeping alert for the gander, a beady-eyed wretch who was more territorial than the Jack Russells, who would draw out his neck and hiss like a traction engine to intimidate family member and visitor alike, and occasionally go as far as to peck at a vulnerable leg. Once, Selina had grabbed the bird round the neck and tossed it across the yard. The other geese were about, among the multitude of noisy poultry, ducks, hens, guinea fowl and turkeys, but there was no sign of the gander. You're learning, Selina thought, grinning to herself.

A terrific squealing started up. Selina smirked to see Jonny herding a trio of escaping sows back into the pig crow. 'In you get! In you get!' Using rapid, athletic, waylaying movements with his long limbs, he got them back inside the pen and shut the sliding doors on them.

'Cunning old swine, aren't they?' Selina giggled at her joke and peered down on the graceless, would-be escapees, their tiny eyes half concealed by their large floppy ears, as they now hunted about eagerly for food. 'You need something to batten down those doors. They get out every other day, from what I've heard.'

'It's none of your business. What are you doing here? I've told you I don't want to see you again.' He shifted uncomfortably, praying no one would witness them talking together. She was very close to him. He could smell her unassuming perfume and smell desire on her. And although he loathed her beyond measure, she had terrifically exciting ways of performing sex and he couldn't fight the fact she was breeding desire in him now. He was ashamed that he had succumbed to her immediately after her first move on him, ashamed he had allowed it at all, and with her words echoing inside his head about his uncle's dreadful end. 'I've told you what happened between us was a mistake.'

'Are you sure about that, Jonny?' she teased, knowing why he was breaking out in a sweat. 'You were outrageously enthusiastic at the time. Now there's no need to get defensive. Once with you was enough for me, you've got too much to learn. Your father and cousin are here, oh, and a girl from Truro called Louisa. A pretty little thing. She seems very out of place here. I must say, I was thoroughly taken aback by your father's dislike of her. It's very strange for him to behave in that manner. What's behind it?'

Feeling more secure now she wasn't going to suggest they slip away to the hayloft, Jonny accepted the cigarette she offered. He bent his head over her lighter, then took a deep, steadying puff. 'No idea.' There was no use denying there was something in what Selina had said. He had quarrelled with his father about his bizarre antagonism towards Louisa. He couldn't understand why he was prejudiced against her, but there was definitely something. He had questioned his Uncle Alec and Aunt Winifred and they had both been reluctant to talk about it, and Polly Hetherton seemed uneasy on the few occasions when Louisa mixed with the family.

'Oh, well, we all have our little idiosyncrasies. Goodbye, Jonny. Good luck with your studies.' Selina drove back to Truro. She intended to call on Gertrude Roberts.

Unless it was a special occasion, food and drink was always served in the farmhouse kitchen. Vera Rose sat on the form at the huge scrubbed pine table, sipping Dolly Rowse's bitter-strong tea and examining her stepfather, as puzzled as Jonny and Selina were about why he disliked Louisa so much. It was more than that: it seemed he couldn't stand the sight of her. It was irrational, and unbelievable in her uncle's case because in every other aspect he was a good and caring man, fun-loving and generous, and totally respectful, but to Louisa he was unapproachable, and when he did stoop to speak to her he was offhand and even sometimes downright rude.

It was no wonder the poor, sweet-natured girl was squirming on her chair and looking down miserably into her teacup. She had asked Tristan, in polite chitchat, how things were at Roskerne.

'What do you expect?' he had replied gruffly, pulling on his black tie. 'We've had a tragedy there too.'

Vera Rose noticed that Mrs Rowse and Tilda were eyeing him quizzically, and because they, like everyone else who knew Louisa, liked her very much, the two women were also looking annoyed. There was obviously something behind all this antagonism. She and Jonny had discussed it over the years and their favourite opinion, the only one that seemed logical, was that his father, her uncle, must know who Louisa's parents were and he had a reason to loathe them.

Vera Rose would have suggested to Louisa that they go outside and find Jonny, but she was eager to see him alone. He would soon be going back up to Oxford and goodness knew when she'd see him again. Jonny had no understanding of it, but the fact that she had given herself to him had left her loving him even more. That would never change.

After the first time with him, on the old couch up in Roskerne's attics, she had lain wrapped up against him, aware that he wasn't satisfied yet, and she had made what she felt to be a necessary explanation. 'I care deeply for you, Jonny. I mean I love you or I wouldn't have had done it with you.'

He had kissed her lips tenderly but also with simmering passion, stroking down her back; her skin, like his, was hot and damp from their energetic joining. 'I love you too.'

He was looking at her breasts and she made a vain attempt to get their eyes to meet. 'What I mean is that I really love you. I'm in love with you.'

'Don't be daft! Vee,' he had laughed as if he'd thought her declaration hilarious. 'Don't make the mistake of thinking there actually is the sort of thing pumped out in storybooks. There's lust and passion and there's friendship and compan-ionship. Some people are lucky to be able to combine the two. If you want children then find someone to marry, but make sure it's someone you can have fun with too, someone who won't try to change or control you.' She had felt herself growing numb in his arms and he must have felt her disappointment. 'Look, my darling, I'll always care about you, always love you, and always be your friend. I find that wonderful and enriching. You should too. It means that whatever happens in our lives we can always turn to each other. And we'll probably need to do so: tragedy links us now in our childhood home and heaven knows what the future will bring. Don't be downhearted. You'll come across other men who'll take your fancy. The trouble is, you've relegated yourself to just the roles of wife and mother. Think again about university. You're an intelligent woman. For goodness sake, get out there and live your life! Don't waste it. Don't waste your talents. Think what you could do in the world. As much as I despise the Bosweld woman, I admire her for doing just that.'

Clinging to him for some sort of consolation, she had thought through his viewpoints and exhortations. And then forgotten them, for Jonny had begun to make love to her again intensely. The first time she had been too nervous to enjoy anything, apart from the ideal of sacrificing her virginity to him out of love and commitment, but now he was doing different things, for her rather than for himself, and she was soon lost to the moment. Despite misgivings on moral and religious grounds, and the fear that their parents would discover them, there had been subsequent unions.

'Louisa,' she said. 'I've decided to apply for a place at university. Wherever I can get in.'

'Oh, good for you, Vee. How exciting.' Louisa looked at her with gratitude for bringing up something interesting. She was angled so Mr Harvey couldn't see her face, which was burning for he was making her feel ill at ease. She instinctively had her hand up over her birthmark, which became even more vividly red when she was uncomfortable. It was such bad luck to turn up here at the same time as him, wretched man. If only he'd go outside or to the den. 'I don't think I'm clever enough to consider higher education. What will you study?'

'I'm thinking of something along the lines of philosophy or social history.' Vera Rose kept up the talk for a couple of minutes, then excused herself to go to the bathroom. She felt awful for lying, but if she had said she was off to seek Jonny, Louisa would have undoubtedly said that she'd join her.

She was thrilled to find Jonny quickly, smoking and looking ponderous by the pigs' crow. She ran to him. He smiled at the sight of her but she could see he was troubled. 'Hello! Is something the matter?'

He could have blurted out, 'Nothing, only that I've allowed myself to be seduced by a vile woman who's little better than a barbarian, and I'm getting the most dreadful, harrowing nightmares about Uncle Alec's last days.' He said, 'Don't tell me you've left poor Louisa with my father? Selina Bosweld was just here asking me what gives over his frosty attitude towards her.'

'I feel awful about it, Jonny, but I wanted to see you alone.' She was curious, and hopeful, about what his reaction would be towards her.

'Why?'

The question, given so matter-of-factly, crushed her to the roots of her being, stamping out her last tiny hope that she would ever come to be more to him than his cousin, his friend, his lover. She dampened down her emotions. 'Oh, I have been silly. I should have brought Louisa with me. I wanted to tell you that I'm going to take up your suggestion about university.'

He put an open hand on her shoulder. All he wanted from Vee now was her friendship and support. 'That's brilliant. I know you'll make a success of it. I'm proud of you. What do the parents say?'

'My mother wasn't happy about it at first. She had hopes for me to follow the traditional path. Your father's delighted. He's making enquiries for me. It won't be plain sailing getting in anywhere, but with a bit of perseverance, well, a few years from now I might be a doctor of philosophy or something. Yes, I think I'd like that.' It was suddenly a thrilling prospect after being let down so badly in the romantic department.

Jonny led them off towards the house to rescue their young friend. 'I suppose Louisa's looking gorgeous. All these continental trips suit her. She already has such flair.'

'I didn't know you felt that way about her.' Vera Rose was jealous. Jonny had never complimented her, except in a carnal way. This made her feel cheap and hurt, and she was glad he no longer seemed interested in her intimately; a certain gleam in his stunning grey eyes was missing. She wouldn't let this mar their closeness though – she'd hate that.

'She's lovely. It's hard to believe she's still a child. I know I'm not usually attracted to someone as unassuming as her, a sweet sort, but there's something about her.' He nodded to reinforce his thoughts. 'I hope she doesn't make the mistake of falling for some cad or chinless wonder. She's always so eager to please, be on the right side of everyone. Damn it, Vee!' He was suddenly angry. 'Why is my father so against her? She's the nicest girl in the world. One of these days I'm going to demand he tells me what the hell's going on.'

Rounding the brick wall of the cattle yard, they saw Louisa perched on the back doorstep, ruffling the necks of Bertie and Hope, the friendliest pair of the numerous Jack Russells. She immediately smiled at them but also fussed with the hair on her right side, bringing it round to cover her cheek, and it was plain she was feeling out of place. Jonny was incensed with his father. He hated seeing her hurt. She was feminine and gentle, delicate and fragile, the sort to bring out the desire in a chap to honour and protect, yet still there was something else about her. Something indefinable. He'd confront his father again but here wasn't the place. His Aunty Em would likely be back from the churchyard any minute – he had witnessed her cutting a bunch of lilies and heading off.

'Hello, Lou-Lou.' Jonny grinned down on her. He wanted to make her happy and he was suddenly back to being a confident youth for the first time in weeks. Louisa was one person who never made demands and she was soothing somehow. 'You look good, even in your old things. What's it like swapping the Cornish Riviera for the far more exotic French one? Not so exciting, I'm sure.'

'Hello, Jonny.' She stayed put because Jonny would likely gather her in and give her an enormous hug and a smacking kiss on both cheeks as a jolly big brother. Gazing up at him, suntanned, brawny, as handsome as a hero in a Cecil B. De Mille movie, she was shy. A young Italian count had made eyes at her at the last hotel she had stayed in and danced with her very closely, and she had become conscious of men in the grown-up sense for the first time. She had not found this uncomfortable, but now things were different with Jonny, she had confused feelings about him and she was afraid to explore them. 'I like travelling and I equally like being at home and back at school. I've come to help. What shall I do?'

'You can budge along for a start. Time for me to take a break.' He made to park himself on the doorstep beside her and she shuffled to make space. Unaware of how nervous he was making her, he fingered in his shirt breast pocket for his cigarettes. 'I'm parched and hungry. Be a good sport and fetch me a mug of Mrs Rowse's best and a saffron bun, eh, Vee? Tell me how your Aunt Polly is, Louisa. Someone mentioned she's looking for a new husband.'

Feeling left out, Vera Rose squeezed past Jonny to act as his waitress.

Louisa fidgeted at his close proximity and nearly stopped breathing when he dropped an arm round her shoulders, even though it was a matey embrace. And she hated talking about her aunt's flirtations. Her aunt was a vital, stylish lady, with grace and wit, who found men easy to relate to. Louisa was aware of the occasional late-night caller being allowed into her hotel bedroom. Her aunt was lonely, it was why she whisked herself, with or without Louisa, off on so many travels. 'She's very well, thank you. Next year she wants to go on a safari in Africa.'

'Africa? Now that's somewhere I intend to go to one day. Bag myself a tiger. You can have the skin for your room. My tribute to a lovely girl who will one day become an even lovelier woman.' He grasped Louisa's right hand. 'No need to cover up your birthmark. Be relaxed about it. Think of it this way. It's a part of you, a way that makes you unique.'

'Uncle Alec used to say things like that,' she said, letting her hand fall away, still clasped in his.

'Well, he was one of the finest men who ever lived. You can't argue with anything he said, can you?'

'I suppose not.'

'There you are then.' Jonny gave her a bear hug. Louisa found she didn't mind very much.

Vera Rose halted at the kitchen door. The two older women were no longer there. Her Uncle Tristan was at a window, his hands pressed down on the sill, shaking his head, gasping in a long, fretful breath. He was watching Jonny and Louisa and his usual kind, calm face was steeped in anxiety.

Chapter Twenty-Seven

Emilia asked the telephone operator to put her through to Reggie Rule's number. 'Hello? Perry?' Since she had spoken to him yesterday her wants and needs had catapulted around inside her head. One moment she didn't want to see him, then she did, but always she thought that she shouldn't want to see him. She ought to keep faith with Alec. She owed it to his memory. She should never have kept in touch with Perry. She had tried to work up greater feelings for Alec, but it hadn't worked. She hadn't looked to fall deeper in love with Perry than Alec, but somehow she had and that was everlasting.

He'd said he'd wait two days for her and then leave. She didn't want him to leave, she could hardly stand the thought of that, and she had his misery to consider as well as her own. She owed him more than her blunt words in the churchyard, when she had treated him as an outsider, as if he had done something wrong. It was she who had kept him dangling on a string, kept his hopes alive. If Alec had not had an illness, if he had lived to some grand old age, there would never have been a future for her and Perry, and he would have wasted his life pining for her. He might have looked for someone else, and even if he couldn't have loved someone new as much, he would have had hope and companionship. She had relegated him to loneliness. And yesterday she had threatened him to endure it for the rest of his life. Loneliness, the very worst thing in life to suffer. She hated herself. She was selfish. She had treated the two most important men in her life very badly. She didn't mind if she suffered as a consequence but Perry didn't deserve to.

'It's Selina. How are you, Emilia?' Lounging on the hall telephone seat, nibbling the tip of one of her nails, wicked lights shone out of Selina's extraordinary eyes. The revenge she was seeking on all those who had belittled her was not far off, not after the enlightening time she had spent with Gertrude Roberts yesterday.

She had taken a bottle of port with her, left it standing innocently in its brown paper wrapping beside her handbag while drinking the weak tea Gertrude served. Her arrival had sent the retired district nurse into a fluster, then into raptures, seemingly, at being called on by a doctor. Gertrude's loneliness and her esteem for those more highly qualified than herself in the medical profession made her easy to manipulate.

'Tell me about your work. Particularly in Hennaford. As I mentioned before, I knew some people there many years ago,' Selina had said, from a matching easy chair set across from the plaster fireplace in the dark-curtained, stuffy front room. Before arriving, Selina had wondered if she was on safe ground with Gertrude, that if, by trawling through her memories, Gertrude would recall a scandal about the Boswelds who had lived in the village, and she would be refused entry, but Gertrude was a bit vague about most things.

A delighted Gertrude had prattled on for ages. Selina couldn't be sure about the accuracy of everything and she would have cut the visit short, but she was curious to learn if the baby with a birthmark and Miss Louisa Hetherton-Andrews were one and the same person. There was definitely something odd about Tristan Harvey's aversion to her; it was worth investigating. Patiently, she pressed for details of the many deliveries Gertrude had made, and as the afternoon wore on and Gertrude showed signs of becoming tired, Selina lifted up the bottle of port.

'If you don't mind me saying so, Miss Roberts, you're looking a little pale. I thought so the other day. I've brought this with me. A small glass will be the perfect pick-me-up for you.'

Gertrude appeared overcome with gratitude. 'Anything you say, doctor. It's most kind of you. I'm so enjoying our little chat.'

'I see you have some glasses on the sideboard. Allow me to pour you a drop now.' She made it a large drop and then it was easy to talk Gertrude into drinking a second glass. Selina fixed the old woman with a confidential stare. 'Tell me more about the baby with the birthmark. I'd be interested in learning what happened to it. Was it a girl?'

'D-did I mention her?' Gertrude was bewildered. She blushed, and Selina sensed it was through the guilt of making a professional blunder.

'Yes, you did. You hinted there was something unusual about her birth. I'd like to hear about that. Was she rejected by her parents because of the birthmark? Some people harbour silly superstitions about such a thing. Of course, you can tell me anything. I'm a doctor and bound to respect the confidentiality of a patient. You don't have to mention any names.' She could work out the characters herself.

'Of course,' Gertrude relaxed. The tortoiseshell bracket clock chimed four o'clock and it could be seen she was pleased to be honoured with a long visit. 'It wasn't anything to do with superstition. It was a terrible tragedy.'

'Really? Was the mother a Hennaford girl? Unmarried? And she couldn't keep the baby?' This could be why Polly Hetherton and her brother had adopted the child. If Tristan Harvey was the father, he and Polly Hetherton would be afraid the girl would discover it. From recollection of the family history, he had been recovering at the farm from battle wounds in the year of Louisa's birth.

'Oh, she wasn't unmarried!' Gertrude exclaimed, eager to get on with the tale now she had, to her thinking, an appropriate listener. 'She was married to an army captain.' Selina poured her another drink and she didn't object.

'I see.' The army captain had to be Tristan Harvey. That was it. Ursula Harvey had died in childbirth. Her baby was reported to have perished too, but obviously it hadn't.

'The baby's father was her lover, a cad, handsome of course, but most disreputable. They were going to run away together and take the four-year-old son of the marriage with them. It was the timely intervention of a young farmer's wife, pregnant herself, and then the army captain, who put a stop to it. Apparently, the lover pulled a gun on them but they managed to overpower him.' Gertrude was warming to this now as if a dedicated gossip. 'I felt sorry for the husband. The wife had run off with her lover before. Now, the unfaithful wife had been in labour for some time, but when she told her lover this he ran out on her. She was so heartbroken she did nothing to help with her baby's birth and tragically she died, a classic case of post-partum haemorrhage. It was one of the most harrowing cases of my long career.'

'Did the baby survive?' Of course she did, she was Louisa Hertherton-Andrews.

'Yes, she was adopted by a young man who had come to the house with the husband's younger brother. The young man had a widowed sister who couldn't conceive and he had a serious heart condition, so he couldn't look forward to marriage and fatherhood – in fact he didn't live for many years afterwards – so he took the unwanted baby away with him. I accompanied him in his chauffeured motor car. It was a most odd thing for me to do, I can assure you, Dr Bosweld. It had already been planned for the baby to be adopted. Until the lover turned up again, the husband was giving his marriage another chance, you see, but he wouldn't accept the baby. It was arranged that I'd take the baby to the adoptive parents but I knew that, sadly, they wouldn't accept a less than perfect child; the birthmark, you understand. The young man had to haggle for the baby, there was quite a row downstairs about it while I was with her dying mother. I think some of the others wanted to bring her up.' Gertrude's wrinkled eyes fluttered. She was drifting off to sleep.

'The others?' Selina went to her and prodded her. 'Miss Roberts, how many people were there? Do you remember?'

'Remember? Of course I do. All three brothers were there, and the eldest brother's young pregnant wife and the youngest brother's weak friend. Such a strange arrangement in the end. The poor husband was talked into it against his better judgement, I'm sure. I remember thinking, there's going to be trouble in the future.' Gertrude closed her eyes.

This time Selina let her drop into a gently snoring slumber. 'You can bet there is.' Selina stoppered the port and put it back in its wrapping. She rinsed out the glass and put it back in its place. Gertrude would probably stay where she was until the next morning and have a headache and little recollection of anything more than a visit from someone she considered a new-found friend. She had the whole cast list of the drama. The secret. A secret which involved Louisa Hetherton-Andrews, Polly Hetherton, Tristan, Ben, Alec and Emilia. Alec was gone, but she could use this information to cause upheaval in the others' lives any time she chose. They were keeping secret the fact that Louisa and Jonny Harvey were half-brother and sister. Jonny Harvey would be devastated and that would be more revenge on him. Did Perry know? Had Emilia mentioned it to him? There was no reason why she should. The news would cause little upset between them, but Emilia was doing that anyway. Perry had muttered that he might be leaving soon and he had no intention of revealing the reason why.

Selina's first instinct at having Emilia on the other end of the telephone was to gloat, but there was something so lamentable about her voice that the part of her that loved Emilia rose to the surface. 'Are you all right, Em? You sound odd. Is everything getting to you? I'll come round if you like.'

'Is Perry not there?'

'Afraid not,' Selina spoke truthfully. 'He's playing a round of golf with Ernest Rule to take his mind off things. Look, Em, I can tell you're troubled. I sense that all's not well with you and Perry. I know I've been perfectly beastly to you both at times but you are the two people I care about most in the world. Would it help to talk? I can be there in a jiffy.'

Talk to Selina? The bitch? Strange as it was, she was the only one she could talk to about Perry. She was the only one who knew about their love. 'I don't know, Selina. I need to talk about him but I can't trust you not to turn on me, to use it against us.'

Now Selina's repressed feelings had surfaced she was anxious to be with Emilia. 'I promise I won't cause any trouble, Em. I swear on… on Libby's grave. Please believe me. I've been muddled, that's all. It's not been easy feeling shut out of your life for so long. I care about you and I care about Perry, I really do. You choose where we meet. I'll do everything your way. Please. I hate to see you so unhappy, really I do.'

'We can't talk here,' Emilia decided. For a start her mother would try to sit in with them. 'I'll come to you. I'll be there in half an hour.'

'Thanks, Em, for trusting me. I'll look forward to it and I swear I won't let you down.' Ecstatic, Selina rushed upstairs to change into her most flattering frock and to put on some make-up and her favourite perfume.

–

'Where're you going, Mum?' Will challenged Emilia as she picked up the car keys from the hall side table.

'I thought I'd pop into Truro. I won't be long. Tilda's got some nice smoked ham for your tea. Be good to Lottie, won't you?'

'You're always popping out somewhere alone.' He was glaring at her, a taller-than-average youth, so much like his father, but his surly attitude like Ben's when he was in an intractable mood. 'You're getting ambiguous, like Dad was, only you're more secretive.'

'What on earth do you mean? Will, how dare you speak to me like that.' The terms of Alec's last wishes had shaken Will as much as it had her. Now he had been placed on the same level as Tom, he had lost some of his haughtiness but it had been replaced with an awkward manner.

'Why aren't you taking Lottie with you? The pair of you used to be never apart.'

'We still rarely are. Lottie's content at the moment to be with Jonny. They've gone down to the woods with the dogs.'

'When's he leaving here? We don't need his help. I mean, *you* don't need his help.'

'Will, I know what this is about. I know you're upset about the unexpected changes in your father's will but there's nothing I can do about it. I won't go against his wishes. You're going to inherit the farm anyway. Why are you being like this?'

'Because it's made me feel small. Some of the chaps at school are laughing at me. They say I'll have to run to mummy for everything I need from now on, and if you marry again and you die first, then all my father's property will go to an outsider. How do you think that makes me feel? Dad had no right to do what he did. Harvey property should always remain in Harvey hands!'

'And it will!' Emilia raised her voice, getting as cross as he was. 'I doubt if I'd ever marry again, and if I did I'd sign the farm over to you. To you and Tom that is, and I wouldn't forget Lottie. You're selfish, Will. I love you, son, but you are far too selfish to ever let you have everything. I'm in no mood for this now. Get on with your homework and don't you ever bother me with this again.'

Will looked beset with fury. His mouth worked, he wanted to say something more, but when his mother made her mind up about something nothing would shift her. 'Am

I allowed to know where you're going? Just in case someone here needs you?' he hissed sourly.

'I'm going to Truro to see a friend. That's all I'm prepared to say. Don't stand there in my way, Will. Don't ever behave like this again.'

Their eyes clashed, hers uncompromising and dark brown, his hard and slate grey, and with a sinking heart Emilia knew she would never be really close to her eldest child again.

–

After the golf, in which Perry had been trounced by Ernest Rule, for his eyes, heart and concentration had not been on the round, the two men went to the Red Lion Hotel for a drink. In the plush surroundings, Perry downed another double whisky.

'You'll never forget Libby but time will help you to bear it,' Ernest said. 'I'll order you a soda water. Take it easy for a while before you have another drop of the hard stuff.' Ernest had been the best of company, staying silent most of the time, saying the right sort of thing when he'd spoken, not trying any sort of jollying-along humour. Perry accepted the soda water, he had no fight in him to object to anything. He tried not to say it but it came tumbling out. 'I wish I was dead.'

'No, you don't. You're not a coward. Your charities need you. Concentrate on them, it'll give you something to live for.'

'You don't understand, Ernie. I've lost more than my daughter.' Not having eaten properly for days, the whisky had taken its hold on Perry. He fiddled clumsily with his glass, his head becoming welcomingly muzzy.

'What do you mean, pal?' Ernest tugged at his beard.

'I've lost the woman I love too. Well, I'm pretty certain I have.'

'You're in love? Well, that's good news. So you don't need to wish yourself dead then, do you? Go back to London and fight for her.'

'I haven't left her in London. The reason I came down here was to be near to her.'

'Even better. Fight for her. Hang on a minute, to be near to her, you say? Ah. I take it she's not free? Not so easy then.'

'Oh, she's free.' Tears of grief and frustration slid from Perry's eyes. 'She doesn't want me, at least she's not sure she wants me. It's complicated.'

'I see. Shame. Do I know her?'

'Yes, very well. You wouldn't approve of our love. You were a very close friend to her husband. I think I've said enough. You've been good to me, you're the father of one of my old friends and I don't want to lose your friendship.'

Ernest was drinking vodka and tonic. He whirled the ice round in his glass, thinking. Not thinking for long. He whistled under his breath, not caring he was in a classy establishment where the staff and clientele wouldn't approve of such a noise. 'Are you telling me you're in love with Emilia Harvey?'

Perry toyed with his glass and kept looking down at the table.

'Blood and teeth!' Ernest hissed softly. 'You've astonished me. Emilia? And she feels the same way? Did Alec know? Of course not, he wouldn't have changed his will. Were you carrying on under his very nose and he had no notion of it? Yes, that's it. That's why she took the reading of the will so badly. If you weren't suffering a bereavement yourself I'd throw you outside and pound you into the pavement. But, well, to be honest, although I've got a happy marriage I have… well, looked elsewhere over the years. When did all this start?'

'Soon after baby Jenna died. I fell for Emilia at once, the day I moved into Ford House to be exact, and there was nothing on earth I could do to stop myself from loving her. She never stopped loving Alec. She never would have left him for me.'

'It's a sorry affair.'

'Yes, it is. Mine and Emilia's feelings mean it's been more than just an affair. My love for her has cost me everything. I accept that I deserve it. I'm relieved that Alec died without finding out about us. When I think how much more he would have suffered. Now I must bow out of Emilia's life again. Allow her to sort out her feelings. Allow her to grieve properly for Alec. And hope… and hope there might be a place for me in her life one day.'

'I'd have made sure you'd go, but I honour your decision. Alec was a good man and he was complex, mysterious at times, and I believe he was never really comfortable with life. He'd had troubled times and had known loneliness that had almost broken him. I think he'd have been sorry to be leaving his family but glad to be away from this world. His thoughts were often on a higher plane. Yes, you're right to go. Emilia will never know peace until she's sifted through her emotions. My advice is to say goodbye but don't put any conditions on it. Wait for her. If you love her as much as you say you do, you'll wait. Find something useful to do and keep your hopes alive. That way, if she decides to see you, she won't want to find you a mess of a man.'

'Thanks, Ernie, I can't tell you how much that has helped. I don't feel that I deserve it.'

'Oh, life's a funny old thing. Throws us all a rock or two. Can't see the point in you and Emilia staying miserable for the rest of your lives. And you're a likeable bloke, Perry. I know you'd have done the decent thing and walked away if Alec hadn't been terminally ill.'

'Don't put that much responsibility on me, Ernie. Emilia would have sent me away, I know that much.'

'You only have to give her time. Don't languish and waste it.'

'Let's have another drink, then I'll pack and let Emilia know. I owe you a lot of thanks, Ernie, I can go with some hope in my heart. It's time I got my sister away too. Time for us to visit Libby one last time and leave Hennaford in peace.'

—

'I thought we could sit out here, Em?' Selina showed her out into the back garden, where the lawn was cut but was the colour of straw after so many years of neglect, the shrubs were woody and the high boundary hedges out of control. Bees and butterflies and other insects were gaily collecting nectar in their God-appointed territories. The nettled ground beneath the half-dozen apple trees was heavy with windfalls. 'I enjoy the wildness here, the sense of abandon. I hate anything uniform.'

Emilia cast an eye over the borders. As well as camellias, azaleas and peonies, Perry had planted new rose bushes. He'd mentioned that those he'd discovered among the tangled jungle had been beyond saving.

'Take a seat.' Selina was unusually flustered and eager to please. 'Are you all right sitting in the sun or would you prefer a shady spot?'

'Out in the sun will be fine for a while. I can't stop long.'

That's a shame.' Selina gazed at her. She looked winsome in her black clothes, tired and weighed down, but her reserves of strength also filtered through. And Emilia could never look anything but beautiful. Selina wanted to hold her and have Emilia respond by putting her arms round her too. In her daydreams she gave Emilia the love she longed to, and there was no selfishness or cruelty in it. It was just a dream and would only ever be so, but it was one she allowed herself to float with now. 'Would you like a glass of wine?'

Emilia realized that she hadn't had a drink for hours and her throat was uncomfortably dry. 'I'd rather have something like lemon tea if you've got it.'

'Whatever you wish. You relax, I'll just be a minute.'

Emilia pulled off her hat and shook her hair free. The sun was hard at work in this sheltered spot. She closed her eyes to feel the warmth, to bid it to ease the tension in her head, to halt her tortured thoughts. She was tired, so tired, having not slept more than two or three hours each night for a long time.

Too soon, Selina came back with the tray.

Without thinking, Emilia said, 'I wish you were like this all the time.'

'Like what, Em?'

She cursed herself. Why on earth start something like this? 'Sociable, I suppose, and kind. When there's not the impression you're about to pounce with something shocking or unpleasant.'

Selina looked straight at her. 'Would you like me then, Em?'

'Yes, I think so. There'd be no reason not to like you, would there? I keep in mind the times when you have been compassionate.' Even as she said these words Emilia knew Selina was incapable of ever being a good person. There was something dark and twisted inside her, and not of the sort attained by abuse or bad luck. There was vindictiveness in the very essence of her. There was no denying that the instant Selina entered a place the atmosphere dimmed and grew heavy, as if the good, breathable air had been cut off, and the instant she left, the oppression lifted and the wholesomeness of the surroundings re-established itself.

What am I doing here? This is foolish. To be here now, to be considering Selina, of all people, to confide in and seek advice about her rent feelings for Perry, Emilia realized just how disturbed and vulnerable she was. She had placed herself at this woman's mercy and would have to be wary of her every second, keep her wits sharp. A short while ago Elena Rawley had called on her, and in terms of passion that went against her nature she had begged Emilia to try to send Selina away. 'I haven't the slightest clue why, but she's out to cause trouble for Jim. I know he had an association with her but that was years ago and I don't care about that. She hurt Jim very badly and now she wants to do it again. I daren't tell Jim of my suspicions, he'd go after her and goodness knows what she'd do then. Lead him on to becoming violent or something and tell the police. Emilia, can't you get rid of her? Nobody in the village wants her here. Certainly not your mother, she's spoken to me of her concerns.' Dolly Rowse warned continually, 'That woman's evil, a she-devil.

We must never forget it and watch her carefully. Very carefully.'

Emilia knew a moment of panic. Selina threw out traps for unsuspecting prey, and here she was probably within touching distance of one.

Selina handed her a frosted tumbler of lemon tea. 'I'm glad you can think kindly of me. I've been so horrible to you. And Perry. I know you hate me for that. But we're brother and sister and we've always had an uneasy relationship; my fault mostly. Shall we sit on the bench? It's shady there.'

Emilia followed Selina to where she carried her own drink. There was only room for two on the ancient, weathered wood, set against a trellis crawling with honeysuckle. It made Emilia's flesh creep to be seated in such close contact to Selina. Emilia's life felt like how this garden had been, a shameful mess and horribly complicated. But here and there were signs of weeding and pruning. Perry's caring touch: he was attempting to bring cherishment and harmony to the chaos. On the ground by the water butt was a touch of colour. It was an abandoned hat, a dark tan trilby with a royal-blue band. Perry wore lively clothes. He was a life-giving man. Had been. Now he was a grieving father. And she had crushed him. Because of her guilt, she had sent him away as if he was the only one who had betrayed Alec. He had walked away from her in the churchyard an almost broken man.

Emilia felt her heart falling apart, one tiny chip at a time. It filled her with dismay, with a sort of chilling horror. She'd had no right to lay the blame she felt on Perry. She had kept part of herself back from Alec and offered it willingly, lovingly to Perry, and although it was in no way right, Alec had not known this and it had never hurt him. Yet the man she loved more than the breath in her body she had treated as if he had no feelings at all, as if he was someone she could take up and throw away at a whim. Perry loved her with the same hopeless depth that she loved him and that meant she could so easily destroy him. She was as hateful as the woman she was with.

'Bottoms up,' Selina said coquettishly, with a silly giggle. 'Let's drink to a new friendship.' To add to her turmoil, Emilia recognized that the other woman was flirting with her, had reformed her hopes for her and was even a little self-conscious, but Emilia also knew just at that moment that she had gained power over Selina, and if she used it wisely she might be able to defuse any looming nasty situations. If Selina really was in love with her then perhaps that faulty love could be used, but Emilia knew it was a dangerous situation and could all too easily go against her.

'To friendship. Thank you, Selina.' Emilia clinked her glass against hers. It took an effort not to blink in disgust.

'You're thanking me for what, Em?' Selina leaned towards her. This sudden development in having Emilia all to herself, needy and pliable and willing to start over again, was beyond her craziest hopes. She longed to tell her how beautiful she was. Her dark eyes were large and jewel-like in her colour-drained, flawless face. Yet she retained her earthy strength. It was such a powerful draw. She was a combination of fragility and magnificence, a little primitive, a little imperial; a goddess. It was no wonder that Perry loved her, that Alec had loved her, and that Ben – she had not missed – wanted her back. Selina had filed away that fact to add to the trouble she would cause, but now Emilia was here, it was trouble she only *might* cause.

'For being available.' Her next words made her feel sick. 'I know we've had bitter differences, but you've always been big enough to set them aside when I've really needed you. You were there for me over Jenna, and Alec. And again now, when I'm so very unhappy and I need someone to talk to. Someone outside the family and my usual friends.' Her mouth nauseatingly dry, Emilia sipped her drink, without tasting it.

'Go on, Em.' Selina's eyes were shining like violet stars.

Emilia coughed on the lemon tea and rubbed at her throat. Was she really taking Selina in? It would be worth it if trouble could be avoided and some sort of peace for herself and Perry was gained. 'You're the only one who knows about Perry and I. We're the two women who love him. Who only want what's best for him, aren't we? We're all he's got and that frightens me. Perry deserves so much more. I've made him miserable and now I don't know what to do. I think I'll soon go out of my mind if I don't get some sort of arrangement settled with him, something we can both live with.'

'You don't know how happy and honoured I feel to have you unburden your heart to me. What exactly is causing you such distress? How have you made Perry miserable?'

She wasn't going to tell this woman anything personal. 'It's hard to explain, Selina. I've been shutting him out. I love him so much, but I feel so guilty about Alec. I guess I need to see Perry and talk to him. I can't bear the thought of him suffering. We shouldn't ever do that, should we? Make him suffer? You're his sister, I'm the woman he loves. If we worked together we could make him content.'

The hope in Selina was blazing out of her. 'And how could we do that?'

'By working for his best interests.'

'And you really mean it about us, working together?'

Selina had moved a touch closer to her again. Emilia thought she'd suffocate on her heady perfume. If she agreed with the question, goodness knew what she'd be letting herself in for, she might never be rid of Selina's over-whelming, revolting presence. And if she did not, Selina would probably be offended and turn malicious. Emilia swallowed some more lemon tea. 'Would you like that, Selina?'

'I'd like nothing more. Honestly, Em.'

'You wouldn't be jealous of any involvement I have in Perry's life, in the future?' Suddenly Emilia knew she could never go on with her life without him being there sometime, not too far in the distance.

'No. We could share him.' *And we could share you. I'd settle for that, even if we only ever remained as platonic friends. We'd be close and I could dream...*

Emilia's expression was part of an inward scream. 'What?'

'What I meant was we could form a partnership. I'll provide him with a peaceful home until the time is right for you both to reveal your feelings to the world. If I make the effort to reform, hopefully people, through our friendship, Em, will see me in a different light.'

The battered wooden gate to the back garden was opened and Perry appeared. Emilia felt her heart lurch. Her whole bearing moved towards him. She wanted to run to him. Selina gripped her hand. Tightly.

Perry raised his dejected head and his brows lifted in delight and puzzlement. 'Em...?'

Selina bawled down the path to him, 'Perry, isn't it wonderful? Em's here and she loves you. She's agreed to be my friend. We're all going to have a lovely future together.'

Chapter Twenty-Eight

'Em, you can't be serious! What are you thinking of, for goodness sake, to be making friends with that woman.' Ben slapped a hand against his forehead. 'Selina Boswed's a witch! She's a troublemaker. She's immoral and she's cruel. You can't possibly want her near your children.'

'Ben, stop shouting at me.' Emilia turned away from him. They were in the drawing room of Tremore House.

'Yes, Ben.' Brooke had come down from upstairs. 'Stop it. What's going on? Why were you shouting at Emilia?'

Ben ignored his wife. He hurled himself across the few steps of brick-red Tabriz carpet to face Emilia and startled her by hauling her into his arms and hugging her. His expression, his voice were of the utmost tenderness. 'I'm sorry, Em. Forgive me. I just cannot agree with what you've just told me.'

Emilia shrugged him away. 'I've not made friends with her. I've agreed to be friendly, for Perry's sake. Reggie's due back from Switzerland soon and he's asked Selina and Perry to stay on so he can spend some time with them, well, Perry at least.'

'Why are you so concerned about Perry?' Ben searched her eyes. 'He's a jolly nice bloke but he comes attached to that conniving witch.'

Brooke did not like the way the questions were heading – Emilia might give away her true feelings for Perry under interrogation like this – and she did not like the familiar way Ben was behaving towards her. Emilia looked so fragilely beautiful in a black dress of beaded jersey. 'Ben, for goodness sake! Leave Emilia alone. You've no right to give her the third degree. Perry's a close friend of the family. Alec liked him. Lottie likes him a lot. He's good for her now she's just lost her daddy. For Lottie's sake it's worth putting up with Selina. We're all on to her and her nasty little ways, so she won't easily be able to cause any more trouble.'

'That's easy for you to say,' Ben rounded on her. 'You're about to go off to the other side of the Atlantic and won't have to put up with her.'

'If you're worried about Emilia then keep a watchful eye on her!' Brooke snapped back. This was a good tactic – Perry would be kept at a distance if Emilia had a brother-in-law in close attendance. Next moment Brooke regretted her suggestion. Ben was gazing at Emilia from large, shining eyes. Adoring eyes.

Brooke felt a dreadful truth dawning on her. She wanted to sit down but pride and the preservation of her dignity made her fight to keep her head clear and remain standing. Ben adored Emilia. Need and desire for her flooded out of every tiny part of him. Talk of Emilia and her circumstances were never far from his lips. Brooke had been thinking it was due to the constant jealousy he had maintained over Alec's superior position, but now she knew differently. Ben was in love with Emilia. He measured her as female perfection and he wanted her. He had probably never stopped loving her, even during the time of their estrangement. Why hadn't she seen this before? He'd always made her feel second best, had kept her out of the running of his farm and businesses, while Emilia had been allowed to be involved in all matters concerning Ford Farm, and Ben, damn him, had praised her nearly every week for it.

'I'll do that,' Ben replied simply, but there was a triumphant smile widening his handsome face. Brooke wanted to raise a hand and slap away his smugness. 'Tris is the elder brother now but he's too far away to offer urgent help, and Will's too young. It's my duty to look out for you, Em.'

'I don't need looking out for,' Emilia stated firmly, unsettled by the tension between Ben and Brooke. And she didn't want Ben coming to the farm and constantly interfering. 'I'm perfectly capable of running the farm and I'd be insulted if anyone thinks otherwise. And before you argue with me, Ben, remember I do have my father as manager and Ernest Rule to turn to for other advice. We're here for a send-off dinner for Brooke. Let's concentrate on that.'

'Yes.' Brooke's tone was hard and sour. 'Can we enjoy the evening? It's supposed to be *my* evening.' The way she was feeling now, left out and spurned, she wasn't sure if she'd come back from America. She was leaving with Faye first thing in the morning for the railway station, to start the journey up to Southampton to join the liner. She just might pack more of her things, including the copy of the photograph of Alec she'd taken at Roskerne. Ben had loved her in the early years together but now he treated her with contempt. He deserved to live his life without his child. She was grinning now. She felt lighter and free, and suddenly she felt she had her own identity again and was not just a part of her husband's. And the best thing was, the child growing inside her body was Alec's. It was going to be fun to watch Ben lording it in his house tonight, fawning all over Emilia, not knowing he was about to lose his wife and children – not knowing that Emilia had given her heart to another man. She clapped her hands gaily, making the others wonder about the swift change in her mood. 'Ah, sounds like the others have arrived. I am going to enjoy this evening very much.'

It was meant to be a family dinner and the three in the drawing room were surprised to see Tristan and Winifred had brought Polly Hetherton with them. Brooke despised Polly, who had marble skin and coiffured fair hair and who unjustly looked years younger than the forty-one she had attained. She was socially witty and was grace and sophistication personified. Polly was a former lover of Ben and she never missed an opportunity to be superior about it.

Polly was a member of the classy set Alec had mixed with in his pre-marriage days to Emilia and she had often, but in vain, tried similar treatment on her. But badly shaken at hearing of Alec's death before her return from France, she had been kind and sympathetic towards Emilia. She took quick, nimble steps to her. 'Oh, my dear, you look enchanting. A grieving widow as if from some tragic Arthurian legend. I beg you to be careful. A beautiful young woman, especially with property, will be seen as prey by ruthless men. How are you? How are the children? I can't even begin to imagine what it must be like for you without having a man like Alec.'

'We're doing quite well, considering.' Emilia was embarrassed, for all eyes had flashed to her, examining her with that awful understanding reserved for the bereaved when they were considered unable to cope. Why couldn't any of them see she had recovered from her moments of weakness

274

in Ernest Rule's office? Also, she had again experienced the twist of guilt at being unfaithful to Alec. But she accepted it. She should feel the shame of what she'd done to him.

Her thoughts swept to Perry. To his reaction in the garden at Highertown when Selina had blurted out about them all having a lovely future together. Perry's drooping shoulders had squared, he had lifted his dropped head and his gorgeous dark-blue eyes had lit up as if by a celestial light. His love, like a living entity, had winged across the few yards of neglected path and wrapped itself around her. An exquisite warmth had touched her then and spread throughout her. The depth, height and strength of his love made her dizzy at first, then it had calmed her, filled her with utter joy and wholeness. And her love for him grew ever more powerful. It was right, meant. They were soulmates. She couldn't send him away. Not ever. Life without Perry would hold no significance; it would make no sense. She would be an automaton, and she would dry up and be of no use to her beloved family. Lottie would look at her and grow up believing that all there was to life was to be half a woman, half alive.

A smile did not have to fight its way through her guilt and unease. It had formed and it was there, chasing away all the shadows in her face and the doubt in her heart. Perry was to stay in Cornwall for good, and if it meant being friendly with his horrid sister, so be it. The others saw it and all, except Brooke, thought the smile was fashioned out of her strength. Brooke thought, *How lucky you are, to have so many men in love with you. Perhaps one day I will find true love too.* She wished Emilia no ill will. Emilia had many problems ahead, for Will was becoming very difficult, and if she did end up permanently one day with Perry then Selina would ensure she was part of the package.

'Good to see you, Polly,' Ben said, handing her a sweet martini. 'Tris, why haven't you brought Jonny and Vee?'

'There's a very good reason for that, and it's why I've taken it upon myself to invite Polly here tonight. I think we should all take our drinks and sit down.'

Brooke chose a seat a little back from the company, as if she didn't belong in it. Ben didn't notice. He stretched out on a sofa, to where he had managed to guide Emilia. 'Sounds ominous, Tris. Don't tell me Jonny's decided not to go back to Oxford.'

'He's going up at the weekend. I've talked him into taking Vera Rose out to a lifeboat fundraising do. I didn't want either of them here.'

Emilia had been studying his, Winifred's and Polly's faces. 'This can only be about Louisa.'

'Yes, indeed it is.' Tristan sighed weightily. 'I'm sure most of you have noticed that she and Jonny have been getting rather close. There's an undeniable attraction between them, and they of course haven't any idea it's because they're half-brother and sister. There's no particular problem now – Louisa is only thirteen years old – but in a few years' time there may well be. I wouldn't be quite so concerned if I thought Jonny would only view her in the same free way he does most other young women, but it's obvious he sees her as someone special. So we're in a fix. What do we do about it? Keep our secret and ensure that if they meet up in the future they never spend time alone or go out on a date? I, for one, don't ever want the truth to come out and be reminded of the hell of that time all those years ago. Or do we come clean? No doubt we'll face their wrath for keeping it from them, particularly from Jonny. He believes his half-sister lies with his mother in Kenwyn churchyard.' For other views, his eyes fell first on Emilia.

'I hadn't noticed there was any special relationship forming between them,' she said. 'But I've had other things on my mind. Over the years, I've thought about the possibility of telling Jonny and Louisa the truth. I think if it were me I'd like to know. Jonny might be angry but he'd probably be pleased to learn he has a sister, and Louisa pleased to learn that she's got a blood relative, to know about her origins. I promised Ursula on her deathbed that I'd look after her baby, but of course I'm not the closest one linked to Louisa.'

'And what do you think Alec would have said?' Tristan asked.

'Alec would have wanted the secret kept,' she replied at once. 'He mentioned it to me several times, that he thought nothing good would be gained from the truth. I believe that if he had become aware of any attraction between the two young people he'd have worked to keep them apart.'

'They may only have a rapport because of their blood link anyway,' Ben announced, before Tristan could ask for his judgement. 'They've little in common. They're hardly each other's type. Louisa's overseas a lot. Jonny won't come home every vacation. He's had a terrible summer, he'll probably immerse himself in his studies and kick up his heels before enlisting. He and Louisa might not meet up again for years, and if they do she could be engaged or married by then. I think you're worrying over nothing, Tris.'

'Thank you for that, Ben.' Tristan nodded, visibly relaxing now he had another firmly in his camp. 'Winnie's of the same mind as me, to keep quiet. Brooke?'

She shrugged. 'I wasn't here when all this happened. It's really nothing to do with me. It's the decision of the rest of you. I'll respect whatever you decide.' She was pleased to be getting away from such a problem-riddled family. She and Faye and, if her baby was a boy, as she was certain it was, young Alec would soon be enjoying an unbound life. The first thing she would do in America was to seek a good divorce lawyer. She'd sting Ben for all she could get. She had just spoken and he hadn't even glanced at her, aiming encouraging little smiles instead at Emilia. When she was out of the way, no doubt, he would move in on Emilia. Boy, was he in for a surprise.

'Your turn, Polly,' Tristan said. 'You're probably the closest one involved in this.'

'Absolutely, I am.' The pale glaze of Polly's skin mottled over in vehement shades of red as she turned her fine head in each listener's direction. 'I emphatically don't ever want the truth to come out. If it did, whatever Louisa and Jonny's initial reactions would be, I'm worried that they might not agree to it remaining a secret between them and us. It would mean telling the younger children in your family, which would inevitably lead to talk and then gossip and scandal. Louisa has a good position in life, but after that she'd be pointed at and laughed about. She has the romantic belief that her mother was some unfortunate engaged girl who got pregnant while her fiancé was on leave and that her father died a hero's death on the battlefield. If the truth was revealed she'd want to know about her real father, that beastly Bruce Ashley! People still whisper about his affair with Ursula. Louisa would be in grave danger of being socially shunned. As it is, she finds things hard at times owing to her birthmark. And she might want to try to find

Ashley. He's a horrid lounge lizard, a con man, he mixes with criminals. He threatened to kill Tristan. How would she feel, knowing that sort of man was her father? I say let things lie, and if one day, in the unlikely event we're forced to, we'll do everything in our power to keep Louisa and Jonny apart.'

A long, thoughtful silence prevailed in the drawing room. When Agnes, Ben's pole-thin housekeeper, announced dinner was ready to be served, she found the incumbents, all except her mistress, stirring as if from some deep, troubled dream.

'Thank you, Agnes,' Brooke said. She was in no mood for formality and led the way to the dining room without an escort.

For a moment no one noticed she had gone on by herself. 'Well,' Tristan said, with observable relief. 'That's decided then. Shall we follow Brooke?' At the table, he apologized to her. 'I'm sorry to have put the dampers on the evening. I thought if we could get that little matter out of the way then we'd be able to wish you a jolly *bon voyage*.'

'No need to be sorry, Tris. I'm pleased to see your family of one accord,' Brooke replied sweetly.

'You must send us a postcard soon and tell us all about the great skyscraper,' Winifred said.

'Oh, I can't wait to communicate with Ben from New York,' Brooke said, eyeing her husband, engaged up at the other end of the table in pestering Emila to drink more wine. Forgetting convention, she rose to her feet and raised her own glass, 'I'd like to propose a toast.'

'For goodness sake, Brooke.' Ben was horrified. 'What on earth do you think you're doing?'

She smiled, the widest, the prettiest, the most meaningful smile she had ever given him. 'I'm just saying goodbye to everyone. To you, Ben.'

Chapter Twenty-Nine

Lottie was milking Bryony, the quietest cow in the thirty-strong herd, a skill her mother had taught her recently, when Emilia had judged she was responsible enough to learn. While Bryony munched on cowcake mixed with barley, Lottie was perched on a stool, wearing a specially cut-down white coat and a grown-up's cap, the peak turned round to the back to avoid it being knocked off. Her face was pressed in near the cow's underbelly, her small hands nimbly pulling on the mature, light-brown and white Guernsey's long, even teats. Bryony never kicked at her milker and her udder bucket could be quickly filled with creamy, frothy milk. Lottie's expression was set determinedly. She was in the end stall of the cowshed, working alongside her mother, her grandfather, Midge Roach the cowman, and Linda, the sparky, fifteen-year-old dairymaid.

It was early October and the weather was still warm and the flies were prolific and bothersome. Countless biting tiny creatures were attacking the beasts and there was a steady flicking and thrashing of soiled tails to swipe off the pests. Suddenly there was an angry shout from Midge Roach. 'Bleddy cow! Bleddy flies!'

Without pausing from the double stream of milk she was producing, Lottie bellowed out, 'What's he so mazed about then?'

Her regional observation, delivered so workmanlike, struck the others as funny and they all laughed loudly.

'He got a shitty tail 'cross his face,' Linda shrieked with hilarity, making her gangly frame rock.

'Language, please,' Emilia chided good-humouredly. She had been busy with Willow, a Jersey-Guernsey cross. She took her full bucket of milk and put it aside. It would be taken to the dairy and poured into wide, shallow pans to stand overnight so the cream could rise for butter making. It was good working like this, the next generation eager to learn all about the dairy, yard and fieldwork. Tom had helped drive in the cattle from the fields and was now grooming the plough horses. Will was the only dissenter. He did as few jobs as he could now and concentrated on his homework, saying that he wanted only to follow Jonny's example into high academic achievement and the Royal Air Force. Emilia understood his sense of hurt and rejection at not being named next in line for his father's property and she allowed him his churlish moods, hoping to be able to talk to him soon and bridge the gap that had opened up between them.

Perry had asked to try his hand at milking a few days before, but due to his disability had encountered difficulty at getting down on the stool.

'You can do it,' Lottie had encouraged him as if she was the adult, while trying to guide him. She was pleased he was at the farm often.

''Tisn't a good idea,' Edwin had counselled. 'You wouldn't be able to jump back quick from a kicker and if the bucket was knocked over, as happens sometimes, well, there'd be a right old mess and you in the thick of it.'

'I know,' Perry had given up gracefully, not at all disappointed. Lottie had fed her grubby little hand into his and he had beamed down on her, before smiling at Emilia. 'And I'd take too much time trying to get up every time. Think I'll stick to the mucking out, the feeding rounds and paperwork.'

Thankfully, Selina did not venture much into the yards or animal houses, preferring to go riding and turning herself out to look her best in the evenings. Jonny, who had decided not to return to his studies until after the threshing, which was due to start tomorrow, kept himself occupied by doing mundane jobs, like clearing ditches, and Emilia knew he was trying to make things easier for her, while keeping away from Selina. Ben spent a lot of time at the farm, making it known that he did not approve of Selina's presence; she seemed unperturbed by it. Perry and Selina had given a meal at Highertown and Ben had invited himself there. To Emilia's surprise, so had Dolly, who had rarely gone past the village limits after dark. 'I want to see what the house is like where they live,' she had explained staunchly, somewhat mysterious. She had watched Selina throughout the evening. It had amused Emilia to see Selina struggling to remain polite to her mother.

The times Emilia spent alone with Perry were infrequent, both of them content to stay more as if just friends until the future dictated the time when they could make a formal announcement that they had decided to step out together. This time next year perhaps, after the first anniversary of their loved ones' passing. It was enough to greet and bid farewell with a kiss, to pass an affectionate touch of hands, to smile into each other's eyes. Indeed, their future together had already begun.

'Mum!' Lottie piped up. 'I'm finished here.'

Emilia went to her to carry the bucket, which was too heavy for her. Lottie stayed put for the bucket to be brought back. She tilted back her head and gazed up, with a cheeky grin, at her mother. A look of devotion passed from one to the other. Lottie crinkled her bright brown eyes and there was a strong likeness of Alec about her. Emilia missed him so much at that moment. But she felt a glow of happiness. Her life was on a happy course again. The only blot, the only thing to cause tension, was Selina.

'Missus,' Midge Roach said in his thick accent. ''Tis Mister Ben come t'see 'ee.' Midge, a married man, ruddy-faced, of small stature, who spoke as he found, glowered for a second before getting on with his work. Years ago he had worked at Tremore Farm, but when Ben had underhandedly gained purchase of it, while Alec had intended to buy it, Midge and another labourer had left Tremore in disgust and had asked Alec for jobs.

Ben didn't care a jot for Midge's opinion of him. 'Hello, Em. Thought I'd drop in, see how things are.' He was pleased not to have spotted a Bosweld about the place. It was hard to get Emilia to himself.

'We're fine,' she said, emptying Lottie's bucket in a churn and returning it to her. Lottie didn't care for her uncle, who had never really bothered to speak to her, and she got on with the milking, humming a jaunty tune. 'Have you heard yet from Brooke?'

'Nothing apart from the telegram to say she and Faye had arrived safely.' He peered down at Lottie, impressed with her industry yet torn, for a rich farmer's daughter shouldn't be attending to menial tasks. Nor should his widow. But Em looked entirely in the right place here, in her work clothes. And so lovely. So appealing. 'See you've an eager beaver there. Need another pair of hands? You've got a busy day tomorrow.'

'Not really, and you've got your suit on. Your shoes are already mucky. Been to a business meeting?' Emilia made her way back to Willow.

'The suit and shoes can be cleaned. I've just had high tea with Dougie Blend. Nothing interesting. I might slip over to Paris soon. Why don't you come with me?'

'Don't be daft!' Emilia looked at him as if he'd suggested they fly to the moon.

'What's so daft about it? It would do you good. What do you say, Edwin?'

'Same as my maid. Don't be daft.' Edwin's tone was softer and polite to the young man who had been his superior when Ben had lived here. 'Emilia doesn't need to go gadding off.'

'Pity. It was just an idea.' It would be ages before Emilia would be free from here and Ben withdrew reluctantly. With Brooke out of the way he'd thought it would be easier to get closer to Emilia, but there was always a family member with her, or she was going about her duties as before as the squire's wife in the village, and oh, those damn Boswelds... speak of the Devil...

Their Daimler pulled up outside the house, next to his sporty model. Selina got out. 'Hello, Ben. Be a dear and help me with these.'

'Help you with what?' he demanded ungraciously.

'These packages. I've been shopping.'

'Who for?'

'Does it matter? I've bought a few things Emilia mentioned she wanted. She hasn't got time to go scouring the shops for bargains. I'm pleased to help out a friend.'

Ben went on ignoring her request. 'You aren't fooling me.'

'Can't think what you mean,' Selina said brightly, lifting out a stack of shopping from the back seat.

'I mean this sudden act that you're a nice person. You've always been an evil bitch and always will be. Emilia isn't fooled by it, you know, and people are watching out for her. Specially me. If you try to hurt her I'll see you out of this world.'

'A death threat, Ben? How very Hollywood. You and these anonymous people had better watch out that you don't upset me.' Selina smiled. A sarcastically innocent smile.

'It won't be long before you show your true colours again, and Emilia will send you packing. You're only tolerated for your brother's sake. How does that feel?'

Selina went up close to him and narrowed her eyes into two purple darts. 'Don't taunt me, Ben Harvey. I know things.' She ground her heel into the gravelled drive and flounced off to the house, sweeping past Dolly Rowse with a forced convivial smile on the way.

'I saw her face, Mr Ben. What's she up to?'

'I don't know, Mrs Rowse,' he replied, his expression as dark as a storm. 'And I don't like it.'

'She'll cause trouble, big trouble. She can't help herself. I wish Emilia wouldn't entertain her so. It's keeping her here. That woman's even talking of going to Miss Rawley's wedding, saying she and Emilia should buy outfits together. She's a parasite. She uses people. She presumes too much. I wish I could think of a way to get rid of her. It needs doing. Don't you agree?'

'I certainly do. I'll try to think of something.' His answer was grim. His position and perhaps Emilia's and even the whole family's could be grim. What were these things that Selina knew?

Selina placed a brown paper carrier of food stuffs, all delicacies, on the kitchen table, which was laden with a mountain of food preparations. She didn't bother to ask Tilda why she had done so much extra baking. She then returned to the sitting room, where she had dropped the rest of her shopping. Her meeting with Ben was the second hostile confrontation she had received in the last two days, but she was too happy to care all that much. The day before, she had been returning to the farm on her borrowed pony. Passing Ford House, she had seen the two Annear children chasing about in the front garden and had reined in at the stone wall. 'Hello there. It's Alan and Martha, isn't it? My name's Dr Selina Bosweld. I'm a friend of Miss Rawley's.'

The children had come to a stop and stared up at her. 'How do you do,' Alan said, giggling.

'I'm very well, thank you. It's nice to meet such a polite little boy. Your sister is very pretty.' Selina wasn't at all interested in them but she hoped to get on better terms with Elena, who, having seen through her earlier ploy to cause trouble for Jim, was being cool towards her. If Selina wasn't intent on trying to establish a closer link with Emilia, she'd have tried to ruin Jim's professional reputation by now.

'What's the pony called?' Alan asked, climbing up on the wall, helping Martha to follow him. 'Can we stroke it?'

'Of course. Her name is Fern. She's very gentle.'

The children were stroking Fern's dark brown mane when a van was driven up the hill. It was brought to an unhurried stop so as not to startle the pony, but Jim had thrown himself out of the van. 'Alan! Martha! Go inside the house at once. Go on, do as I say.'

Alan had frowned and Martha had looked unsettled, but their trust in Jim was infinite and they had jumped down off the wall and ran round to the back of the house without glancing behind.

Jim had hissed many a swear word at Selina, 'Don't you ever dare go near those children again! Do you hear me?'

'I was only talking to them.' Selina had nudged the pony forward, not wanting a scene overheard by Elena. She was anxious there would never be anything that would make Emilia change her mind about her. 'But I won't do so again.'

–

'It's here, Mummy!' Lottie burst into the sitting room. Her brothers followed her in, their faces excited, even Will's. Selina was surprised to see Lottie was still up.

'I've been waiting to see this,' Perry said, offering Emilia his arm. 'Shall we?'

Sensing something momentous, Selina hastily pushed her arm through Emilia's free one. 'Has this got something to do with the threshing tomorrow? Whatever's happening it sounds thrilling. Lead the way, Perry.'

Selina found herself outside with the entire family and workforce and she was genuinely fascinated about what she learned. Ford Farm had its own thresher, which was loaned out to the smaller farms; the farmers and labourers working in turn on all the farms. The thresher, which had the appearance of a vast wooden box, had several wheels and gadgets attached to it, and the power would come from the source of the mysterious noise, the smoking, coal-fired, visiting traction engine, which was now, like some fearsome beast, chugging and clanking and clattering, still at a good distance along the lanes. In places where low hedges and gateways allowed, belching smoke and steam could be seen.

'It will be settled in the mowhay for a very early start tomorrow,' Emilia explained to Selina, wishing she could think of something to free the woman from her arm. She would have picked Lottie up, but she had grabbed Perry's hand and was dancing about in a state of anticipation. She and her brothers would be allowed the day off school tomorrow to help out.

Emilia tightened her grip on Perry's arm to convey that she was glad to be able to share these moments with him. She always enjoyed this hectic time ahead, when the women did all the milking and animal feeding, and made the most of the female companionship, laughing and joking while they prepared and served the food for the three feasts the workers would consume throughout the day.

As the traction engine got closer the earth seemed to start shaking and the more Lottie danced about. The thick smells of burning coal, smoke and grease overwhelmed the farmyard's usual ripe smells. When the immense, green-painted mechanical beast, with great puffs of smoke and many a shrill blast on its whistle, finally clanked and jangled its way heavily into sight, Perry tightened his grasp on Lottie, afraid she might plunge out in front of it and get crushed. It was a glorious sight. The engine driver and his mate, an ageing father and middle-aged son, wearing overalls, caps and red-and-white-spotted neckerchiefs, kept all the metal parts well oiled and highly polished, and their pride of the *Cornish Belle* was firmly on display. After they had brought the engine into place, the usually merry pair jumped down and solemnly gave Emilia their condolences over her loss.

'Mr Harvey was a fine gentlemen,' they said in unison, their declaration given in heavy dialect.

'Yes, he was,' Emilia said, her eyes misting over. Alec had also favoured the threshing.

'He was,' Perry echoed her words.

'See you've got plenty of help.' With his raddled old eyes, the father looked over the gathering. Jonny was lurking in the background. At his side was Ben, who had just arrived. Neither liked seeing Emilia in between the Boswelds.

'Yes, I'm a lucky woman,' Emilia said. 'We'll all work hard this year as usual and honour Alec's memory.'

–

With the father and son seated around the supper table, Emilia thought herself very lucky, but later in the evening she was concerned to see her mother, Ben and Jonny whispering together in a little group. It could only be about one person. It seemed they were plotting some sort of campaign to rid the farm of Selina. But in successfully doing so they might inadvertently take Perry away from her too. *Please God, don't let anything go wrong tomorrow.*

Chapter Thirty

The time of threshing was a pleasant time of camaraderie between the men, but not so for Perry. He soon regretted joining the throng, wearing, like them, a cap, a touser round his waist and more hessian sacking tied to his trouser legs, as protection against the unavoidable, sometimes choking, flying dust and chaff. He felt out of place, and Ben, Jonny and Will, usually so chummy with him, were so cross at Selina insisting she'd take part with the women, they all more or less ignored him. The farmers and labourers, and Jim Killigrew, who was helping out, were bemused to see him there and didn't know how to relate to him. Perry was as able as any man to heft the sheaves from the corn-rick, which were fed beard first into the top of the thresher, but his disability made him slower and he fancied he heard more than a few impatient sighs. To withdraw now would draw derision on his masculinity, and he didn't want to appear to Emilia to be less of a man than Alec had been, so he blundered on, thoroughly miserable.

The amount of grain, as it passed through the various sieves in the threshing machine and was graded into different sizes for different uses, grew satisfyingly nonetheless. As Emilia and Selina appeared with the tea urn, and the women and Lottie carried the food for the crib break of saffron cake, thickly buttered splits and hevva cake, Tom sought Perry's company. 'How are you getting on?'

'To tell you the truth, I think I'm getting in the way.' Perry lifted his cap to pull chaff out of his hair, its blackness dulled by the dust.

'You're not. People are a bit quiet because my father's missing this year.' Tom rubbed an itchy spot on his neck. The tiny flying debris irritated the flesh of every worker.

'The first year will be particularly hard for you. Everything will be a constant reminder of him.'

'It's how I want it. I'll never forget him. It's good to see my mum coping so well, but there's no one quite like her.' Tom set his keen brown eyes on Perry. 'You know that, don't you? How long have you been in love with her?'

If Perry's face wasn't red from his efforts to keep up with the demands of the work it would have been now. 'Tom, I...'

'Don't be afraid to discuss it. It's not Will you're talking to. He's not so receptive as I am or he'd have noticed the way you look at her. The grandparents and Uncle Ben would have done so too but they're so worried about your sister being around.'

'Do you mind? About the way I feel about your mother? And is Selina getting to you too?'

'The answer to your first question is that I don't mind as long as you don't rush things or compromise my mum. As for your sister, well, again, I think I'm the only one to realize what she wants.'

'She wants to be near me, that's what, worse luck,' Perry said with feeling.

'She wants more than that. She wants my mother. Do you understand, Perry?'

'What do you mean?'

'Watch.'

Perry gazed at the interactions of the two women. Selina was floating around Emilia. She was very close to her all the time, seeking her eyes, seeking her approval. Seeking her. 'Dear heavens! I had no idea.'

'Mother knows,' Tom said simply. 'And I know that she cares for you. Why else would she tolerate that sort of thing?'

'Oh, bloody hell.' Perry brought his hands up to his face. 'Of course, now it all fits into place. Why Selina stopped insisting we move away. I'll have to get her away from here.' He nearly crumpled. He was going to lose Emilia after all. He couldn't stay. He'd been hoping that sooner or later Selina would get restless and fix herself up with a new position far away. But she wouldn't leave Emilia any more now than he wanted to, and inevitably, because Selina was Selina and a bitter, twisted woman, she'd make a determined play for Emilia, and she'd take some sort of terrible revenge over the rejection.

'Perry, I'm sorry,' Tom said. 'I wasn't happy at first when I knew there was something between you and my mum, but after my father, there's no one else I'd consider suitable for her.'

'I can't do anything right now,' Perry said feebly. 'I don't want a scene in front of all these people. I'll tell Selina we must pack up and go tonight.'

Emilia came over to them with two mugs of tea. 'All right, son? Enjoying it, Perry?'

'Yes, Mum,' Tom said.

'Yes, Em,' Perry lied.

Jonny and Dolly were watching Selina, who was distributing tea with a sickening jollity, but Ben's dark, brooding eyes were on Emilia. Why did she spend so much time with Perry Bosweld? She always seemed to be fussing over him. The death of his daughter was sad, but – but! Ben felt he had been dealt the biggest blow in the world. No! It couldn't be true! A few more moments of surveillance and he was certain that his horrible suspicions were not misplaced. Emilia and Bosweld were in love. They were attempting to disguise it but it was plain in his wistful, longing gaze and the overcaring way she was with him. Ben strode over to them. 'If you've had enough,' he all but hissed at Perry, 'why don't you call it a day?'

'Ben!' Emilia rounded on him. 'Don't be so rude.'

'I think he should go. You both know why! My brother's hardly cold in his grave.'

Selina was there. 'Ben, your foreman's brought this letter for you. It's from New York. He thought you'd rather have it now than to wait until you get home.'

Ben snatched the envelope out of her hand. 'And you can get away from here too. Now! Everyone's had a stomachful of you.'

Emilia glanced at Perry and they exchanged a look of helplessness. 'Shut up, Ben.'

'Yes, Ben,' Selina scowled at him. 'It's in your interests that you keep your mouth shut, or I shall open mine.'

Jonny and Will added themselves to the gathering. Dolly and Jim were not far behind. Will demanded, 'What's going on?'

'It's nothing,' Emilia replied, distraught.

'They're all getting concerned about me.' Perry forced a brightness. 'My leg's not up to it. I'm about to leave. Selina, I think you should come with me.'

'I don't want to go,' she retorted. She was rigid with wrath. Obviously, the game was up over Emilia and Perry, but she wasn't about to be run off by these wretched people again.

'Now, Selina. I'm sorry, Em. Goodbye. I'll ring you tonight. We need to talk.' Not least about Selina's feelings for her. Perry began to walk away.

'Don't ring her at all,' Ben hurled at his back.

'You haven't got the right to say that, Uncle Ben,' Tom turned on him.

Perry whirled round and clutched Selina by the arm and dragged her with him. 'Don't say another word. We're going before we cause this family any more trouble.'

With the cosy future she had been looking forward to ripped from her and all her hopes crushed, she struggled against him. 'I won't go unless Emilia says I must.' Lashing out at Perry's face and kicking his good leg, she made him stumble and got free. She ran up to Emilia. 'What do you say, Em? Do you want to me to leave?'

Her heart down in her feet, mindful that her children were listening and Lottie was running to her for reassurance, Emilia drew away from the gathering, her expression pleading for understanding. 'I don't want this, Selina, but I think you'd better go.'

'To leave you for good?' Selina asked, a mounting assortment of emotions and demands fusing in her mind. She looked injured and this made Emilia afraid. Never was Selina more deadly.

'I hope not.'

But Ben hadn't finished having his say. 'Of course she wants you to go for good. No one in their right mind would want a poisonous bitch like you anywhere near her home and children. The same goes for me, and everyone else here.'

Selina was roused to hate-filled passion. There was only so much humiliation she could take. 'You'll regret this, Ben Harvey. Emilia, ban me from coming here and I swear your whole family and others too will regret it.'

Ben nudged Emilia, making her jump. 'Tell her, Em. Her reign of fear, of disgusting everyone, is over. And he, her brother, must never set foot here again either.'

Dolly had no idea what Ben had against Perry but she was eager for her daughter to put a stop to Selina's visits. 'Go on, Emilia. Tell her exactly where she stands.'

'Yes, Mum. Do it!' Will exclaimed.

Selina stared into Emilia's eyes waiting for her verdict. Her abusers, including Jonny Harvey, Edwin Rowse and Jim Killigrew, had taken up a stance that was threatening towards her and protective towards Emilia. 'Well, Em,' she said dangerously. You have the last word. What's it to be?'

'Selina, don't...' Perry begged. With his life falling apart yet again he was finding it hard to keep steady on his feet. The repeat of Selina being publicly hounded out of these people's lives, and now he also, was almost too much to bear.

'Still your tongue, Perry! It's up to Emilia to speak.'

Emilia swallowed the hardness tightening her throat. What could she say? With her family making demands she had no other choice. 'I'm afraid you'll have to leave here for good, Selina.'

She expected more argument, a hurl of abuse, perhaps a scream of rage. But Selina considered her very coolly. Then she simply turned round and walked away. She would take her revenge when Perry wasn't present to witness it, for he was all she had left now. When she reached him, she enveloped his wilting body as if aiding a frail patient. 'Come with me. I swear on Libby's memory that these people will never hurt us again.'

Standing still, Emilia cried at the sight of Perry's dejected figure, at the man she loved being ejected from her life. An arm was brought over her shoulders. She thought it would be Ben's and she would have pushed it away, ordered him to go too. He was the main instigator of this new heartbreak for her and Perry. But it was Tom, and she leaned against him for support. When she looked at Ben she was shocked to receive a stare as hateful, no, even more so, than when he had blamed her for his partial blindness. He stormed off.

'Come on, Mum,' Tom said softly. 'I'll take you to the rose garden.' Lottie went with them and her younger son and daughter were her only comfort.

As the day wore on, the corn-rick dwindled in size and a new straw-rick grew. It was thatched, roped and reeded, all without Emilia seeing it, for she could not bring herself to face those at work. She left it to her father to thank her weary neighbours, whose eyes would be watering and scratchy, only to have to start all over again the next day and the next until all the farms had been serviced, as well as their necessary jobs morning and evening at home. When the mammoth activity finally came to an end, and the traction engine clattered on its way back up the lane to Druzel Farm, taking the thresher and the bundler rattling and bumping with it, she finally broke down and wept, going off to be alone. With no comfort at all. Just a sickening worry over how Perry would cope and what Selina would do now.

Chapter Thirty-One

Ben didn't read his letter from New York until the following day, while having a lonely breakfast. He glanced first at the other end of the table, and now his hopes for Emilia were extinct he was feeling betrayed and cheated, and he was missing Brooke and Faye and looking forward to seeing them again. He took consolation in the fact that he had another child on the way, perhaps his longed-for son. It was cold and he shivered. It was raining hard, it had been lashing down all night, and everything was dark and gloomy, almost sinister.

The words from the American lawyer swam in front of his eyes. Brooke was divorcing him for mental cruelty and demanding a huge financial settlement, and it was stated she and Faye were staying in a secure place where he would be unlikely to find them, and if he did he would be jailed because she had taken an injunction out against him.

He put the letter down, numb with disbelief. Mental cruelty? He hadn't been the most attentive of husbands in the last year or two, but how did she work that out? He might have been rather aloof, insensitive and perhaps a little controlling, but cruel! He had never been cruel to her. This was the excuse of the card-sharp American lawyer. Americans looked after their own. There was nothing he could do. Brooke had turned against him. She must hate him to deny him another chance, and his daughter and coming child. Seconds later, he didn't care. About Brooke, about anything. He knew hatred. He shook hands with it, welcomed it. He had despised people before, but now he felt he knew hatred by its first name in capital letters. Everything else was forgotten and above all else he was happy to concentrate on the hatred he had for Emilia for loving another man.

Agnes disturbed him out of his anger and desolation with the announcement that he had a visitor. It was the last thing he wanted, but this person he could deal with and he didn't mind seeing her too much. It was Louisa Hetherton-Andrews. Her sweet company, and hers alone, would lift him a little.

Are you all right, Uncle Ben? You appear quite shaken. I've heard there was quite a disturbance at Ford Farm yesterday,' Louisa said, joining him for tea and toast. 'I telephoned there to say I was going over to say goodbye to Jonny before he goes up again, but Aunty Emilia advised that I should stay away. She said everything's unsettled. Would you mind telling me what happened? Did it have something to do with that dreadful Bosweld woman?'

'It was, but it's nothing for you to worry about, my dear,' Ben said. At least Louisa was one person the evil witch couldn't threaten. Unless… no, surely not? Suddenly, Ben was very afraid for her and some others.

–

Perry had written a letter to Reggie Rule apologizing for not staying on for his return from Switzerland. Forsaking his mac and hat, he was becoming soaked in the downpour as he dumped his suitcases in the motor car. More carefully, he put in Libby's things. He was about to make a sad journey home to London with all that he had left of his daughter. How he regretted having her buried in Hennaford churchyard, where it would be impossible to visit her grave; the heartbreak would be too great.

'When are we setting off?' Selina asked tonelessly, when he made a wet trail into the hall.

'Straight away. Have you packed?'

'Yes. I'm about to bring my things down. It's chilly. We need something to set us up. Before we leave, let's have a cup of tea, and I'll make some sandwiches to eat on the way up.'

He sighed in relief. 'I was afraid that you'd refuse to come with me. That you'd stay behind, intent on wreaking vengeance.' But as soon as they reached London he'd turn her out of his life for good. He loathed her. He felt sick at the mere thought of her. He was only taking this last journey out of Cornwall with her to make sure she was out of reach of Emilia.

'What's the point?' Selina shrugged, appearing defeated for the first time ever. 'I'd only end up hurting myself again.'

By the time she'd prepared the food and cleaned up the kitchen, Perry was sleeping deeply. She had drugged his tea. Taking the car keys out of his jacket pocket, she left. For Hennaford.

–

Dolly Rowse was collecting Lottie from the school gates, and because Alan Annear was spending dinner time with her granddaughter, she was collecting him too. Dolly stopped long enough to fasten the last buttons on the children's coats. 'Martha's already at the farm, Miss Rawley's paying a call on the rector. Your mummy's gone into town, Lottie. Come on then, best foot forward, the pair of you. The wind's picking up.' Taking a hand of each child, she set off determinedly with them down the village hill.

–

Selina parked the Daimler in the town and took a taxicab to Hennaford. If she pulled up in Perry's motor car there wouldn't be a door opened to her. She was wet through. Her shoes were ruined, the hems of her trousers were muddy and uncomfortable. Water dripped off her hat and the tip of her nose and stung her eyes. She didn't care. She was hardly aware of it. All she was intent on was getting to Ford Farm before Jonny Harvey was collected by his father, and gloating over the truth about the parentage of Louisa Hetherton-Andrews. And when she'd done that, she'd tell Emilia, Perry's precious Em, who had so cruelly rejected her again, that she'd keep Perry away from her for ever, even if it meant taking his life.

She had directed the cab driver to drop her off on the outskirts of the village, where she would take the lane that led past Ford House. All seemed quiet in the house, there were no lights on to offset the deepening murkiness. She had no time now to make some sort of attack on Jim Killigrew and his sickly sweet fiancée, but she'd think of something at a later date. Something to tarnish his professional reputation and put an end to his business. She could suggest he had been making approaches to the housewives in the homes he'd worked in. Mud stuck and, hopefully, enough of it would make the self-righteous Miss Rawley break off with him and then he'd have nothing, just as he deserved!

Carrying on down the hill from the house, splashing through the running little muddy streams, she came to the fork in the road, but on hearing voices she crept back round the bend until she was out of sight. She didn't want anyone to know she was about and ruin Emilia's horrified surprise as she forced her way over her doorstep.

She recognized one of the voices. It was Dolly Rowse, the horrid old hag who despised her so much. Why was she out in this weather? She prided herself on her good sense, so it was a strange thing to pop down to the village shop. Then she heard the giggle of a child. Lottie Harvey. Emilia's precious brat! Selina's heart turned to ice. Then it warmed over strangely and she didn't view anything in a right and proper manner any more.

–

The Daimler wasn't outside the house in Highertown and Emilia's heart beat in fear that she had missed Perry. It was understandable that Perry would want to leave here today. Was she too late? Perhaps he or Selina were shopping or saying goodbye to Ernest Rule and one of them was still here, packing. Praying she wasn't too late to see Perry, she knocked on the door. It was an awful risk to come here – if Selina was inside she would undoubtedly cause a dreadful scene – but she couldn't just do nothing, to let Perry go away without trying to talk to him. She didn't know what she'd say to him, what promises she could make, but he meant far too much to her to let him go without a word. With nothing. Although that was what Selina had left them with. Yesterday she had telephoned here several times but the phone had been engaged every time. If they were leaving, arrangements would have been made with Perry's housekeeper and perhaps with others, but someone couldn't have been using the line all night. Had Selina sabotaged the telephone this end? If she met Selina now, if she mocked her, insulted her, if she had done anything bad to Perry, Emilia felt she could actually cause her harm.

She knocked again. Silence. She was too late. She'd have to go. She might never see Perry again. All she would be left with was telephoning his London number tonight. Or she could go up to London herself. Now it was general knowledge, thanks to the spite of Ben, that she and Perry were, at least, attracted to each other, she could wait a while and travel up and see him. People liked Perry, and hopefully they wouldn't hold on to any disapproval for too long. Tom didn't mind about her and Perry. And her mother, usually so tartly outspoken about what she considered was right from wrong, had only said it was a shame that Perry had such an unfortunate relation. Lottie loved him and would miss him. Why care about what the others might think? It was none of their business. And she could only pity them if they had never known the love she and Perry shared. Perry was all that mattered. If it meant having a loving, secure future with him, she'd settle the farm on her sons, leave her father there as manager, and move away to be with Perry. She'd send a message on to London ahead of him.

She left the house for her own car. Then looked back at the house. Something made her feel she should try the door again. The house didn't seem shut up. Some of the curtains had been thrown back, not left neatly for Reggie Rule's return. It wasn't Perry's way to be slapdash. She ran back to the front door and tried it. It was unlocked. She went inside.

'Perry! Are you here?' There was warmth coming from the kitchen, so someone had cooked food in there recently.

She went into the kitchen. Everything had been left neat and tidy.

She made her way to the dining room. And gasped to see Perry slumped in a chair. 'Perry!' She dashed to him and threw her arms round him. Her thudding heart slowed a little when she felt he was warm, breathing regularly and seemed only to be fast asleep. For one terrible moment she had thought he'd sunk into such deep despair he had harmed himself. She shook him. 'Perry! Wake up. Wake up, darling!'

She had to shake him again and again, call down his ear before she got a response.

'Mmm.' He let his head loll on his chest. 'Em...'

'Yes, it's me, darling. Why are you like this? Did you take some sleeping tablets? Where's Selina?'

Perry tried to open his eyes, the lids were so heavy. 'I... I don't know. Em... why are you here?'

'I had to see you. Perry, try to wake up. We have to find out what's going on. Where Selina is. Oh, my God, she's done this to you. She wanted you out of the way for some reason and that could only be to cause trouble. Perry, do you think you could walk to my car? We have to get to the farm.'

—

Selina stepped out from her hiding place to meet Dolly and Lottie in the fork in the road. Better still! Alan Annear was with them. She could get her revenge on Jim Killigrew in the same way as she would Emilia, and Emilia's suffering would make Perry suffer too. They all deserved it so much.

A chill ran down Dolly's back which had nothing to do with the weather, a chill that had fear edged greatly round it. Instinctively, she drew the children back and got in front of them. 'What are you doing here? Didn't you understand what my daughter said to you yesterday? You're not welcome. Go away!'

Selina kept coming towards her, with her hands stretched out in front of her. 'No! You get away. Move away from those children.'

'What? No! I won't. Don't you dare come near us. Children, run! Run to the village and get help. Scream! Scream at the top of your voices.' Dolly pushed them hard in the direction they had come from.

Lottie teetered a few steps but stopped. 'Granny!' she cried.

'Lottie, run!' Dolly shrieked. Then she ran at Selina, her own arms out, aiming to push the woman in the chest.

Lottie grabbed a stunned Alan by the hand, but instead of running to the village, she thought – as a child would – that she would be safer at home, and she hared with the boy towards the ford with the intention of running up the hill. Selina stepped smartly to the side and seized hold of her. Lottie screamed and struggled. Alan fell to the ground, screaming in fear. Dolly screamed for her granddaughter.

Selina was running, running with a struggling, shrieking Lottie, back up towards Ford House. She'd take the captured child into the woods. She hadn't got the boy but the girl was her main target.

Dolly had always been a strong, fit woman and she drew on all her reserves to chase Selina, shouting all the way. She got just in front of Selina and reached out to get Lottie back. Selina whirled sideways and avoided her, then backtracked, this time heading towards the ford.

Lottie kept fighting. She clawed and scratched Selina's neck, then managed to rake her nails across her eye. Selina howled but did not stop. The water was running fast and was two feet deep above the road. Selina halted. The ford had a bridge at the side, tight against the tall hedge, but with the child beating on her it would be a precarious passage and Lottie might manage to get a grip on the foliage. So she began to splash through the muddy water.

Dolly went after her, screaming in the furious need to save her grandchild. She flung herself off her feet at Selina. She hit Selina in the middle of her back and sent her hurtling frontwards. Selina and Lottie hit the water with a heavy splash. The momentum took Dolly after them and she fell on Selina's waist. Selina still had a grip around Lottie, and while trying to beat Dolly off her she pushed Lottie's head in under the water.

'No! No!' Dolly screamed in terror. 'Don't you dare hurt her. I won't let you!' She couldn't do anything from where she was, so she got up and climbed over Selina and faced her. Selina was pressing down on Lottie with all her might.

Dolly bent forward and swung her fist up high. With a howl of rage she brought her fist forward and smashed it across Selina's jaw. Selina's head swung to a right angle. But she went on trying to put an end to Lottie's life. Next, Dolly kicked out. Her boot got Selina's cheekbone and this time she was stunned almost senseless. As her hands let go of Lottie, Dolly's were reaching to save her.

She brought Lottie's head up out of the water, and crying in fear she wiped the wet and dirt off her little face. 'Lottie! Lottie. Speak to Granny.'

Lottie had clamped her mouth shut and had not swallowed any water. She was desperate for breath and gasped some in. Then she was crying and scrabbling to get out of the water to her grandmother.

Dolly hauled her out and gathered her into her chest. Shaking, drenched from the rain, muddy and crying, Alan crossed over the bridge and went to Dolly.

'No, no!' she cried. 'Alan, run up to the farm. Get Mr Rowse. Get Mr Jonny. Get anyone!' It took another few seconds to break through Alan's fright and need for comfort before he staggered away.

Dolly looked down on Selina, stirring now, crawling on her hands and knees to get out of the ford, coming in her direction. 'I won't let you hurt my family!' Dolly shouted. Lottie was cradled against her, sobbing, her eyes tight shut. When Selina got close, raising her dripping head, a maniacal expression of deadly intention glaring from her once beautiful eyes, Dolly lifted a foot and brought it down fiercely on her head. Selina was knocked senseless. Her face was under the water.

Dolly rested her foot on the woman's head and kept it there long enough so she could never raise it again.

Chapter Thirty-Two

There was a gathering of Harveys and Rowses. The only one there not related by blood or marriage was Perry. He felt everyone's eyes on him. 'I'm glad she's dead. My sister was evil. I'm sorry I didn't get her away earlier, that Lottie was nearly… don't worry, I won't have her buried anywhere near here. How's Lottie now?'

Emilia had just come down from Lottie's bedroom. 'She's badly scratched and a bit shaky. Tom's reading her a story. I'll go back up to her in a minute.'

'I can't say how relieved I am that Selina's dead,' Ben said vehemently. He had told Emilia and Tristan his belief that Selina had intended to reveal the secret to Jonny about Louisa being his half-sister. 'There's no big black cloud hanging over us now.'

'I'm sorry about your troubles, Ben,' Perry said, eyeing the other man uncertainly.

'I don't need sympathy from you,' Ben replied, dismissive and hostile.

'If you're going to take that tone with Perry then you won't be welcome under my roof, Ben,' Emilia said, unarguably.

Ben got up from his chair in the sitting room. 'Your roof? That should never be. I don't intend to ever darken your door again. As for Brooke, she's welcome to stay in

America for good but I won't let her keep my children from me. I'll find them. I won't be back to Hennaford until I'm able to bring my children with me.'

'Ben.' Tristan was grim. 'Be very careful or you'll end up a lonely old man.'

Ben shot an angry glare at Emilia before turning on Tristan. 'Congratulate yourself on being the only truly happily married brother. Goodbye.' He left.

Jonny shook his head, appalled at his uncle's behaviour.

Emilia found Ben instantly forgettable. 'Mother, are you all right? You took quite a few bruises. I'm so proud of you, and like Elena and Jim, so grateful for what you did.'

Dolly pictured Selina's head floating lifelessly on top of the water of the ford. 'I only did what any other good woman would have done to protect her young.'

'You mustn't blame yourself for being unable to get Miss Bosweld out in time to prevent her from drowning, Mrs Rowse,' Winifred said.

'No, indeed,' Perry added. It was justice, his sister dying like Libby had.

'I don't,' Dolly said. 'Like I've said, I only did my best.'

Emilia was looking at Perry. He needn't go back to London now, at least not straight away. She'd talk to him alone tomorrow. From now on he'd be wonderfully unencumbered, free at last to grieve properly for Libby and think of the future. With her. She would have it no other way. 'If you'll excuse me, I think I'll slip back up to Lottie.'

'Why don't you go up with her, Perry?' Dolly smiled kindly at him. 'The maid would be delighted to see you. Eh, Edwin?'

'Yes, dear. She would,' Edwin agreed.

'You don't mind, Mother, Father?' Emilia was surprised and delighted. 'That Perry and I…?'

'We did at first,' Edwin said. 'But after all that's happened today, well, nothing's to be gained by us climbing on a high horse. And at the back of it, well, I believe Alec would only want you to be happy.'

Emilia glanced at Tristan, who gave an open-handed gesture. 'You never left Alec like Ursula did me. You didn't break his heart.'

She turned to Will. 'Son?'

Pleased to have been invited to sit in with the grown-ups, he had taken everything in quietly. 'I nearly lost my little sister today. It's made me aware how fragile the barrier is between life and death. I find this situation hard but I won't do anything to make things difficult.'

'Thank you, Will.' Emilia hugged him. 'You've just shown me that one day you will be worthy of your father's farm, but Tom and Lottie will get a joint share too.'

She held out her hand to Perry. 'Shall we go up?'

'I'd like nothing more.' At the door, he said, 'Thanks, everyone.'

Hand in hand, Emilia and Perry climbed the stairs, to the little girl who meant so much to both of them. Climbing at last to a future together.